I0628232

Matt Shea Books Presents:

Judge Alvin Wong

In:

'The Mouse That Roared'

PLUS

'Lauratown And Other Short Stories'

AND

'The World's Greatest Rock Star And Other Short Stories'

"Judge Alvin Wong in 'The Mouse That Roared' plus 'Lauratown and other Short Stories' and 'The World's Greatest Rock Star' and other Short Stories," by Matt Shea. ISBN 978-1-947532-76-2 (softcover); 978-1-947532-77-9 (eBook).

Published 2018 by Virtualbookworm.com Publishing Inc., P.O. Box 9949, College Station, TX 77842, US. ©2018, Matt Shea.

All rights reserved. No part of this publication may be reproduced, stored in a retrieval system, or transmitted in any form or by any means, electronic, mechanical, recording or otherwise, without the prior written permission of Matt Shea.

Table of Contents

About the Book

Matt Shea Books Presents: Judge Alvin Wong in: 'The Mouse That Roared' Plus 'Lauratown And Other Short Stories' And 'The World's Greatest Rock Star And Other Short Stories' is a 3-in-1 book by author Matt Shea.

It's the union of two successful Kindle projects with a Judge Alvin Wong story thrown in! This is Matt's response to the many who wanted to have all of his writings available in paperback.

Our feature story, *'The Mouse That Roared,'* illustrates a crossroad every teen faces somewhere in life: *What do I want to be when I grow up?*

William Randall Stokes IV is our main character — a humble young man who was cursed by being the youngest, smallest and shortest boy in his graduation class. Like any impressionable youth, our star begins his quest through trial and error *with the wrong crowd.* A rollercoaster ride that came with its share of heart aches, harsh lessons, and occasional embarrassment . . .

There was another side to the fence, however. The side where the grownups hung out *with the Bible being part of the equation.*

From there, our magnificent Creator makes His presence more prevalent with a spiritual path waiting for one William Randall Stokes IV.

The result?

Our Lord has once again performed in *mysterious ways!*

The other two stories: *Lauratown* and *The World's Greatest Rock Star* have many stories attached to them as well. You will find them and the lessons they teach, as you go from one story to the next.

When ready, get comfortable and enjoy!

Matt Shea

Special Thanks

Ella Ray (left) and Renée Klause.

Regardless of how simple my stories appear, I still need those who assist me. If they weren't there, my stories would have peaked out as dreams, wishes and thoughts that were never to be printed. Please let me introduce two fabulous ladies who have contributed to my projects and made a difference.

Renée Klause of Artistic Xpressions has always been there for me when it comes to my writings and being a *special friend*. Her wizardry in painting and photography has already graced three of my book covers, with many more to follow. In fact, the happy golden retriever in some of the pictures is non-other than her once wonderful companion, Dolly. Most important, Renée encourages me to stay on my path and gives wonderful ideas that often lead to a great story.

I highly recommend anyone and everyone to look up her site on Facebook. I guarantee that you'll be impressed and *she even allows viewers to contact her!*

Artistic Xpressions by Renée Klause

◀◀ ◀◀ ▶▶ ▶▶

Ella Ray is a wonderful friend who does a meticulous job proofreading and editing. There is always an education for me when she addresses my rough drafts. Sometimes this is accompanied with a little embarrassment, *but only a little . . .*

My friend, Ella, along with Renée, also joins in on many of my radio interviews to kick things up a few notches. I'd be lost without them.

Thanks for being there for me Girls!

Matt

Are two Brattons Better Than One?

Ric Bratton

Sean "Boomer" Bratton

But of course!

Many of you are quite familiar with radio talk show host *Ric Bratton* and his national broadcast. *This Week In America* is a renowned talk show that truly covers both ends of the spectrum when it comes to interviewing amazing people who represent all walks of life — creative beings who have an interesting point of view to share with an abundance of good will attached.

The apple doesn't fall far from the tree.

Have you heard about his son, *Sean*? This guy has been doing some pretty amazing stuff himself.

Most people in Fort Wayne, Indiana certainly know of this personality very well: *he's been around for over twenty years!* Sometimes you can hear him on 97.3 WMEE-FM cutting it up with Ron Mellencamp. Other times his leash is extended when he unmercifully unloads *'Boomer's Wacky World,'* a one-of-a-kind show that would definitely cause cars to pull over in traffic.

"Why?" you ask.

To further your education by learning important stuff like:

The Moron of the week-
Worse Joke Wednesday
and

Only In Indiana
That's why!
It's all fun and interesting to say the least!

(I wonder if it's time to promote Ric and Sean as the newest tag team in professional wrestling?)

Tune in to Ric and Sean when the opportunity presents itself; it will make your day!

And:

Keep up the good work, guys!

Matt

Dedication

I'd like to dedicate this compilation to Amber, my publisher's autistic daughter who graduated this year! Amber, you are a special girl with a family that loves you very much. I think it's appropriate that your confirmation verse was Philippians 4:13 — *I can do all things through Christ who strengthens me.*

Judge Alvin Wong

in

The Mouse That Roared

Introduction

The stocking feet of William Randall Stokes IV rested on the antique desk that dignified his bedroom. The cherished family heirloom made of polished oak and brass was a perfect fit for the room that never allowed any dust to gather. Looking around his perfect world, the sixteen-year-old studied the bed one could bounce a quarter off and smiled.

It was *here* that the conservative lad with thin black hair parted to one side found peace. A place of refuge for the dainty young man who wore the classic wire-rimmed geek glasses that all modern-day science fiction movies have come to know.

Standing at 5', 5" and weighing a flimsy one hundred and forty pounds, this harmless specimen was cursed even further. He had distinct, nervous brown eyes rivaling that of none other than Deputy Barney Fife himself! In the automotive world, he would have been the first AMC Gremlin off the assembly line.

There was more.

This cruel hand dealt by nature was knocked down a few more notches. Somewhere, someone in early childhood referred to him as *Mouse*—and the name had stuck ever since.

It was a menacing label that never allowed the humble soul to get off the ground socially. One that made others double up with uncontrollable laughter. In fact, it could

2

always be used endlessly, whenever anyone chose to ramble on with the *play on words game*:

It was synonymous with cheese; *a product that goes with almost any food group*. It was also affiliated with computers, what a professional photographer might ask a subject to say, what the moon was once thought to be made of, an undesirable amount of drama, etc. . . .

No one could ever argue that his life had started out with little or no chance at all.

True, the boy did have a cavalry that came in the form of a rich uncle. A strong, handsome stud who was once the local high school football star. A well-respected businessman who had the most popular car dealerships in two counties!

"Show them your real power," he advised. *"Use your brain to excel so high that you advance yourself to the next level and leave them all behind in the dust!"*

The nephew did just that. In fact, *twice!*

The result?

Each time he advanced to a higher grade, he was dwarfed by his new classmates even more. Thus making him *even more mousey* . . .

Today was a new day, however, and those trials and tribulations *were to be all behind him now.*

Looking straight ahead, he marveled at the room that had just become more enriched. It now boasted an all-important document that hung perfectly centered against the wall his desk faced. It was his high school diploma; the ever-important deed that emancipated the teen who stared at it!

The 'academic wonder boy' was now in a trance, reflecting on the years of *hell he paid* to achieve this milestone.

The many parties he was never allowed to be invited to . . .

School dances where he couldn't find a date . . .

Hearing loud comments in town with the name 'Mouse' or 'cheese' being exaggerated for all to hear . . .

It was a long time coming, but his perseverance had finally paid off! It was now his turn to have the last laugh:

He was able to get out of prison early based on hard work and good behavior.

Suddenly, it entered his mind about the carrot that once dangled in front of him. The one he was about to receive from his rich uncle *if he graduated early with honors.* Without warning, an uncontrollable Cheshire grin with a devious undertone began to cover his face. Hand in hand, a famous quote modified to his liking played through his mind.

They won't have William Randall Stokes IV to kick around anymore!

And now our story begins.

Chapter 1

It was early morning in the dusty town of Hangman, where all stood still.

This all-American town nestled in the dry plains was surely embraced by our Lord's favor. It was graced by a river, along with a few nearby lakes that boasted fish, eagles and other natural residences. In fact, one side was protected by a ridged mountain range that extended for miles.

This was truly *'home on the range'* for those who settled here. Every night, this humble town was embraced by a dark sky that revealed a galaxy of stars. A marvel that seemingly served as a heavenly canopy promising further blessings—even if clouds were passing through . . .

It was a typical morning, where God's magnificent creation would continue its pace. The summer sun would again begin its natural encroachment on this spiritual setting, a phenomenon that initially introduced itself by casting a mild hue of sunlight that triggered such sounds as chirping birds and a lone rooster. Soon a single star would be remaining, as many households would already be up and about to start their day.

It was the daily 'changing of the guard' where the animal kingdom received their wake-up call first—only to be followed by the awkwardness of the human species.

The flawed race that can't evolve unless it forgives its own kind.

Off in the distance, a set of headlights could be seen. They were driving up a spiral dirt road that led to a bluff overlooking the main section of town. A once—and still—sacred outlook where many congregations prayed, worshiped and performed the sacrament of marriage. It was named Indian Pointe, with many word-of-mouth stories about Native American culture attached to it. A place that also served as a breathtaking viewpoint featured by postcards and a few nature magazines.

Soon, additional daylight exposed the brand spanking-new, American-built 4x4 pickup truck with all the bells and whistles one could ever imagine.

Then it happened.

Its lone occupant opened both side doors, as if the truck were a battleship ready to open fire. A frightening scenario that proved to hold true, as the loudest, most powerful sound system that *any* vehicle could ever pack began its assault on the unsuspecting village below.

Within milliseconds, the entire town was outside in disarray, realizing that they were under attack. In a state of panic, the locals scattered about taking shelter while trying to find where the thundering noise was coming from. An intrusion that shook homes, spilled coffee, and rattled windows.

Instinctively, all looked toward the source where the amplified fire was coming from. It was way up high on Indian Pointe, where all could see none other than William Randall Stokes IV himself; alias *Mouse*! His glistening teeth and folded arms could be seen as he watched with apparent satisfaction.

There was something wrong with this picture.

This local high school grad was never known to bother anyone, *ever*. In fact, it was *he* who was teased and picked on his entire life for being the smallest boy with the highest grades. The guy who was nicknamed 'Mouse' because of his non-threatening stature and cowering demeanor. A nickname he *absolutely detested* beyond words. One that he would quietly shrug off in public and cry himself asleep over at night, cutting a deeper wound every time it was thrown at him.

One would have to ask oneself:

Q) *How could a young man just out of high school ever afford such a vehicle?*

A) *Easily! It was a 'deal' set up by his rich uncle, if he were to graduate on time with honors. A condition set for the boy who never had a father.*

It was a sight to see (and hear), with locals scratching their heads and pondering, *"What's gotten into that boy?"*

William was now addressing the entire town of Hangman like a conductor standing tall at the pulpit. His ultra-conservative image was thrown to the wayside that morning. To make his statement even more clear, he was wearing the latest in Western fashions, complete with hat and dark shades!

This was the boy's proclamation to the entire township. He was telling all that he had adopted *a new image*. A well thought-out presentation that would launch the career of any professional wrestler.

Judge Alvin Wong was on the scene and knew what to do. The Chinese-American man who stood at 5', 7" was waving his arms in a downward motion in order to calm down the irate citizens. "It's just a dumb kid saying *Hello* to everyone," he yelled. "I'll drive up there and see what he wants . . ."

Everyone in Hangman knew William Stokes as a good person and agreed that Alvin would yield the best results. They also knew that soon, the disturbance would come to a stop.

It did.

As the forty-seven-year-old man drove to the historical viewpoint, William wisely turned off his stereo. Soon they were face to face, with Alvin making the first move. "You're up kinda early today; does your mom know that you're here?"

A tidbit of valuable information was exchanged. The adolescent shrugged his shoulders, and in a timid voice said, "She's gone for the weekend."

That explained *everything* about the boy with a guilt-ridden face. The adult rolled his eyes and mildly shook his head. Maintaining his upbeat tempo, Alvin changed to a more important subject. Leaning forward, he began to whisper as if he were telling a secret. *"Can I let you in on something?"* he asked in a friendly tone.

The question piqued William's curiosity, compelling him to lean closer. *"What?"* he whispered back.

Alvin then repositioned his body and pointed toward the center of town. "Do you see that old, old wooden building down there with the big cross in front of it?" he asked.

William looked at the church below and said, "Yeah, I see it."

Turning to the boy who needed guidance, he got a bit closer and whispered, "It's a neat place to hang out—*and they accept guys like us . . .*"

Alvin's message was delivered with perfection, causing the young man to think. After a short pause and a dry swallow, William responded, "Yeah, I guess it's a good place . . ."

The good judge was fast on his feet and found a common ground that would fit at that moment. "Would you like to join me for breakfast this morning?"

His approach was *perfect*. The good man knew when a good kid was reaching out to be accepted. He also knew how to tactfully nudge someone in the *right direction*. The youth extended his hand with an ear-to-ear smile, realizing that his day was off to a good start. "That would be great!" he countered.

They were now on the same page. "This will be fun!" said Alvin as he pushed William on the shoulder. "I'll meet you at Ric Bratton's place. He has a breakfast spread that all the truckers are talking about; and don't worry—this one's on me!" In the same motion, Alvin threw in a condition to address the morning's problem. "That is, if you can come along peacefully . . ."

William knew exactly what he was talking about and immediately apologized for the mayhem he created. "Sorry about that," he said with a slight laugh.

Alvin pushed the issue a smidgen further. "You will probably see the road better if you took off those glasses . . ."

The young man realized that *looking cool* at that time of day wouldn't work well with a county judge. Besides, he greatly respected the man. He placed the glasses in his shirt pocket and removed his hat.

The shiny new truck followed Alvin to the well-known spot in town. Parked side by side, they walked to the front doors, where Ric's country humor took over. Waving both hands over his head, the shop owner stepped outside, pleading, "Don't shoot!"

All present laughed, knowing of the teenager's escapade that morning. William loved the attention he was receiving and joined in on the laughter. "Sorry about that," he said to Ric.

"I can't hear you," replied Ric with a theatrical twist. "My ears are plugged!" More laughter followed, with knees being slapped.

Alvin playfully grabbed William by the hair, as if he was punishing him. *"What are we gonna do with you?"* he said, using a ring of laughter.

At that moment, Ric took over and introduced his friend *William* to all who were present.

It was music to William Stokes' ears!

From there, he and Alvin ate breakfast with a couple of local truckers. Ric would join in when time allowed. More introductions were made as hungry drivers entered the famed general store, with amusing stories circulating.

It was possibly the greatest morning in the life of William Randall Stokes IV. Unlike the cruel comments that surrounded him throughout his school life, this day would be different. Here, he was NOT *Mouse;* he was William! More important, he was being spoken to and treated *the way friends do to one another.*

9

He did, however, make *one* tactical error. The young man got ahead of himself by formulating an early conclusion:

He was convinced that his bionic stereo did indeed update his image to the entire valley.

How right he was . . .

Chapter II

News travels fast in a small town.

Those who weren't rudely awakened that morning by the industrial-sized woofers and tweeters heard about it before noon. Soon, all attention was focused on the boy with the monstrous new truck that almost required a step ladder to climb into. The one that alerted all wildlife in the surrounding area before it came into view.

Just then, without any warning came a faint vibrating 'thumping' sound off in the distance. It was the black and chrome marauder with tinted windows, approaching fast. At the controls was the feeble lad on a mission. With cowboy hat and shades in place, he beamed with pride as he watched his own reflection in the rear view mirror.

Years of mental cruelty had taken its toll, but the Valor Victorian *who was denied the honor of presenting the valediction* had survived the odds, and had something to show for it! He would now parade around town, showing off his monetary reward. The consummate dream ride that *any* cowboy could ever want—and a 'chick magnet' to boot! All while using his discretion as to when to announce his arrival by blasting neighborhoods to kingdom come. A sure-fire gimmick that was already proven!

Proud as a peacock, he knew one thing: *It was now his turn to play catch-up with life.*

Matt Shea

For the rest of the day, William played the role of the ice cream man. He would simply travel about, letting all know that *he was there.*

Can we say, *"Power"?*

Like any one-hit wonder, William was certainly the talk of the town. A spotlight he initially thought he always wanted . . .

◀◀ ◀◀ ▶▶ ▶▶

The next morning arrived, with one William Randall Stokes IV plotting his next course of action. Knowing that the previous day's experiments yielded quick results, he elected to expand his menu by further penetrating the town he grew up in. It wasn't long until he was parked in front of the famed Lazy Trail Saloon with windows down, thumping away . . .

Then it happened. His first customer confronted him, a towering man by the name of Blaine Wolf who looked like a former offensive lineman. Normally, a friendly town such as Hangman rarely had much in the way of a public outcry. But the high school grad who commandeered the speakers with gargantuan range had been, in effect, violating many. Including the controversial rancher with wild blond hair and matching blue eyes. "You don't want to be doing something like this!" he barked. "You're reminding me of myself not too long ago, and that's a bad place to be . . ."

The teen knew when he was outmatched and turned off the system completely. "Thank you," replied the baritone voice that all knew. Sticking his head into the window, the big man displayed his gentle side. With a smile that resembled Santa Claus, he softly said, "I actually like you a lot; in fact, I love you!"

William was taken by the big man's compassion and said, "Thank you."

Blaine then handed the boy something. "Here, take this. It's full of everything you'll ever need to know."

The young man was now holding a Bible.

"If it can do wonders for a guy like me, it will certainly lead you down the right path as well. Look through it when you have the time and have a good day!" The two-hundred-seventy pound man then gave encouragement by patting him on the shoulder. Blaine Wolf left with a gratifying feeling, knowing that he'd done his good deed for the day.

William held the book with both hands, realizing that it was a gift from one of the most respected people the town had ever produced. In time he would come to understand the spiritual guidance that was known to come with it. Regardless of his good fortune, our star was just young enough to have a learning curve to address the hard way. William was still in the woods and could not see that his gift was lightning in a bottle; the cure to all his problems. He placed the Good Book in the glove box of his truck and continued his path in life.

At that moment, his world came to a screeching halt. Across the street walked a former classmate whose natural beauty included shoulder-length blonde hair and striking blue eyes. It was the lovely Amber Johansson, in the flesh! The class princess that every boy competed for. That classy, wholesome Miss America material who treated everyone with a special respect that included her charm, smile, and sense of justice. Even those who rated at the Mouse level were always welcomed to be a part of her day.

Wasting no time, he threw his truck in gear while turning the knobs that would amplify his mating call. Next he made a semi-legal U-turn as his thump-thump vehicle quickly pulled alongside his prey, almost skidding to a complete stop. His impromptu visit and primitive method caught her off guard and scared the hell out of her!

Fortunately for our victim, she had reached her destination. Catching her breath, she gave William a look of disappointment, recovered and turned to enter the neighborhood church without saying a single word.

Strike one.

The boy in the cool glasses felt his heart sink to the floor. Mouse buried his head in the steering wheel and, in time, quietly drove home. He spent the rest of his day scratching his head, wondering what went wrong. True, he was fully aware that there were those who didn't appreciate the racket he was making. However, there were also those who tipped the scales even by serving as a cheering section. Boys his age, whose actions weren't always approved of, either.

William Stokes was at the proverbial crossroads in life. It was to be a decision, however, that required no concentration whatsoever. *He wanted the girl!*

A question now arises: *What is the best way to win her over?*

Foolishly, he would regroup within himself and allow the blind to lead the blind. Convinced that his present tactic was the best method, he would simply use trial and error to see how best to channel it. The young driver would simply experiment with the many ways one could force a square peg through a round hole . . .

◀◀ ◀◀ ▶▶ ▶▶

William continued his ways by forcing all to hear him wherever he drove, getting many mixed results. There were those who cheered him on; but they were also the very ones who used him as a punching bag throughout the school system. Then there were the grownups, who were getting more assertive by yelling things like:

"Turn that thing down!" and *"I hope you run out of gas!"*

Their opinion really didn't matter, though; it was Amber the lovesick boy was trying to impress. William Stokes would continue spending his time trolling through town and changing bait by blaring out a variety of recording artists who were known worldwide. Still, he got no nibbles; only an occasional gesture from an adult who was getting pelted by the friendly fire.

In time William realized that he could use some good advice. Without any hesitation, he drove to Ric Bratton's place ,where he knew *real friends* awaited.

Soon he walked through the main doors where Ric, Blaine Wolf, Judge Alvin and Sheriff Chesterfield himself were all gathered. "Just the guy I was looking for!" commented the old-time lawman who seemed to come out of a western movie.

William froze. "You mean *me?*" he asked.

The seventy-year-old local who spoke with a whistle through his mustache pointed his index finger directly at him and replied, "Yes, *you!*"

William and the lanky man with silver hair and twinkly blue eyes would spend the next hour having a heart-to-heart. The many complaints about the 'Darth Vader truck' that was shaking homes and making dogs hide under beds were finally being addressed. "Look," said the compassionate elder. "We've all been there, but enough is enough . . ." The good man said what had to be said. He then gave a parting handshake, tipped his hat and left the establishment.

It was now Alvin's turn. Taking the seat that was occupied by the sheriff, he leaned close to William and whispered out loud. *"What's her name?"*

William was initially embarrassed and pretended that he did not know what he was talking about. "I don't understand," he replied softly.

"C'mon," said Alvin as he brushed William's arm with the back of his fingers. "I once had an old Pacer with a tape set-up to play my stuff for the whole neighborhood to hear. Who's the girl you're after?"

Blushing, he buckled down and gave the information. "Amber Johansson."

Alvin gave a wolf whistle as he looked upward. *"Amber Johansson?"* he asked. "Wow, you got good taste!"

"Yeah," agreed William. "But she can have any guy, and I'm not the best choice," he said, lowering his head.

"Says who?" asked Alvin as he motioned with his hands, palms up. William looked at Alvin with an expression of hope. It was obvious that he wanted to hear more. "Just find out what she likes; *what she believes in,*" the seasoned judge replied.

William wisely digested the advice given by his friend as he stared out the window. Seeing the light, he turned to Alvin with a smile and said, "Thanks!" He then shook hands with the beloved man and left to reassess his conquest.

Chapter III

That evening, William looked through all of his high school yearbooks to study the life of Ms. Amber Johansson more closely. It was mind-boggling to see the many committees, charities, community services and other extracurricular activities the homecoming queen was involved with. *There must be a favorite,* he thought to himself.

It was then when he made what was possibly the most important move his life would ever know. Bowing his head, he closed his eyes and made a sign of the cross. From there, he simply asked the Lord for guidance. Once done, he took notice that there was still some daylight left and decided to clean the inside of his truck. It was there when our Savior's mighty hand extended Itself. When he opened the glove box, he saw the Bible that had entered his life through a well-known, respected man.

Bells and whistles went off in William's head. *Church!* he thought to himself. *She's always going to church!* Then it occurred to him: *the very walkway she recently chose to part ways led to the place she reverend most. The House Of God!*

Without any thought, he ran to his vehicle in an attempt to do his impersonation of the Pony Express. Initially, he would have made it there in record time with loud instruments and screaming voices echoing from his truck.

Something *peculiar* happened on the way to church, however.

Approaching the sanctuary, his four-wheel-driven beast seemed to get tamed rather quickly. For whatever reason, it idled down immensely, with its imposing sound silencing. Like the old sitcom *My Mother The Car,* the ride seemed to rebel with a mind of its own. Frantically he pumped the gas pedal while switching his stereo on and off, but to no avail. Regardless of his new dilemma, his heart told him to stay on course. Befuddled, he arrived in front of the community church *quietly and legally.*

William was gradually fitting the pieces of the puzzle together, but still needed some help. His interest in Amber did take precedence over the unexplained glitches his new ride displayed.

Unfortunately, William was like most impatient guys. He overlooked the utmost important factor which was staring him in the face:

Why the lovely Ms. Amber went to church.

The mammoth wooden structure with stained glass windows appeared to be dark and empty. Regardless, all knew that its doors were never closed. Upon entering, the lad immediately felt a warm presence that let him know he wasn't alone. Standing still inside the main entrance, he felt a warm aura of love and acceptance. In awe, he gazed above at the wood beams that were built over a century ago. He then looked around at the many statues, portraits and verses that all seemed to reach out to him with a touch of encouragement and understanding.

It was a feeling unlike any he had ever felt before. One that brought an everlasting message of peace and comfort.

Pastor Jonathan Smith had arrived undetected and broke the silence with his dry humor. "It's so nice to see you here," he said in a charming voice. *"I didn't hear you coming."*

William was startled at first, and then laughed at the pun the pastor had made. Turning toward him, he said, "I guess I've been doing that too much lately." It was easy for

William to joke around with the man in the robe; he'd attended many services with him since the day he was born.

"We've all been there," chuckled the non-judgmental man as he walked towards him. Playfully, he shook the parishioner's shoulder and said, "Welcome!" Calmly, he placed an arm of fellowship around William's shoulder and escorted him toward the altar. Soon the two shared a pew, where they could talk without any interruptions—*without anyone else hearing a word.* It was an open conversation with no boundaries that was allowed to go any direction and off into infinity, one guy to another.

Pastor John was known to be a good listener, and had the teen sitting before him open up about the secret pains of his life. "It's all a trial," Pastor John would inject.

William loosened up more and discussed how much the name *Mouse* infuriated him beyond words.

"When an innocent person is teased, *it's because they are greatly respected,*" the man of the cloth pointed out.

The evening continued with intense conversation, laced with occasional laughter. Eventually, a specific topic was addressed when Pastor John told him of the many church activities and community involvement the church was known for. "They are open to all ages, including those just out of high school," he explained.

The middle-aged man with rosy cheeks then delivered an unsuspected twist. Leaning forward, he tapped William on the hand and whispered, *"And that includes the lovely Amber Johansson herself . . ."*

William's face turned a pastel shade of embarrassment, realizing that his secret was out.

Pastor John was two steps ahead. Leaning back, he said, "Don't feel that you're the Lone Ranger. Why, every boy from your class has an eye on her."

"But she goes away from me," he confessed.

"Then you need to figure out where she goes to," said the wise man. Continuing, he said, "Let me rephrase that . . ." Leaning back, he clasped his hands behind his head and reiterated, "I meant to say *Who* she is going to . . ."

William looked up with a smirk on his face, knowing exactly *Who* he was referring to.

At that moment, the room became noticeably darker. The setting sun had quickly diminished the sunlight that once illuminated the surrounding stained glass. "Shall we turn on the lights, or call it a night?" asked Pastor John Smith.

William's mind was wandering at a fast pace and gave the standard answer his age group was known for. "It's getting late; I gotta go now . . ."

"Very well," replied Pastor John. From there, a quick exchange of gratitude was traded with the pastor, reminding the young man that he was always there for him. The pastor then summed up their evening. *"Remember, there is a reason why you're in other people's lives and why you really came here today . . ."*

That final message did hit home with the impressionable youth and would be stored away in his memory banks forever. It would be pondered on whenever he felt all alone, or when moments of disparity arrived.

William drove home in deep thought. Mentally preoccupied, he forgot all about playing his music and didn't notice that his truck was no longer restricted to the posted speed.

Chapter IV

Around town, William Randall Stokes IV was straddling the fence publicly. On one hand, he was under lots of scrutiny by his critics. On the other, the boys he graduated with approved of his abuse of power and encouraged more. Some were even beginning to refer to him as *The Mouse.*

He didn't like that one either.

None of that seemed to matter to the boy, who had bigger fish to fry. All he wanted was to be with Amber.

◀◀ ◀◀ ▶▶ ▶▶

The next morning had our hero cruising around town, on the prowl. William hadn't forgotten the recent warning he received from Sheriff Chesterfield and the many like him, who also threw in their two cents' worth. Today his volume was turned down considerably, but poised for a quick blast when the opportunity presented itself.

Boys will be boys.

Such an occasion arrived when William spotted the girl of his dreams walking toward the local park. His approach this time would prove to be one of a more sophisticated nature. Having done some research, he knew that she played various instruments and performed not just in the school orchestra, but for various events throughout the valley. Using this vital information, William devised a game plan.

It would be timeless classics that he would bombard her with!

Approaching the love of his life, he twisted the dial to an abnormally high setting and watched her almost jump out of her pants! Recovering quickly, she walked in the other direction while fixing her hair.

Strike two.

William was shocked to see that his selection of music didn't appeal to her. Feeling dejected and fresh out of ideas, he began to fall into an emotional tailspin. He was now desperate to lick his wounds within the comfort of friends. To find those who truly loved him and gave good advice.

The lost soul instinctively knew that he needed *special assistance,* and that it was time to send a signal flare to a Higher Power. A silent prayer was launched.

Lickety-split and out of nowhere came what seemed to be an angel sent from Heaven. "Well, at least you're not getting around in a Pacer . . ." It was a relief for William to hear the forgiving, low-keyed voice of his friend, Judge Alvin. The public official was going for a walk and just so happened to witness the event. Leaning into the truck's cab, he asked William permission to ask a question. "Can I ask you something?"

"Sure," replied the young man.

"Why do we guys do stupid things like that?" he asked.

The blind fool answered the other by responding, "I don't know . . ."

"Me neither," agreed his fellow male as he shrugged his shoulders. "You know what?" he continued. "This guy is thinking about hitting Ric's place for a good breakfast. Wanna join me?" he asked.

William was saved. "Climb in!" he yelled. Alvin got in and fastened the seat belt. Next, he lowered his head while plugging his ears. "You don't have to worry about that!" laughed William.

"What?" asked Alvin. *"I can't hear you!"*

Soon William was sitting with the guys at Ric's place. The constant influx of customers and familiar faces came and went while their table gradually increased in numbers. Some additional key players who'd missed the last roundup were now in attendance.

21

It was a meeting of the minds, with the topic being *women* and young William being the focal point. Feeling comfortable amongst friends, he spilled his guts about Amber Johansson. He then elaborated further by reflecting on the school life he barely survived, and the trial-and-error attempts he had made to win her over.

"Wow," commented Otto. "You must really feel for her . . ." The thirty-nine-year-old who stood well over six feet tall with black hair and green eyes expressed sincere compassion.

"I bet you two have a lot in common that you don't realize," encouraged Ric's forty-five-year-old son, Sean. The famed radio talk show host from Fort Wayne, Indiana, had more to say. "She probably sees some wonderful things in you that you're not aware of."

"I second the motion," commented Ric.

"I third," agreed Alvin.

William looked at the champions that surrounded him and began to feel pretty good about himself. "What should I do?" he asked.

Mayor Marcus Hipple was present and heard everything. The homegrown product who socially set *nerd records* could definitely relate to William's dilemma. "You are certainly approaching this in the right matter," praised the man who could pass as his biological father.

Grant Wolf, another resurrected misfit, was in tune. "You're doing just fine, William!" The local with blond hair and blue eyes was just a few years older, and knew when he saw his own kind. "You are respected far more than you'll ever know," he proclaimed.

"I'll cheer to that!" said his uncle, Blaine, as he raised his coffee mug up for a toast.

"Hear, hear!" called out Alvin as he stood tall with mug held high. All at once, everyone followed suit with the good judge calling out: "To a good man!"

William was overwhelmed. He had *never* in his life been celebrated before. What made this milestone special was that it came from the best Hangman had to offer! Blushing with pride, he said, "Gee, thanks guys!"

Ric Bratton addressed William. "Have you ever heard that old saying: *It takes one to know one*?"

"I've been told that my entire life!" exclaimed William.

"Good, because when you knock yourself, you're actually describing *all of us!* laughed Ric. In one motion, the shop owner placed his arm around the teen's messy hair and affectionately applied a headlock that lasted all of three seconds.

"Come on in," cried out Alvin. "The water's fine!"

"Hey!" called out Blaine Wolf. "You're just as lost as the rest of us . . ."

'I'll drink to that!" said Sean as he raised a mug.

It was a moment of truth. At once, every male extended his steaming cup of java high up in the air.

The mother/daughter-in-law team of Shannon and Kara Bratton were sitting down in the opposite corner. In his usual diplomatic manner, Ric pointed at their table and made a gesture that implied:

Why don't you go see what they'd have to say about all this?

The brilliant suggestion didn't require a single word. Soon, the lovesick youth was sitting at the table that hosted two of the most respected women the valley had ever known. It was to be a great dose of medicine from the women, who cared for William. Motherly types who had a special place in their heart for the teen they'd watched grow up.

Shannon, who stood gracefully at 5' 2", was the epitome of having a sound mind and body. In fact, the classy lady was known to walk five miles a day when conditions allowed. The striking senior, who by many standards was too young to fit into any senior category, also possessed beautiful brown hair with matching hazel eyes.

There was more:

It was evident that her broadened character could only stem from being raised in a large family. A blessing that gave her great values with an understanding that she would carry them throughout life. Standards that went on to gift the world with:

The proverbial good man who went further because of the good woman behind him—and the pride of the Fort Wayne, Indiana, airwaves himself; her handsome son, Sean!

Kara Bratton, the wife of Sean, immediately thought about her home life. The woman who barely cleared 5' even definitely had compassion in every sense of the word. They were the *fun residence* in the neighborhood who opened their home to rescue abandoned cats that would otherwise have little or no chance of survival. The dynamo with sassy short brown hair and blue eyes always *felt the calling* when it was time to nurture a good life that was reaching out.

Greetings were exchanged in the true Bratton fashion as each stood up and hugged the bewildered youth. Once seated, Kara chose to be the lead-off batter. "You seem down," she commented.

"I am," responded William with his head hung low. Looking up, he fought back the tears and asked, "Do you know what it's like to *never* be good enough?" From there, the controversial figure told one story after another about being the joke of the valley, sniffling all the while . . .

After hearing a multitude of horror stories, Shannon's knuckles got white. Immediately the courageous woman began the process of tipping the scales *more than just even*. Utilizing the truth, she chose words that lifted him beyond the stars. "What you are really known for is what you've always been: *a decent person who will always be there for us.*"

Startled with a ray of hope, the boy looked up with dignity. "I have to agree!" added Kara.

William's undivided attention was now solidified. With the stage set, it was now time for the Bratton women to go to work. The girls started off their campaign by using a *tit-for-tat method*: They took turns reminding William of the countless times he made a positive impact on the community.

One episode after another was brought to light. In fact, it was a series of noteworthy events that were basically delivered in chronological order—accounting for most of the boy's life. Accolades ranging from the times his picture made the local newspaper for being involved with another worthy charity; to the time he immortalized town history by winning the state's High School Chess Tournament. An unselfish act that required hundreds of hours to build up to. A rare achievement that made Hangman more noticeable on the map.

No one could ever argue that William Randall Stokes IV was entirely respected in his hometown—*until he graduated.*

Shannon soon shifted gears by initiating a topic to build on. "Let's talk about what *really* attracts a good woman . . ."

William's facial expression lit up like a Christmas tree! Leaning forward, he gave every indication that he wanted to hear more.

"And what they *don't* particularly like . . ." added Kara.

"You mean things like playing a car stereo too loud?" he muttered while laughing at himself.

"Very good!" applauded Shannon.

The ensuing conversation covered a broad area that basically spelled out the difference between well-respected intellects; and the childish macho wannabes who need to make a public spectacle wherever they go.

In essence: *the difference between men and boys.*

William tensed up as he stared back down at the table. Sadly, he knew he was guilty of leaving his side of the fence for the seemingly greener pastures on the extravert side.

In other words: *being weak.*

The girls continued by occasionally throwing in a few cornball jokes that pertained to the subject. A brand of harmless humor designed to loosen things up a bit while driving the point home a little further.

It was a comfortable lesson that never made the patient feel vulnerable or outcast. Feelings that could never transpire when spending time with the magnificent Shannon and Kara. It was just like being with Ric:

It was all fun, with lots of positive things going on.

In time, the subject was strategically advanced to William's main concern: *Amber*. "What is it about her that you like so much?" asked Kara.

William's age showed when he responded with an unoriginal answer. "Everything . . ." Shannon rolled her eyes, then motioned her fingers back and forth to express that she wanted to hear more. "It's not just her beauty," he confessed. "She's always happy and doing wonderful things, whether or not she's with someone else."

From there he elaborated further, giving one example followed by another. Finally he pointed out a very impressive fact about the girl he wanted to spend the rest of his life with: "She even goes to church, regardless of what day it is." Looking across the table, he saw two smiling, pretty faces looking back.

"Sounds pretty healthy to me," commented Kara.

"I like it!" added Shannon.

The mother figures were impressed, knowing where William's head was at. They also realized that the young man's plate was already overflowing with emotions. It was time to put a close to their first session of therapy and leave their patient feeling good about himself.

"Well, I know one thing," said Shannon with a smirk on her face as she stood up, looking at Kara. "If everyone was as sweet and considerate as you; this whole, wide world would almost be Heaven!"

Shannon winked at Kara while the husbands watched. All at once, the like-minded duo stood up on either side of William — kissing the teen's cheek at the same time. The sixteen-year-old froze in place and turned every shade of red know to mankind. Walking away, Shannon called out a friendly command:

"And don't change a bit!"

Ric and Sean were receiving discrete gestures when William wasn't looking, as a way to cue them in that they were wrapping things up. Knowing what the wives probably had in mind, they watched in great anticipation. Once the play was executed, Ric turned to his son and said in a harmless voice, "I didn't see anything . . ."

Sean volleyed back in the same tempo. "See what?"

William looked at the Brattons and was fully aware how much they loved him. From there he uttered out the best words he could possibly assemble at that moment and said, "Gee . . . Thanks guys!"

The two couples left to go outside as William went to the restroom.

Watching the crowd disappear from the room where so much love was spent compelled Alvin to cry foul. Standing up, he pointed at himself and yelled:

"Hey! What about me?"

Chapter V

William Randall Stokes IV left the general store with plenty of wind in his sails. After all, he'd just topped off his tank with an abundance of love and encouragement from the finest Hangman had to offer. What seemed like a path to endless happiness was actually a calm before the storm: *Mother Nature was about to intervene with some unfinished business of her own.*

The acid test of peer pressure would be next: A very important, perplexed, emotional existence of mass confusion that creates the final touch needed for one to complete the stage of adolescence. A dichotomy in the making; one that would soon have our hero hanging in the balance.

On one hand, he was 'in' with the wise old elders who built Hangman. On the other, it was becoming evident that his former classmates wanted to hang out with the guy who possessed the most powerful stereo in the county's history!

Soon, conflicting offers from opposing social circles would play tug-of-war for his favor. On one side, he could become *Joe Popular* by allowing his youth to give in and play catch-up with his age group. On the other, he could spend his Saturday nights playing horseshoes while getting a further understanding of politics and Medicare.

Decisions, decisions . . .

◄◄ ◄◄ ►► ►►

Hangman had the typical back roads that led to *here and there.* Desolate land out in the middle of nowhere, where a sense of freedom could be felt *and rules did not apply.* Riding with the wind, our hero traveled on such a road with his sound system echoing in all directions.

Not far ahead was an old county park off the beaten path, where a lesson in life was about to unfold. Parked cars with dents and faded paint jobs told the story. It was summertime, with a group of teens trying to find something—*anything* to do . . .

This low-budget refuge may have been restricted to just an outhouse with a few picnic tables and campsites; all surrounded by overgrown grass. Still, it was at least *somewhere* to go. A getaway that would have been forsaken years ago if it were in a big city. For a small town like Hangman, however, families have been known to spend their entire weekends right here.

It was apparent that the *glitter people* from his graduation class had found the dried oasis first and lay claim over it. Regardless of their find, the monotonous pace of another unproductive day was taking its toll. Boredom had overtaken the group that could only reminisce about their high school glory days and randomly gossip. In desperation, renditions of worn-out jokes were being recited for the umpteenth time. A cavalry was needed to save the day.

All of a sudden, new life entered the picture!

Out of the West came a mild thumping sound that was getting louder and louder, causing heads to turn. Hopeful faces transformed into glee when a fast-approaching cloud of dirt could be seen. An excited Bernie Westbrook stood up first and exclaimed, "It's the Mouse!" Immediately, all stood up waving their arms frantically while cheering, as if they were marooned on an island and saw a would-be rescue ship.

The class reject who had been menacing the entire region with unequaled sound waves was now their *rock star.* William's polished white teeth glistened as his fans beckoned him to join in.

29

William Stokes looked at his past and weighed what he was most hungry for. Years of denial had him succumb to opening up the proverbial Pandora's Box that consisted of high school cliques. It was time to discover what he *really* missed out on. The tiny male with the super truck and outfit to match did the only thing he could do: he picked the *popularity route*. It was as if he were a sunburn victim in the desert and had found an Aloe Vera plant.

It was now William time!

◀◀ ◀◀ ▶▶ ▶▶

Back in town, Ric Bratton was in the process of leaving a message on William's cell phone. It would be an invitation to watch a few Roy Rogers reruns with popcorn and hot chocolate. The offer was capped off by: *"We'll play charades later!"*

◀◀ ◀◀ ▶▶ ▶▶

William Randall Stokes IV was now straddling the fence socially, but for how long? He would periodically keep in the loop at the famed general store while cavorting with his new friends when away, a combination that could *never* mix. Eventually, the young man was faced with a fork in the river and had to make a choice.

Jaded by the newness of being accepted by the very crowd that used to torment him, William drew the short straw first. The adult half of Hangman knew that this was just a phase that he should recover from. In the meantime, they patiently waited for his return and prayed. "He's just being a dumb kid," commented Alvin.

On occasion, *The Mouse* could be seen with his vehicle resembling an old phone booth, containing as many bodies as humanly possible. Teenage fun that was greatly enhanced by having everyone forced to hear their presence.

There were times when William thought he was happy, knowing that *he finally fit in*. Deep inside, his conscious mind felt quite the contrary and begged to differ. Guilty feelings churned his stomach when familiar faces watched him parade through town *with the wrong crowd*. It also bothered him that his nickname had been modified to 'The Mouse'. For William, that upgrade was no upgrade at all.

30

He felt like a kid who didn't want to eat his vegetables: *When mom cleverly buries them under a sauce, he knows that they're still there!*

Subtle controversies arose when the other 'William Stokes' from the community were immediately scoffed at because they weren't good enough. Guys who were just like him and considered friends. There were also times when someone would reach over to crank up the speakers when they drove by elders. *An intentional act to show disrespect.* Often, he was talked into doing donuts in loose gravel as a way to wrongly display the power of his monster truck.

It only took a few days of this gallivanting for things to come to a head. On one of their escapades, William's close friend, Charlie Mays, was spotted walking down the sidewalk.

Charlie Mays was a wholesome boy who would graduate the following year. Despite having blond hair with blue eyes, he was practically a clone of William Stokes himself. If each wore a matching hat, they'd look identical from the back. More important, they shared some things in common: each was picked on for being too small, too kind, and too studious. It was common to see both of them having lunch together in the cafeteria – alone.

The square pegs had formed a friendship from day one, a bond of respect that would last a lifetime.

It was Brian Sherwood who spotted Charlie first and yelled, "Stop the truck!" Immediately, William hit the brakes just shy of skidding to a stop. In a split second, the all-city linebacker jumped out of the vehicle and confronted the mild-mannered student while spewing insults.

Brian then grabbed Charlie's hat off of his head and flew it like a Frisbee over a cliff. The smaller youth just stood still and remained quiet. William knew that he'd be getting the same treatment if his hat wasn't attached to a truck. This was the breaking point for him. He turned off the engine, got out – and flew his own hat over the cliff to show unity with his *real friend*. Brian looked angrily at William and said, "So, you're only a mouse after all . . ."

William had won that round by sticking to his principles. In adult fashion, he utilized the fewest words possible: "Let's get back to town." He encouraged Charlie to climb in the back with the others. In time, it was just William and Charlie riding through the vast prairie land. The same way they shared lunch when they attended school together.

William's fling with high school fame was over, but a valuable lesson was delivered in the process. One that he would carry with him throughout life.

Chapter VI

William Stokes spent the next few days alone, licking his wounds.

Ironically, his experience with the wrong crowd actually did him a service: it made him yearn to be with the *right crowd*. This in turn led him to a very important crossroads that every young man must face:

What do I want to be when I grow up?

This soul-searching trek would have him start at 'square one'. It was time to go to the general store and reach out to his *real friends*.

Initially, William was a tad bit embarrassed dropping in on Ric and the guys. Being the decent folk that they are, not one mentioned anything about his brief absence. In fact, it was as if it had never happened.

"Great to see you, William!" was Ric's greeting as he entered the store.

Friendly exchanges were made between Willliam and the regulars, who were there to hobnob over the famous coffee. The ambitious grad wasted no time and addressed his concerns about his future.

"You are being very wise," commended Ric.

"I wish I'd put thought into my future when I was your age," said a customer at the counter.

Soon, many within hearing range added their two cents' worth. Sean Bratton was in the room and, being the successful radio personality he was, *listened*. It only took a moment for a smile to slowly come across his face.

"What is it?" whispered Kara.

His mentor looked at him with a directness that undoubtedly shared the same thought. "The airwaves certainly have a way to help communities, don't they?" commented Ric.

"They most certainly do," replied the son in agreement.

"I have to agree," said Otto.

Shannon picked up on their wavelength and telegraphed great approval. Kara was right behind her and beamed with love at her man. The Bratton

family was tuned-in to one another *with a greatness in the works*.

"I'll assist you in any way possible," offered the dad.

"Count me in," said Otto.

"I appreciate that," said Sean. "When you guys give something a boost, you really give it a boost . . ."

William stared at the renowned family with a puzzled look on his face. He knew something was up, *but what?*

Within a short period of time, the news was spreading that 'Boomer Bratton' himself had been conducting job fairs throughout the state to help guide young people to a rewarding career. His traditional live radio broadcasts given at fairgrounds and community centers drew many near and far.

Hangman was just added to his tour!

⏪ ⏪ ⏩ ⏩

Within two weeks, the sleepy town was highly populated, with the center of activity being conducted at the rodeo grounds. Several bands, along with vendors and representatives from many trades, made their presence known. Most of all, *Boomer* was on the air playing great music, announcing the latest news, and randomly sharing the microphone with anyone within reach. Electricity filled the air!

William not only attended that weekend's spectacle; he volunteered to help set it up. The two days of entertainment and presentations helped hundreds find a direction in life. It also gave praise to that very small, all-American town that personified the values this great country was built on.

When the festival was packed up and put away, Judge Alvin asked William a question. "Well, what did you think about all of that?"

William was like a child who'd just attended his first circus. He stared off into infinity as he mentioned one display after another that grabbed his interest. Trades that ranged from computers to long-haul trucking. "Anything specific that called out to you?" asked Alvin.

A blank facial expression covered the face that had no whiskers. The young man slowly turned and looked at Alvin with no answer. The good judge was ready and delivered his Sunday punch. "Hey, have you eaten yet?" he asked.

"I'm starving!" replied William.

"Great!" he exclaimed. "I know of a place where people like us can find what we're searching for—and the food isn't too bad, either . . ."

For some reason a tingling sensation began to ring throughout William's entire body. It was as if Alvin was taking him to an enchanted place *that would forever change his life.*

True, the judge *did* have an ace up his sleeve. He knew that the local church always held a Sunday evening open house. It was a gathering to meet interesting people and learn about the many programs the church was involved with. It also featured an array of food that included desserts and beverages.

It was a given that the young man searching for a meaningful direction would do the driving, with Alvin navigating. Within a short period of time, the spiritual landmark came into view as Alvin winked at the driver. William's unexplainable inner peace began to surge off the charts. It was like a metal detector that increased in intensity as it neared priceless coins.

"We'll get all of our answers right here," said Alvin as William parked his truck.

"Let me comb my hair first," said William. He leaned over Alvin to open his glove box, where such things were kept. Reaching in, he felt a gift that was recently forgot about. It was the Bible that Blaine Wolf had given him: a gift that would *lead him down the right path.*

"Well, look at that!" Alvin pointed out. "Those things certainly have a way of guiding us."

How right he was . . .

Once inside, they were immediately greeted by Pastor John. "Welcome, my brother!" exclaimed the good man as he spread out his arms. A group hug was initiated as the red carpet treatment continued.

William felt a tapping on his shoulder and turned around. It was his lifelong friend, Charlie Mays. "I knew I'd find you here!" exclaimed Charlie. Soon others emerged around William and Alvin as the jubilation escalated. In time, the entire room was in line at the buffet table. Everything from casseroles and salads, to cider and apple pie was staring at them!

After dinner, all were channeled to the auditorium to visit booths that displayed specific causes. Later would come a series of slideshows, films and guest speakers who traveled from near and far. It was all a conglomeration of spiritual programs designed to help those less fortunate, while spreading the goodwill of our Lord.

The Bible that Blaine Wolf had given him worked like a charm! *It brought the lost boy to God the Almighty Himself.*

It was that evening when William felt an *epiphany.* He could relate to everything he witnessed and believed in. It then occurred to him that he wanted to get more than just involved. He felt compelled to dedicate his life to being a soldier of God!

William Randall Stokes IV had undeniably received his *calling* that evening. He would now direct his life to serving our Lord.

Chapter VII

The following week had William spending most of his time at church. Volunteering by day; Bible study at night.

Throughout the community, the enlightened teen was frequently spotted assisting seniors, visiting the local hospital, and wearing a smile on his face. His merit had promoted him to becoming the talk of the town *in a more favorable light*. Even Amber Johansson had taken a closer look at him.

William Randal Stokes IV: *the boy at recent church functions who didn't even notice her . . .*

It was apparent that young William Stokes' stock was skyrocketing. Slowly, he was being slated as an eligible bachelor in the town of Hangman.

Like all women, Amber possessed an unfair amount of arsenal which constituted unfair play. Realizing that soon there would be an entire parish of single women competing for him, *she declared war!*

The following month had the prized beauty hitchhiking—just before the glossy truck rounded the corner where she stood.

"Amber, it's great to see you!" William cried out. "Hop in!"

Despite showing respect, she could detect that he seemed to have lost some of his interest. "Thanks for giving me a ride," she would comment.

At church she would approach him and compliment on the great job he was doing. Again, he expressed appreciation while diligently focusing on his task.

There were Bible studies where he often sat by someone else who was new to the program.

Amber was aware that she wasn't being rejected for another woman. She knew that it was because he was being consumed by his faith. *Her man* was simply honing in on how he could serve best.

The following day, William accepted an offer to have a picnic with Amber. It would be at the little park in the town square. "Great!" he responded.

Just as Amber set the picnic table, a car drove by with its occupants screaming out, "Mouse!" *It was the guys he used to drive with.*

"Don't pay any attention to that," she said.

"I love it," exclaimed William. "Don't you see; the Lord has them following me. In His fine time, *they'll be sitting with us in church."*

How right he was: such an event *would* take place in the future.

Amber could only love him more.

They spent the afternoon walking through town while looking at shops and bumping into friends. Innocently, someone would call William, *Mouse.* He would shrug it off, knowing that they meant no harm by it. Deep inside, it matched a set of fingernails scratching a chalkboard.

Finally, the day arrived when he hit the nail on the head: *William Randall Stokes IV realized that he was meant to become a pastor!* Upon that revelation, he immediately contacted Pastor John. "I knew that the day we first met," remarked the pastor.

It was time for round one of the celebrated announcement. The famous general store would be *Pastor Stokes'* first stop.

"I'm so proud of you!" exclaimed Ric with a bear hug that brought tears.

"You're my kind of guy!" exclaimed Alvin Wong.

"Seeeee," exclaimed Blaine Wolf as he pointed at him. "Didn't I tell ya that your Bible would guide you!"

"I see it!" cried out Shannon as she hugged William.

Sean, Kara, Otto, and all present were elated by the news. One by one, each hugged the devoted soul who always graced them.

An hour later, the jubilation died down with the shop returning to automatic mode. Normal topics came into play, like the day's grain report and the construction going on a block away. On occasion, a joke would filter in.

It was around that time when Alvin noticed William staring down at a table, deep in thought. His facial expression showed signs of a problem. "Okay," said Alvin as he patted William on the head. "Out with it."

Looking up to the man who always brought magic, the pastor-to-be didn't hold back. "You guys probably don't know about this, but throughout my life I've been called a name I don't like . . ."

"You mean *Mouse?*" replied Ric.

"That's the one," answered William after a long pause.

"William," called out Shannon. "A nickname usually isn't a bad thing. Even if it seems a bit insulting, they are actually a form of distinction that carries a respect with it."

Alvin went to bat. "My ruling is in favor of Shannon!" he injected. "Want to hear the nickname I got as a kid?"

All eyes were on Alvin with an anticipation of humor. Using a clean white towel he found on Ric's counter, he covered his head. Next, he did his imitation of a baby in a stroller looking up. "My mother always thought that I was cute like a blueberry ready to be picked. Guess what she kept calling me in front of all my friends, long after I was out of diapers?" he challenged. Alvin then got on his knees, looked up and cried like a baby.

The room broke out with laughter.

Standing up, he took off the towel and continued. "You know what?" he asked. "In time it got shortened to *blue,* and I liked it! Mom will always love me—and my friends mean well!"

The comical judge finished by saying, "There!" Next he held his arms to his side and bowed in all four directions.

How could anyone not love Judge Alvin? He received a standing ovation that lasted over a minute.

Blaine Wolf went next. "Long ago when I was in grade school, a group of hippies were making fun of me because I was different and wore my cowboy hat. It really bothered me when they called me *Tex,* making matters worse . . ." The big man took a deep breath, as if he were at an AA meeting sharing his story.

"When I told my parents about it, they praised the name. They pointed out that whether or not I liked those guys, they'd just associated me with the origin of this great country. From there, they named many famous Americans with that same nickname. They even pointed out country western stars and great athletes! I began to like that name—a lot!"

Sean weighed in: "Boomer Bratton here."

The shop had many disclose their nicknames, and a few volunteering their *pet name.*

"It's all a special form of tribute," explained Kara.

"Let's get to yours," said Ric. "Don't you have friends and acquaintances that have called you that name a few times?"

William digested what Ric was getting at. Things were beginning to fit together, with William sitting up straight and answering with a smile on his face. "Most people who called me that were actually friends who didn't know that it bothered me."

"Because they are comfortable with it and like you?" questioned Shannon. The comment registered deep, causing William to gleam a bit.

The name 'Mouse' was starting to sound *not too bad . . .*

Throughout the store, everyone stressed that the name carried a noble tone to it. "They are meek and always reliable," added Otto.

It was Alvin who best summarized what a nickname meant in Hangman. "Hey, I got one for you," he said. "Haven't you noticed that it's only the older half of this town who carry nicknames? It's never the younger crowd. *It only exists right here—with us!*

William looked around the entire room and saw friends who'd earned nicknames throughout their lives—*and he was one of them!*

Chapter VIII

News spread throughout the valley that Hangman had a popular pastor in the making. Church attendance was not only up, but an extra Sunday mass was added to fill the demand. Weekday family gatherings intensified, as did Bible classes and baptisms.

It would be an understatement to say that William Stokes had a busy schedule. He was even taking the mandatory classes needed to get ordained. He was definitely burning the candle at both ends—*and loving it*.

Amber Johansson was proud of the man who had committed to our Lord. A career decision she was about to make . . .

◀◀ ◀◀ ▶▶ ▶▶

One evening, Amber offered to cook dinner for William and just have a quiet evening together. He accepted.

That evening the young man noticed how beautiful his high school crush was. He also realized how much she admired him. A point in time was reached when the woman he once prayed for *addressed him* about having a family. A marriage that would be dedicated to their faith while serving our Creator.

"We have a start," his would-be wife pointed out. "You already have a truck."

"I hate that truck!" he said. "I am getting paid as a full-time staff member for the church. My goal is to buy a simple car with *my* money, and let the church raffle off that loud piece of metal. That is, after I remove the sound system from it!"

Amber was further impressed.

William's life seemed to momentarily pass in front of him like a man drowning in holy water. He was relieved to have survived the early stages of his life and the horror stories that accompanied it. William Stokes was now at the opposite end of the spectrum. He was in God's favor, with the most beautiful creature he'd ever known. *A blessing for being faithful through thick and thin.*

William knew that the entire county respected Amber and began to realize how fortunate he really was. He thought about his many friends at the general store and how much they liked her. It was all 'perfect'.

Amber's patience was beginning to wear a little thin. Hugging her man, she popped the question. "Well, how about it, William? Could you accept a life with me?" She then gave him the first of many kisses.

What else could our hero say at a time like that?

He looked at his wife-to-be and said:

"Call me Mouse!"

Lauratown and Other Short Stories

About this Collection

Lauratown And Other Short Stories is a collection of writings by author Matt Shea.

The theme story, Lauratown, is about the town's oldest senior taking the County Assessor to an overgrown trail leading to the ruins she once called home.

Laura O'Shea is the *Dorthy Gale* of the valley and relives a battle that initially put them on the map with national recognition. A display of courage and faith that resulted in a town being named after her.

In time, newer surrounding communities attracted droves of people. From there, little Lauratown was eventually cut off from the main stream and left to die. Overgrown and abandoned, the senior approaching age one hundred has a final visit to where she grew up. It is there where she gets an enlightenment that intensifies the fire in her soul. This spiritual phenomenon unites Laura with her past — confirming her faith.

Dedication

I have the blessing of being a father and, equally important, a dad. My one and only child, Laura, has always encouraged me and is my number one fan in life. As mentioned in my past books and interviews, Laura bought me a state-of-the-art computer when I retired. This was done so that I could pursue my dream of becoming an author. She would entice me to read my stories to her and constantly build my confidence. In time, with a lot of effort and her support, this dad made it!

Thank you, Laura, once again for inspiring me. You are not only my daughter, you are also a special friend. There were many nights when you took me out or called just to see how I was doing.

Laura, I dedicate this book to you. *You are 'Lauratown'!* Love, dad.

Laura Shea with her dad, Matt Shea.

Old People

Lauratown

County Assessor Kris Wills was faced with a harsh decision. Heavily populated towns needed to expand their territories. This would hinge on whether it was justifiable to extend their boundaries over the few ghost towns that they neighbored. These abandoned homesteads held much history that the current cities spawned from. The middle-aged man in wire-rimmed glasses was searching for past residents from these forgotten communities. He would interview them to understand what significance their town had.

His quest would have him meet the county's oldest citizen, Laura O'Shea. Laura was the sole survivor from the town she was raised in. This ninety-six-year-old was bright, spunky and had a story.

The letter addressed to Laura O'Shea had an immediate response. She was more than happy to meet with the County Assessor and verify the territory she once knew as home. The letter included her phone number and address. Kris called her upon opening the letter.

The assessor dialed the ten-digit number and connected with an operator. A happy voice answered with a cheerful greeting. "Golden Hills Retirement Home."

"Hello!" Kris acknowledged. "I would like to talk to Laura O'Shea."

"One moment, please," said the operator as she transferred the call. The phone rang twice and was answered.

"Hello," called out the voice of an aging woman.

"Good morning," said Kris. "Is this Laura O'Shea I am talking to?"

"Yes it is," answered the woman.

"I am, Kris Wills, your County Assessor," he replied. "I was happy to receive your letter and would like to coordinate a visit. We can go to the town you grew up in to verify if it is, indeed, 'Lauratown'. I will also need you to share that town's history. It has been abandoned for years and is subject to annexation. This would probably erase the town's name altogether."

There was a long pause, and then came her answer. "I would like that very much," she said.

"I appreciate that," exclaimed Kris. "Could you let me know when it would be a good time for us to do this?" he asked.

Without hesitation she said, "How about right now?"

Kris was overwhelmed. He detected a lot of character in this senior. "Well, great!" he said. "I can arrive at your residence this morning at eleven o'clock. We have vans for senior citizens that cater to wheelchairs; you'll be in good hands."

Laura O'Shea gave a quick response. "That won't be necessary. I can walk just fine, thank you."

The woman was feisty and Kris loved it!

The day was perfect for this field trip. The sun was shining, with a few scattered clouds. It would be warm enough for the scouting, but not too hot. The assessor, who always wore a white shirt with black pants and suspenders, canceled all appointments for the rest of the day. He donned his hat and went to the parking lot to meet history. The bleach-white vehicle with state emblems on the doors found its way to the Golden Hills Retirement Home. Kris pulled into the home's valet parking stall that was directly in front of the main entrance.

51

He then saw something that would stay in his mind forever. Just beyond the automatic doors was an elderly woman with piercing blue eyes. She wore a beige outfit with a matching straw hat that suggested a safari. Her facial expression showed dignity as she marched up to the truck. Kris smiled in amazement as he rolled down his window. The woman stood next to the driver's side door, looking at Kris. She spoke, "Laura O'Shea, at your service!"

Kris grinned at her spirit and knew that he could treat her like a regular guy. "Well, get in here!" he volleyed back. "Let me open the door for you."

"That's quite all right," she said, "I'll get it myself." The ninety-six-year-old woman took her time walking around the van and proceeded to get in. Once inside, she closed the door and fastened her seat belt.

Kris marveled at her and extended his hand. "Kris Wills," he announced. "Pleased to meet you!"

"Laura O'Shea," replied the passenger as she shook hands. "The feeling's the same."

Kris put the vehicle in drive, and the journey began.

The assessor initiated a conversation. "According to our records, you are the oldest person living in this county."

"But I'm not that old," replied the quick-witted woman.

"I have to agree with that!" said Kris. He then changed subjects to address business. "This morning I studied the map to find Lauratown. I am a bit confused because apparently, there are no signs leading to it. Maybe you can direct me there."

The elder spoke, "Drive down Main Street, and take a right on Prosser. From there, drive straight until you leave the city limits. You will travel about a half-mile and will notice an overgrown field on the right. There will be a set of tire marks that are almost hidden under the tall grass. That road leads to Lauratown."

They drove to the outskirts of town. Kris found the desolate trail that Laura described. It cut through the dry plains and dissipated over a hill. He turned a sharp right, leaving the asphalt behind; continuing on yesterday's dirt road. Kris Wills drove slowly for about a mile. He approached the remnants of a wooden shack that was once someone's home. "We're here," said Laura.

He came to a stop and studied the county's first map.

Memories danced in Laura's head as she spotted a tattered rope hanging from an oak tree. "I used to play on that tree," she said.

"Do you get out here often?" asked Kris.

"Not as much as I used to," replied Laura.

"When I do, it's to visit the cemetery."

Laura motioned Kris to a dirt path that led down an embankment. Together they took the brief walk that unveiled Laura O'Shea's past. What Kris Wills saw made his jaw drop.

It was a rustic, abandoned homestead from last century. Tall grass, overgrown bushes and the wicked branches from a dried-up orchard hid this once-mighty town. Creases in tall, wavy grass revealed where a road once was. Its few wooden structures bent with the contour of the ground as a traditional windmill peered over the isolated territory. Empty grain silos gave tell-tale signs of yesterday's prosperity. A rusted water tower bearing the town's name stood, proud defying time. The outskirts of this ghost town had a crudely maintained, fenced-in lot with monuments. This was home for everyone who had ever lived there; everyone except one.

Kris surveyed the ancient civilization and gave a long whistle. He felt an aura that surrounded Lauratown. Despite being a town of yesterday, there still seemed to be spirit here. Kris's eyes followed the indentations that passed through the vacant main street. Traveling west, they rolled over a hill and united with Prosser Street. At one time, the town of Prosser did exist. In the opposite direction, the hidden path led to the outskirts of the Mule Shopping Center. The town of Mule once neighbored Lauratown.

Kris Wilds looked at Laura O'Shea. Her gray hair waved slightly in the gentle breeze as her weathered face broke into a smile. She walked toward a small, condemned two-story house. It listed slightly to one side, with the doors and windows missing. Faded white paint had surrendered to the elements years ago. Wooden steps led to a deteriorated porch that had tall grass growing between its decking. Next to the structure leaned a wooden post that held a dilapidated mailbox.

She sat down on the steps and said, "I was born in this house."

"It looks like there was a battle here," said Kris.

"There was," replied Laura.

Kris looked at Laura and asked, "Well, tell me; who won?"

Laura turned and looked at Kris. With enthusiasm, she said, "We did!"

◄◄ ◄◄ ►► ►►

A windmill spun from the Frontier Valley breeze, pumping precious water. Acres and acres of farmland covered these rolling hills, where the O'Shea family survived. The freedom of this American homestead was alive, but being challenged.

The family land was being threatened by an emerging small town. There was a conflict in the making that would control the water and roads in this valley.

The decisive battle would be over the location of new grain silos. The government accessed the grain reports in that area and vowed to create a central terminal in that state. It appeared that Frontier Valley would be the most likely choice, being in the middle of the state. But where?

A young girl in dark brown pigtails bends over to pick up raspberries. A straw hat shields her from the sun as she carefully inspects every berry. The coveted berries would be the key ingredient for a raspberry cobbler that her family was famous for. It even won a blue ribbon at the county fair. Her loyal female companion, Luca, stands nearby wagging her tail.

This was the O'Shea farm, and eleven-year-old Laura was proud. They were known for feeding travelers and assisting those who wanted to settle down in that peaceful valley. Soon, she would have to join the fight to keep their dream.

A masculine voice broke the tranquility. It was her father, Mathew O'Shea. The Paul Bunyan sized country man in blue coveralls leaned out the front door of their home. "Laura," he called, "the Grain Report is about to start. Do you want to listen to it with us?"

Laura hastily picked up the pail of raspberries and ran to the house, with her dog following. Upon entering the living room, she took off her straw hat and handed the pail to her mother. The room was silent as the family of three sat at the dinner table to listen to the radio. The familiar music theme for the Grain Report began to play. The family all stared at one another with excitement. Then came the announcer:

"Live from New York City, The American Grain Report featuring Sam Rockford!"

The host of the broadcast began to speak. It was none other than Sam Rockford himself, Chairman of the National Agricultural Department. "Good morning to the American farmer, this is Sam Rockford."

The Grain Report gave hope to their homestead. It was a nationwide report that reached out to their humble farm. Sam Rockford was their guiding light. He gave the progress of American farmlands across the country and told which crops were in the most demand. Every farmer listened to Sam's reports and plotted their course.

There was a special surprise on this week's report. A decision was made to honor the productivity in Frontier Valley. High yields, along with an increasing population, drew attention. The Agricultural Department voted to place grain silos in that area, as a way to centralize the many harvests. This would bring in more buyers and encourage more farming. A radio telecast was scheduled to transmit from the City of Baxter to New York the following day.

The town of Baxter was almost fifty miles away, where the county's public auctions took place. It also had a courthouse and other public services. There would be a debate from various towns with many representatives. They would all lobby to be home for the grain silos.

The O'Shea family was overjoyed with the news. The painstaking work of farming in that valley was finally recognized.

Mathew O'Shea turned off the radio and heard Luca barking. He looked out the window and saw a car traveling down their road. A closer look revealed that it was Father Grechin, the most beloved man in the entire valley.

He visited every home in that region. It seemed that he had a special liking for the O'Shea family, always making them his last stop. He usually brought a gift when he came by and often stayed the entire evening. Sometimes, he even stayed the night, like family. Laura loved to hear Father Grechin's stories. He even allowed her to wear the necklace that held his crucifix whenever he came to visit.

The Father's car parked in front of the house. Mr. O'Shea opened the door as the holy man got out of his vehicle. Luca ran up to Father Grechin and stood up on two hind legs, extending paws on the Father's waist. Luca's smile showed every tooth as her tail wagged violently. The visitor resembled Santa Claus. The short, heavyset man with the jolly laughter looked down at the affectionate animal and scratched the dog's head. He looked over at Mathew and gave his signature wave.

"Well, this is a wonderful surprise, Father!" said Mathew O'Shea.

"Good afternoon, Mathew," said the Father. "Now where is that precious daughter of yours?"

Laura ran out of the house with her mother following. "Father!" she cried out. "It's so good to see you!"

Father Grechin replied, "It's always good to see you!"

"Father, we'd love to have you for dinner, and please stay the night!" said Mrs. O'Shea.

Laura's face lit up as she raced toward Father Grechin. "Please, Father! Please stay with us tonight!"exclaimed the little girl.

"We'd love to have you," said Mathew.

The proud Father looked at the family and said, "I'd love to."

Laura cheered, "Yeah!" as she hugged the holy man. Luca barked with excitement as the happy dog jumped in circles.

Father took off the necklace that held his crucifix and placed it around Laura's neck. "Why don't you wear this while I stay here?" he said.

Laura stared at the crucifix in awe. She was honored. "Thank you, Father," she said. "I promise to take care of it."

Father Grechin continued, "I also have something for you." He unzipped his jacket and reached inside. A paper bag was exposed as he handed it to Laura. The little girl's eyes lit up with excitement. "This is something special that I made myself. I want you to have it," said Father. "Go ahead and open it."

Laura opened the bag and put her hand inside. She felt a soft, spongy object. With enthusiasm she pulled out the gift. It was a doll made out of old cloth; just right for cuddling. Laura held the doll with both hands as its Raggedy Anne smile looked back. The little girl hugged her new friend and said, "Thank you, Father!"

"I had old patches that I just couldn't throw out, and then I thought of you," said Father.

"What are you going to name her?" he asked.

"Patches!" cried out Laura.

The parents gleamed at their daughter; they had never seen her so happy.

Mrs. O'Shea said, "I'll get dinner started."

"I'll help you, Mom, after I feed Luca," volunteered Laura. Together they turned to enter the house. Luca's dog house was next to the front porch. Laura picked up the shiny metal bowls that lay in front of the small structure, signaling her dog that it was time to eat. Luca positioned in front of the tiny home in anticipation.

Mathew O'Shea was now alone with Father Grechin. "You certainly are a blessing," he said.

"I am only serving our Lord," replied Father. He then changed subjects. "There are rumors floating around that this valley is in competition to accommodate new grain silos."

"That's true," said Mathew. "We just heard that news on the grain report."

Father looked at Mathew with a concerned look. "There is more to the rumor than that. Your neighbor, Greg Mules, wants those silos on his property. As you know, he is trying to control this entire valley. Word has it that he will be in Baxter tomorrow to actually talk on the radio with Sam Rockford. I have a funny feeling about this."

Mathew shook his head in disapproval. "So do I," he commented.

Mathew digested the information. He then looked at Father's car and was reminded of something. "Oh, Father, before I forget; we have

extra produce from our garden that can feed the hungry families you visit," he suggested.

Father's face lit up with a huge grin. "Mathew, you have no idea how much help that would be. Most families I visit are struggling. How much do you have?" he asked.

"Enough to fill your entire car, and then some!" he said with pride.

Father's face contorted as he thought. "Do you mind if I leave a few personal belongings here to get maximum capacity out of my car?" he asked. "I can spend this week delivering to the needy."

"We can place all your items in our barn for as long as you need," said Mathew. "That's where the produce is. Why don't you back your car up to our barn, and we can get this chore out of the way?"

"Bless you, son," said Father.

Mathew walked to a post that held a mailbox. He opened the box and reached in with one hand. He seemed to be pulling on something. Then he removed a piece of wood that was cut to the same squareness of the mail box. It was obviously a barricade to hide a hidden compartment inside the mail box. Reaching in a little further, he pulled out a sealed coffee tin. He opened the container and grabbed the set of keys that it held. Looking at Father, he waved the keys and said, "I'll open the barn doors." Father entered his car as Mathew walked across the dirt road and unlocked the mammoth doors, swinging them open.

Father Grechin drove to the open doors and backed up his car. He parked, got out and opened the trunk. Laura noticed the activity when she brought dinner to Luca. She walked to the barn and saw Father carrying a large metal box with wires.

"You can put that right here," said Mathew O'Shea as he pointed at a table.

"What is that?" asked Laura.

Father Grechin placed the bulky object on top of the table. He looked at Laura and explained. "I received a gift from the University this week," said Father. "It's an abandoned science project. They attempted to build their own transmitter that would have the capacity to communicate across this country. Hundreds of hours that involved hundreds of students were spent on this project. They just couldn't get it to work. I asked if I could have it to use for my sermons. It would serve as an example to illustrate how prayer is always transmitted to the Lord. They gladly gave it to me, and commented that at least it could serve a good purpose somewhere."

Laura was in awe. Science was always her favorite subject in school. She was fascinated by radios and wanted to know more about transmitters. She asked, "If it did work, what else would be needed to transmit across the country?"

Father Grechin replied, "All it would need would be an electric current and a tower to transmit from."

"A tower?" asked a puzzled Laura.

"Yes, a tower that's at least as tall as your barn," said the Father. "The tower will act as an antenna. The higher it is, the further you can transmit." He then turned the

Matt Shea

transmitter around, showing the back side. He pointed at a black- coated wire that exited the back panel. "This wire needs to be connected to a transmitter tower. They even gave me a spool of wire that could be used as an extension."

Next he pointed at a much longer cord with an electric plug. "This is your power source. All you have to do is plug it into a wall socket." He held up a microphone that was fastened to a cord. "This is how you transmit. You turn it on here," he said as he touched a knob on the front of the transmitter. "This knob also controls the volume." There was a dial next to it that was four inches in diameter. He placed his hand on the dial and turned it back and forth. "This dial is used to find the proper frequency to hear the transmission from a radio trying to communicate with you. You keep turning the dial until you can receive their transmission. When you do," he then picked up the microphone. "You simply press the red button on the side of this and speak through the microphone. You release it to listen. It's that simple!" he said.

Laura glared at this modern technology. She continued to ask more questions. "What is a tower made out of?"

"Metal, just like any radio antenna," said Father.

"Do you mind if I play with it?" she asked.

"Why, sure, I don't see any problem with that," he said. "Maybe God wanted you to have it," laughed Father.

Laura stared at the transmitter and started to think . . .

Mrs. O'Shea was on the front porch. She wore the same yellow dress every day, with her brown hair tied up in a bun. "Dinner will be ready in ten minutes," she called out.

The hungry men looked at each other with eagerness. "That will give us enough time to load your car and wash our hands," said Mathew. They began to place baskets of corn, squash, peas and carrots in the automobile. Soon they entered the house with the aroma of a home-cooked meal greeting them. They entered the bathroom and washed their hands. Moments later, all were seated at the dinner table, with the reverent Father leading grace.

A country dinner was prepared from what their farm produced; the fruits of their labor. Fried chicken, warm bread with butter, corn, peas, carrots, and mashed potatoes with rich brown gravy covered white porcelain plates. A glass of fresh milk accompanied each plate. Father Grechin commented, "This is the greatest family to have dinner with, and the food is excellent!"

The conversation rotated with Mrs. O'Shea discussing her quilting circle, Laura talking about school, and Father sharing the goals their church had. Mathew watched with satisfaction as his household shared another rewarding evening. Soon, Mathew O'Shea brought up the controversy with Greg Mules.

"Father," said Mathew. "I am aware that it is wrong to judge others, but I cannot trust Greg Mules."

"I can't blame you for that," said Father. "I don't trust him either." Father took a bite of chicken and continued. "The impression I get is that he wants to have the silos on his property as a way to control the valley, and us."

"That's exactly how I see it," said Mathew. "If he can pull that off, we will all be at his mercy. I have a hard enough time driving by his farm. He tries to tell me that he owns the roads there and that I need his permission to travel off my property. Those are county roads." Mathew looked at Father Grechin and continued. "He even says that he can block the streams that travel through his property toward ours."

Father Grechin dropped his fork with disgust and leaned back in his chair. "That man needs to be stopped," he said.

Mrs. O'Shea stood up and spoke in a loud voice. "Well, someone needs to do something. Tomorrow's Grain Report will be his opportunity, and he'll probably succeed!" The mother regained her composure and sat back down.

Laura was frightened. "What can we do?" she asked.

All eyes were on Father Grechin. "We will do what we always do in a time of crisis; we'll pray and ask God for direction." All hands united with heads bowed. Father spoke out to the Lord and asked for His intervention.

The tempo changed to a happier feeling. "Is anyone ready for dessert?" asked a cheerful Mrs. O'Shea.

"If it's that incredible raspberry cobbler you are known for, I'm ready right now!" said Father.

"Coming right up!" snapped Mrs. O'Shea.

"Laura," called out her dad. "Would you mind helping your mother and clearing the table?"

"I'd love to, Dad," replied the daughter. "I'll also make a pot of coffee." She then excused herself from the table, kissed her father on the cheek and went to the kitchen.

"Father Grechin looked toward the kitchen and remarked, "You certainly are a lucky man."

Mathew agreed and said, "I am a *very* lucky man, Father."

The evening continued as the foursome enjoyed the award-winning cobbler. Plans for the following morning were being discussed. Father would have church services in the morning. It was agreed that they would have an early breakfast and leave for church together. After the services, they would return and listen to the noon grain report.

It was soon bedtime for Laura as she went to her room with Patches and changed into her pajamas. Her mother tucked her in bed as they said their goodnight prayers. The mother turned out the lights and left the room, closing the door behind her.

Laura was in deep thought as she held her doll. She wondered if all the effort building the transmitter had it close to actually working. Maybe very close. If a simple cure could get the transmitter to work, and if it could be connected to a metal tower, their farm could be represented on tomorrow's Grain Report. She prayed for an answer as she clutched Patches and Father's crucifix. The little farm girl tossed and turned all night, as if she was discussing the matter with God Himself.

Daybreak cast its golden rays through Laura's bedroom window as she rubbed the sleep out of her eyes. It was another glorious morning, as the gift of life continued. The young girl was still in thought about the upcoming grain report. She needed the transmitter to work, and a tower to transmit from.

She followed her morning routine by opening her bedroom window and breathing in the fresh country air. There before her was the solution to one of her problems.

God's magnificent sun gave the answer. It was rising above the windmill. This was a tall tower made out of metal; the highest peak on their farm! A graceful combination of sun and mild breeze comforted her face. It was unmistakably a simple answer directed by God Himself.

The little girl grinned at the sight, nodding with a spiritual understanding. Laura looked up to the clear sky, knowing that her prayer was heard. She looked down at Father Grechin's crucifix. It was still on the necklace she wore to bed. Using both hands, Laura held the cross and kissed it.

Laura changed her clothes and ran to the barn with Luca following. She inspected the antenna wire from the back of the transmitter and looked at the spool of wire resting next to it. She noticed that the spool had a small metal clamp on the end of it. She clamped the metal teeth on the antenna wire that went inside the transmitter. She pointed her index fingers toward one another, pinching the spool in the middle. Slowly, Laura walked backwards to the windmill that was fifteen feet away as her dog looked with curiosity. Just as the spool emptied itself, she was leaning up against the windmill. The end of the wire also had the same metal clamp. It barely reached the closest pole of the sturdy frame; as if it was meant to be there. With ease, she clamped it on. Phase one was complete.

Laura could then hear her mother calling out. "Laura, if you can hear me, breakfast is ready."

"I'll be there in a minute," she yelled back. "Let me feed Luca first." The smell of bacon enhanced the entire home as Laura ran to the dog house and retrieved the metal bowls. In a minute she returned with Luca's breakfast and placed the meal in front of the dog house. The dog buried its head and silently devoured the food as Laura ran into the house and joined everyone at the breakfast table.

"Did you sleep good last night?" asked Father.

"Yes I did," said Laura. "Did you?" she asked.

"I did when I finally went to sleep," said the holy man. "I stayed up late last night and wrote my sermon for today. I think that you will like it," he said.

"We like all of them," said Mathew.

Breakfast was a continuation of last night's dinner. Everything was farm-fresh—bacon, eggs, toast, raspberry jam, and milk.

"This is delicious," said father Grechin. "Around here, you don't have to buy anything at the grocery store; it's all right here!"

"That's how we like it," said Mathew. "Laura," said her dad. "It's important that you help your mother clean up after breakfast. We need to get ready and take Father Grechin to church as soon as possible."

"Don't worry about me, Dad," replied Laura. "I'd never make anyone late for church!"

Within twenty minutes, the meal was devoured, everything was cleaned and the family was dressed for church. Mathew locked the front door to the house as the family waited in their car. "The drive to church is only a half-hour away," said Mathew as he sat in the driver's seat and closed the door.

Father Grechin looked at his watch and said, "That gives me plenty of time."

Mathew O'Shea started the car and drove towards their destination. A lonely dog barked as it trotted down the middle of the road. Soon, its ears dropped with disappointment as the car drove out of sight. A dust haze from the dirt road was all that was left. Luca digested the abandonment. The dog slowly walked back to the farm with a lowered head and motionless tail.

The O'Shea family eventually arrived at church, giving Father Grechin enough time to prepare for the services. Laura removed the crucifix from her neck and handed it to

Father Grechin. "Thank you, Father, for letting me wear this," she said.

"That's quite all right," Father replied. He then left the car to enter the rectory.

The O'Shea family was early and entered the building. They walked up the aisle to the front pews and sat down. The sanctuary was full when the services were about to begin.

Father was in control as he entered the altar. He performed the rituals of their faith and read scriptures from the Bible. Then it was time for his sermon. He spoke about how each person has an independent mission for God. "We all have a calling to do extra work for the Lord, outside of church," he said. "Sometimes we feel all alone. We must always pray to ask for help in these situations."

Laura could relate to that feeling. The early morning sun assisted God in helping her. Still, she needed more help. Father reminded everyone that prayer is always heard and will always lead us to the answers we need to further serve the Lord. Laura bowed her head with the understanding and prayed for more guidance.

Church let out with Father Grechin visiting the parishioners in the lobby. He spoke to Mathew and said, "When I am finished, I will change and meet you in the parking lot."

"Okay, Father," said Mathew O'Shea. "By the way, that was a great sermon you gave today." Mathew extended his hand to shake Father's.

"I am glad you liked it," replied Father Grechin as he shook Mathew's hand.

It was eleven-fifteen in the morning as Mathew O'Shea drove his car back to their farm.

While driving the final hundred yards, the family car was being charged by a four-legged, dark-furred object with its ears pinned back. Glossy black eyes with an open mouth ran full bore at them. A pink tongue waved in the air like a neck tie in the wind. A wagging tail signaled friendly fire. Luca had done her job: the farm was protected. More important, she missed her family.

65

The Grain Report would broadcast in fifteen minutes. Upon arriving home, Laura petted her dog and ran upstairs to change out of her clothes. She then ran downstairs to the front door, only to be stopped by Father Grechin.

"Wait a minute, Laura," he said. Father then took off his necklace with the crucifix and placed it around Laura's neck. "There," he said. "Much better!" Then he smiled at her in approval.

"Thanks, Father!" said Laura. She then went to the barn, to answer a *calling*. Luca followed her master.

Mathew walked to the dining room table, holding their radio. "I hope that today isn't doomsday," he said as he plugged the radio into an outlet. His wife and Father Grechin sat at the table, staring down in despair. The familiar music that introduced the Grain Report began to play. Sam Rockford's voice would soon follow, with every farmer in America listening.

Laura was in the barn, holding the electrical outlet for the transmitter. She looked at a beam next to the table that supported the roof and noticed an outlet at floor level. She plugged it in with no complications. It seemed that everything was fitting together perfect. Almost too perfect.

She held her breath and turned on the 'off / on' dial. It held a small amount of tension as a 'click' sound could be heard, signaling the 'on' position. Nothing happened. Laura scratched her head and jiggled the electric cord that entered the back of the component.

Immediately, glass tubes glowed to life, with a high-pitch humming noise following. Luca's face held no expression as black furry ears expanded like radar. The dog tilted its head at the strange box that produced strange noise. Laura's face lit up with excitement! She found the bridge that would connect their farm to the outside world.

Laura concentrated on the control dial, with the sounds of radio waves changing as she turned it. Dull hums, static, and a whistle ranging in pitch followed her hand movement. Then came the distinct baritone voice of Greg Mule. It was a full, crystal-clear transmission, as if he were in the same room.

" . . . and I am sure that you will like it here in Mule Town," transmitted Greg Mule.

A response came. It was the recognizable voice of the Chairman from the National Agricultural Department, Sam Rockford. "Well, that sounds interesting," he said.

Greg Mule spoke, "The towns of Mule and Prosser will yield good crops every year."

Something needed to be said to defend the O'Shea farm. Laura took a stab in the dark and picked up the handheld microphone. She pressed the lever that would allow transmission and spoke. "There is another farm between Mule and Prosser that also produces good crops."

Sam Rockford immediately responded, "Is that a little girl I am listening to?"

Like Graham Bell, Laura's experiment worked on a dry run. Laura tensed up with excitement; she was talking to New York City! She answered, "Why, yes, my name is Laura O'Shea."

Mathew O'Shea sat up and yelled, "Laura is on the radio!" Immediately, everyone got up and ran to the barn. When they entered the barn, they saw the eleven-year-old girl sitting studiously on a bench that faced the transmitter. They saw the long wire that ingenuously connected the transmitter antenna wire to the windmill. She smiled back with the microphone in her hand. Father Grechin beamed with admiration. All mouths were dropped open with wide eyes. A huge ovation followed as the little girl grinned with success.

"Well, I am pleased to meet you, Laura!" said Sam Rockford. "My name is Sam Rockford. May I ask how old you are?"

Laura spoke, "I am eleven years old, Mr. Rockford."

"Eleven years old?" questioned Sam Rockford. "I am impressed! But please, call me 'Sam', Laura."

Laura smiled and transmitted back, "Okay, Sam."

"Now, where are you located?" asked Sam.

"We are between the towns of Mule and Prosser," answered Laura.

There was a pause, then Sam spoke. "I see Mule and Prosser, but there isn't anything between them on my map."

Laura was quick to respond. "We have existed here as long as the other towns have."

Sam transmitted back. "And what is the name of your town?" he asked.

At that moment, Mathew O'Shea leaned over his daughter and yelled, "This is 'Lauratown'!"

The whole room cheered and said, "We are, 'Lauratown'!" Laura blushed with the honor. Luca joined in with a bark. Her tail wagged as the dog bounced up and down with excitement.

"Well, I'd better mark Lauratown between Mule and Prosser," replied Sam as he chuckled. "Now tell me, why would we want to set up silos in Lauratown?"

Greg Mule interrupted, "The town of Mule will have all you need, right here!"

Sam was offended by the intrusion. "Let the little girl speak," he said.

"We are the central location, not just in this valley, but for the entire county," said a calm Laura. "We also have the land you need to put whatever you want here."

Greg Mules was desperate as he interfered a second time. "We have land too, and will sell it to you at a fair price."

Laura countered, "In Lauratown, you can have all the land you need for free. We will also serve you our homemade raspberry cobbler, with our own coffee."

Sam replied in a warm tone. "Now, Laura, how did you know that raspberry cobbler is my favorite?"

"That town doesn't even have a sign leading to it, or a water tower!" blurted out Greg Mule.

"That's all right," said Sam. "According to our map, Lauratown is the central location for that entire county, and their hospitality is great! We will put a water tower there ourselves, with the town's name on it. We have chosen Lauratown to be the location for the grain silos— and that's final!"

Laura was ready to cry. She held her composure and transmitted back. "Thank you, Sam. Let us know what we can do for you."

Sam was choked up and replied, "Laura, the pleasure is mine. You have no idea how well you have just served us. We will be in Lauratown a month from now and begin construction. And I can hardly wait to taste that raspberry cobbler! Pleased to have met you, Laura."

"Please to have met you, Sam," answered Laura.

Static hissed through the speaker as Sam Rockford signed off. Laura sighed in relief and turned the transmitter off, placing the microphone on the desk. The entire room mobbed their hero in tears; Laura had officially gotten their town on the map.

"I was just fulfilling my mission for God," she said laughingly.

The next day, Mathew O'Shea drove his car toward town. As he approached the Mule farm, a lanky man in coveralls and straw hat stood in the middle of the road, stopping him. The weathered face with a twisted moustache needed no introduction. It was the unmistakable posture of Greg Mules. "Well," said Greg Mules. "I guess that pretty soon I will be calling you 'boss'."

Mr. O'Shea got a puzzled look on his face. He looked at Greg Mule and asked, "What do you mean by that?"

"The silos that are being placed on your property," said Greg Mules. "That makes you the king of this valley."

"I have to disagree with you," replied a compassionate Mathew. "Those silos will be placed here to serve this entire valley, and draw more people here. Now, more than ever, we need to work together." The big man smiled at his neighbor and extended his hand.

Greg Mules did something that he never did before. He smiled at Mathew O'Shea and took off his hat to shake hands. With a charming voice, he said, "I couldn't agree with you more!"

◀◀ ◀◀ ▶▶ ▶▶

Kris was fascinated by the story. "Did you get to meet Sam Rockford?" he asked.

"Yes I did," she replied. "They came down our road three weeks later and knocked on our front door. My dad looked out the window and shouted, "They're here!" A strange man was at the door when my father answered it. I recognized his voice when he asked if he was in Lauratown. My dad said, "Yes you are!"

He then introduced himself as Sam Rockford and asked if he could meet me. I was standing behind my dad and stepped forward. He looked down at me and said, "Sam Rockford, at your service." He gave me a big smile and shook my hand. We were then asked to join him outside. What we saw made our world stand still. There was a caravan of trucks that carried all of the parts to start up this town. A water tower with 'Lauratown' painted on the side was first in line, with the silos following in sections.

"My dad looked at the crew and said, 'You can put those anywhere you feel is best, and that land will be yours!' Dad turned to me and said, 'Laura, make a pot of coffee, and be sure to have plenty of raspberry cobbler for everyone.'"

Laura broke into a laugh and said, "You should have seen the expression on Sam Rockford's face when my dad said that!"

"There was a crew of twelve men who camped on our property until they finished their work," said Laura. "Sam Rockford told us that those silos would last about thirty years. He was right, almost to the exact day."

Laura continued, "The word was out that Lauratown was booming. People came from all over to get their life started. Soon, neighboring communities sprung up to accommodate larger populations. Eventually the county had to tap into our streams to supply their water demands. We lost most of our water with newer roads going elsewhere. We were slowly being choked off. When it was time to replace the silos, they naturally choose a more populated area. We were soon left behind and forgotten."

The old woman had told her story. She broke out from the trance of yesterday and lifted her head. Peering over the horizon, she viewed 'today'. What she saw was tall buildings, factories and freeways outside the valley. This was the offspring of their homestead. Her family's battle brought in industry that caused many to inhabit the area. This resulted in a city that became the state's central location for agricultural produce. The old woman gleamed with pride.

Laura turned and looked at her old home. She couldn't help but notice the old mailbox and felt compelled to open it. She walked up to survey its condition. The elements seemed to warp the box, sealing it on all sides. The door was concaved, with corroded hinges. Moist- rotted wood would allow easy access. The face came off as she pulled on it. She peered inside to discover that it was empty. Laura then had a revelation and remembered the secret compartment that hid the last quarter of the mailbox. Its wooden barrier was curved and loose. Laura reached in and grabbed an upper corner of the decayed wood. It crumbled as she pulled on it.

With the excitement of a child, she reached in and felt metal. She grabbed the mystery object and pulled it out. Laura's face lit up as she held the coffee tin that hid the keys to the farm. The small container was weakened from years of exposure. Its shiny exterior was now darkened with rust and flexed when held. The tarnished cylinder bulged from corrosion. She felt excess weight inside the tin and shook it. A muffled clanking sound could be heard inside.

The once tightly-sealed lid popped off like a flat bottle of champagne. She looked inside. Daylight revealed a special surprise for Laura: 'Patches' and Father Grechin's crucifix were well preserved! Laura reached in and pulled out the past. Like a child waking up on Christmas morning, she knew that she wasn't forgotten.

The old woman sighed like the little girl she always was. She held the heirlooms and marveled at them. Laura hugged the treasures and smiled toward the graceful sky.

Kris was overwhelmed. He was willing to use his position to review any case she might have. "Do you wish to protest the encroachment from neighboring towns?" he asked.

"That won't be necessary," said Laura. "We can leave now."

A compassionate Kris Wills was taken by this unselfish act. He was talking to the last resident of Lauratown, the very folk hero it was named after. He got choked up with the realization of what her battle did for the entire state. "This town will officially be off the map by next year," he whispered.

Laura looked at the outskirts of the property and saw the formation of large rocks that outlined her future burial site. The rocks supported a wooden fence that resembled a corral. She saw the grave markers accompanied by flowers she'd placed on her last visit. They wilted long ago, having fell victims to the dry heat. All was in perfect formation, except the vacant space next to her mother and father. It was obvious that she was the only one who visited, or even knew about this sacred ground.

"That cemetery is a historical landmark, which will be preserved," replied Kris. "The county will post signs giving direction to it, and the story of this town will be displayed at its entrance."

Looking down, she clutched the doll and crucifix. Her feeble body trembled as she began to cry. "Thank you," she said softly. With a slight pause, her tearful eyes looked up to the scattered clouds that shielded the heavens. Laura O'Shea continued. "This town has served its purpose, and anyone who has ever lived here has been taken care of."

The County Assessor nodded with understanding. He casually got up and walked to the truck. Laura O'Shea would now spend a few precious moments alone. It was time for her to pray, say her goodbyes, and part from the ruins.

Soon, she would return and take up permanent residency. Laura O'Shea would once again reside in Lauratown and be with her loved ones.

A day she longed for.

The Battle of Greensborough

There is nothing like a crisis that bonds people together. The unity created when a community has a common enemy is unbreakable. It establishes a common thread for life. Senior citizens look for such battles, giving them an updated sense of value. More important, it brings them back to their childhood—making them feel young again.

Fashionable Bermuda shorts and rich dyed hair swayed in the gentle breeze. Wigs and layers of makeup with permanent tattooed eyebrows also held their ground. This community felt confident that they were winning the fight against the aging process. This was the Greensborough Retirement Home—but it only housed *active* retirees. Like any high school, the 'who's who' strutted their stuff like peacocks during mating season.

"Good shot, Wally!" cheered Mildred Childs. Her lawn bowling partner rolled the ball with expertise, putting their opponents at a disadvantage. Wally turned and, with his prim and proper etiquette, took off his cap and bowed.

Chaos erupted without warning. The loud thumping bass of a car stereo blanketed the area. Wilber Parker took a plastic chair from a table that rested next to a concrete wall. He slid the chair against the wall and used it as a step ladder. The frisky seventy-year-old with a balding head and silver moustache stepped on the chair and peered over the wall. He frantically waved his arms, getting the attention of the intruders.

They were teenagers visiting outside their car with the stereo cranked up. A thin, blond-haired youth reached inside his car and turned it down. His friend with tattoos, dark braided hair, and an army jacket asked, "What is it, old man?"

Wilber was upset and yelled, "You are playing that radio too loud and need to turn it down!"

The boy in the car showed disrespect by turning up his stereo even louder than it was before. Everything was ruined. There was nothing the elders could do but go indoors and weather the storm. Once inside, Wilber said, "I wish there was a way to shut those things off!"

Thomas Banks made a comment that started a movement. "My son can solve that problem real quick. When he was in the military, they would use a simple technique that silenced any radio speaker that was playing too loud."

The room silenced with all eyes focused on him. All at once, each frown slowly broke into a huge grin. The seniors turned their heads and nodded at each other. They wanted to hear more . . .

"Does he live in the area?" asked Sarah Campbell.

"Why, yes, he does," answered Tommy.

"Can you bring him over? We'd love to meet him," said Stanley Moats.

"Well sure, I can introduce him to everyone this afternoon. He and his family always visit me on Sundays," said Tommy.

"We are going to be freed!" proclaimed Edith O'Brien.

The crowded hallway of over forty seniors cheered in hope.

It was just past one o'clock in the afternoon when Brian Banks arrived to visit his father. The son, along with his wife and two children, entered the lobby. Brian followed the normal procedure and checked in with the receptionist. Tommy's room was called and notified of Brian's arrival.

Upon finishing the call, the receptionist addressed Brian. She explained that his father and some of his friends wanted to meet him in the conference room. It was located near the lobby, with instructions given. The young family agreed to split up, with the mother and children going to the cafeteria. Brian would join them there after his meeting.

Brian approached the conference room and entered. Several minutes later, his father entered with a small group of residents. "Hello, Brian!" called out his father.

"Hi, Dad," answered Brian.

"Brian," said the father, "I have brought some of my friends with me. Our community has a problem, and we wanted to see if you could help us."

"I will do whatever I can for you," said Brian.

Everyone introduced themselves, and then the problem with loud car stereos was discussed.

Brian shook his head in understanding of the problem. "I see . . ." he said.

With weary blue eyes, his father represented the retirement home by asking him for help. "Do you know of a cure that will give us the ability to stop this loud noise that's contaminating our air space?"

"Yes I do," said Brian. He noticed a blackboard at the front of the room and motioned everyone toward it. He picked up a piece of chalk, and like a college professor, began to draw a diagram. He explained a simple technology that used batteries and a radio transmission. "This simple setup will give you the power to blow out any car speaker that's being played too loud—from a safe distance.

"Can you build us one of these?" asked a member in the room.

"Easily," said Brian "I have an old citizens band radio from a semi truck and a car battery that can be modified to do the job. It won't take long to set it up. How soon do you want it?" he asked.

"Right now!" said the entire room.

Brian spoke. "How about you go to the cafeteria to visit the family? I will go home and return with the materials needed for this project."

"That's a great idea!" said his father.

"I'll be back here in less than an hour," said the son. "Just show me where you want it installed."

"Anywhere that will stop a car stereo from drowning us out with their speakers!" exclaimed the father.

"Gotcha!" said Brian.

The seniors clenched their fists high in the air with victory. Brian said, "It's been nice meeting everyone, I'll be back in awhile."

Tommy looked at his friends and said, "Oh, you gotta meet my grandchildren and daughter-in-law; follow me!" He led the party to the cafeteria.

Tommy was showing off his grandchildren. He made faces with silly noises to make the toddlers laugh. All present were amused. It seemed that hardly any time had passed since Brian left for home. He entered the cafeteria holding a sturdy cardboard box. He removed one hand from the box and gave a thumbs-up to his father. Tommy looked at the clock on the wall and noticed that an hour had already passed.

"It's all done, Dad." said the devoted son. "All I need now is to know where you want the controls."

"My room would be perfect, son," said Tommy. I have the good fortune of being on the top floor in the far end of the building. I have that birds' eye view of everything."

"That sounds good to me," said Brian. "I also brought some more goodies for you and your friends." He placed the container on the table, where his dad sat, and opened it. He reached in and pulled out a memory from his childhood. Five transistor walkie-talkie radios that he received as a Christmas gift many years ago were displayed. They were especially meaningful to him, because this gift came from his father.

He smiled at his dad and said, "This was my most favorite present that I ever got. My friends and I had hours of fun with these. I am sure that you and your friends will have a good use for these things, too," he said in a laughing tone as he winked at his father. "Let's go up to your room now and take care of your problem."

The proud father led the way to his dwelling. Like the Pied Piper, he had a long trail of followers.

Once they entered his unit, Brian went to work on the project. Amazingly, he was finished in five minutes and had it resting on a portable dinner tray with legs. "There," said Brian as he brushed his hands against each other. "Now, let me show you how to use it."

The students crowded around the elevated tray. With curiosity they looked at the old truckers' radio with the microphone still intact. They saw that it was connected to a twelve-volt battery.

Brian started his presentation. "I placed a large antenna that has sensors to this unit outside. It is fastened on a metal utility pole that the traffic lights are suspended from. It blends in with everything and looks inconspicuous. When a car stereo is too loud and passes by the antenna, we can give it feedback by transmitting back with too much power. By turning our volume to maximum capacity and clicking the transmission button rapidly, it will overload the car's stereo system. The pulsating volume will address the weakest component of their sound system; the speakers. This overpowering surge, along with their excessive loudness, will cause the speakers to blow out. They'll never know what hit them . . ."

"Any questions?" asked Brian. The room had given him their undivided attention and nodded their heads sideways. "And now," said Brian. "It's time for a demonstration."

Brian carried the tray next to the window and turned the off / on volume dial to the 'on' position. In silence they huddled, waiting for an intruder. Finally the thumping of a car stereo could be heard approaching their neighborhood, getting louder and louder. A car with teenagers entered their block without a care in the world.

All eyes were on Brian. He simply turned the volume dial to its highest setting and started to click the transmission button on the microphone repetitively. The booming sound silenced with a thunderous punch. Faces remained still with mouths wide open.

They looked out the window. The ten-year-old high school car with faded red paint and dents had stopped. The occupants were obviously equally surprised, not knowing what happened. The car sat motionless for a brief period. Like a dog with its tail between its legs, it started to drive away cautiously. The seniors looked at one another with a stunning realization. They actually did have a secret weapon, and it flew under the radar . . .

"Okay," said Brian. "The ones who have to learn the hard way deserve this." He said his goodbyes and parted with his family.

The armed seniors had a new life. For years they had been suppressed by the inconsideration of those who dominated territory with loud stereos. Now they could peacefully fight back, and have a little fun with it too.

The next day at breakfast, Thomas held a meeting in the cafeteria. He issued out the walkie-talkies to the top floor rooms that had the best vantage points. The entire community had been victims for years, and now they would form a coalition for a well-overdue counter attack. The residents were aware that such a practice could be considered a violation of law. They agreed to keep their battle a *secret,* and even disguise their identities by dressing up like their favorite television personalities and going by that name only. It was agreed that if anyone got caught, they would only give their name, rank and serial number.

That afternoon, the intense competition of croquet was interrupted by a booming car stereo. It played so loud that it vibrated Arnold Livingston's toupee off to one side. The community was caught off guard by the attack. Tommy Banks took command and called out, "Battle stations, and remember to wear your fatigues!"

In twenty minutes the volunteers were dressed in cowboy hats, army helmets, old thrift store clothes, lavish dresses with matching hats, and vintage space uniforms. With no time to waste, they manned their posts. It was time to protect the fort . . .

A loud static sound of screaming voices entered the atmosphere.

"Look, Thirston, they're ruining our sunny day," pointed out a woman's voice.

"Don't worry, Lovie. The rifleman will get him!" said an unidentifiable person.

" Commandant, do you hear something?" asked an inquisitive bystander.

"Hogan!" came a reply from nowhere.

"Lamont, are those your friends making all this racket, you big dummy?" said a concerned elder.

"No, Pop, I have never seen these guys before," responded an invisible set of eyes.

"Bandits at twelve o'clock," warned a lookout.

"Hey! You sank his battleship!" reported a correspondent.

The car that was penetrating the neighborhood with echoing screams came to a silence and coasted to a stop. The minors with tank tops that bore logos of their favorite bands immediately focused on the radio, fingers hastily turned knobs in a frantic attempt to hear *their* music. The motley crew couldn't revive the sound system and continued their travels in silence.

"Ward, is that Eddie Haskell out there?" asked a woman.

"No, June," replied a firm male voice in control. "Those are just kids playing. Beaver, Wally!"

"Jed," called out the jittery voice of a woman in her eighties. "Can I shoot that varmint that's making all the noise?"

"Granny," answered the voice of a Southern gentleman. "We better tell Mr. Driesdale first. If that doesn't work, we can always get Jethro after them."

"Look, Gilligan," called out an enthused old man. "The professor has developed a way to shut down those noisy car stereos."

"Skip-peeerr!" cried a youthful male in desperation.

"Klingons, Captain!" warned a concerned cohort.

"Put phasers on stun and go to warp seven!" barked a command.

"Felix," said a sharp voice. "Do we want to take any of them as prisoners?"

"Oscar, Oscar, Oscar . . ." rebuked a disappointed counterpart.

"The name's 'Bodie'; Shyanne Bodie," announced a serious voice as another car got silenced.

"Look, Chief," came someone over the airwaves. "I think those are KAOS agents in that car down there."

"Max! That's a police car!" replied a fatherly tone.

"Oh look, Archie," came the sound of an aging woman. "That car seems to be having problems."

"Will you stifle, Edith?" remarked a crusty old man. "You are beginning to sound like 'Meathead'."

The streets seemed to have quieted down. The loud music seemed to pass by in smaller intervals. The enemy seemed to have retreated. Eventually, enough time had passed by to call it a day. The camouflaged army had caught their limit.

"Head them up; move them out," came the final order over the airwaves. The volunteers left their posts and changed back into their civilian clothes.

It was now time to send out scouts to confirm *kills*. Deloris, Benjamin and Curtis left the grounds to inspect the parameter. They were reminded of their oath and knew to act casually. The three walked a short block and saw a car parked with two African American teenagers standing around it. As they got closer, an apparent discussion about the car's sound system could be heard. The trio would further investigate by eavesdropping.

"Marcus, I don't know why it stopped working," said a tall teenager with glasses. "What I do know is that you were playing it too loud."

"Wilson, I will listen to it as loud as I want to," said an athletic companion with hair in long dreadlocks. "Besides, it's my music and my car."

"You are missing the whole point," replied the intellect. "When your own parents don't allow you to play it that loud in their neighborhood, you should never play it that loud anywhere." Wilson then raised his voice. "I also hate it when you do that sort of stuff when I am with you; it makes me look just as bad!"

The seniors were impressed with Wilson's argument. They nonchalantly made themselves noticeable and walked by the troubled teens.

"Excuse me," called out the older boy as he saw the seniors. "I was wondering if I could ask you a question?"

The elders braced themselves to be interrogated about the mysterious silencing of car stereos. They were relieved that they couldn't have been further from the truth.

"Sure," said Curtis, "but let's get introduced first." Names were exchanged as hands were shook.

"Curtis," asked Wilson, pointing at a field across the street. "Do you know if there are any fish in that stream over there?"

Curtis looked at Benjamin. The men seemed to know something that most didn't. They shook heads knowing what each was thinking. Benjamin looked at Wilson and spoke. "There are fish, but there is a trick to catching them."

"Could you tell us?" asked Marcus.

"Do you guys have fishing poles?" asked Benjamin.

"Yes, we do!" answered Wilson.

"How about getting them, and we will meet you over there in one hour?" suggested Curtis.

"That would be great!" said Marcus. He and Wilson quickly left for home.

The young men seemed to have forgotten about their problem. They were now going to catch fish! Deloris looked at the two young friends getting into their car. She then looked at the two old-time fishing buddies and saw the spirit of youth within them come alive. "What a great display of diplomacy," she thought to herself.

Deloris, Curtis and Benjamin returned to the retirement center and told their friends about Wilson and Marcus. "These guys are great," said Benjamin. "You are going to like them!" The good news spread throughout the complex and recruited other anglers for the outing. The elders arrived first and staked out the choice spot where always they caught the largest trout.

Marcus and Wilson could be seen walking toward the group with fishing poles swaying in the air. It was obvious that they had the same sentiments, bringing some of their friends along too. Each group waved at the other as new friendships were about to be created. All at once, an outbreak of introductions and handshakes swarmed the area.

"Marcus," called out Curtis. "Hand me your poll for a minute." Marcus handed his fishing poll to Curtis and watched him put a peculiar bait on his hook. "What I learned in my early days is that the fish will only eat what's natural from this stream," said the old man. He pointed at a wet plastic bucket that had a rope tied on the handle. "I use that bucket and drag it along the bottom of the stream. Then I pull all of the worms out of it. That's their main food source, and the only bait that will work here."

Curtis continued, "It's also important to know where they are." He pointed at a boulder in the center of the stream. "Just cast your line in front of that rock, where the water is calm. That's the deepest part of the creek and where the biggest fish are.

Marcus followed his instructions and made a smooth cast directly in the center of the still water. He reeled some of the slack and rested the pole next to him.

"Now comes the best part of fishing," said Norman Jackson. "We get to be guys and talk about anything."

"Would anyone like a pop?" asked Ralph Simmons.

"I'd love one," said Wilson. "Same here," said his friends, as Ralph threw cold cans to open hands.

The moment was interrupted by a violent yank on Marcus's pole. He picked it up as a large trout jumped out of the water. The young man started to reel it in as Dwight Cox took his vintage wooden net and leaned over the brook. Marcus guided the fish toward the net as Ralph scooped it up. The seventy-two-year-old man held up the mighty two-pound rainbow that was suspended in the net for all to see.

"Nice catch!" said Benjamin.

"Let's get those other poles baited right away," said Curtis.

The new friends dangled their lines in front of Curtis as he baited worms on hooks with expertise. Soon everyone had a line in the water, with an occasional fish striking. Laughter, cheering and hilarious stories rotated amongst the fishing buddies.

A topic was addressed by Marcus's younger brother, Phillip. "Does anyone here know why car stereos don't work in this area?"

There was silence.

"Could you explain that in greater detail?" asked sixty-eight-year-old Walter Johns.

Marcus spoke next. "My stereo stopped working when I drove through this neighborhood today."

"Do you play it loud?" asked retired postal clerk Cliff Hayes.

"Sometimes," Marcus answered back.

Benjamin asked a question. "Has anyone here ever been in a situation when you were forced to hear something that made you feel violated?"

"Well, sure," responded bleached blonde skateboarder Billy Suddoth.

"Tell us about it," asked Benjamin.

Billy took a deep breath as he looked toward the ground. "My mother likes the Lawrence Welk re-runs and will turn up the television full blast to hear the music. That stuff drives me crazy. I can hear it in every room and have to leave home to get away from it."

Jake Fields, a high school wrestler, contributed. "My bedroom is above the garage. My older sister is allowed to use my parents' car at night to go to her college classes. She wakes me up sometimes when she comes home because the car radio is playing too loud. I have talked to her about it, but she still has times when she forgets to turn it down."

One by one, each person had a similar story about loud stereos.

Marcus commented, "I get offended when someone doesn't like my music and tells me to turn it down."

"That's where you are wrong," said his good friend, Wilson. "It's the volume you are playing it at, not what you're playing."

Marcus let the information sink in.

Wilson spoke again. "It doesn't matter why it stopped playing that loud. What's important is that it finally stopped. Who knows, the manufacturer might have a setting that is sanctioned by a government code, and when you play it too loud, it automatically shuts down—as a respect for others. If there is some sort of gadget out there, can you blame them for using it?"

No one disagreed with Wilson's logic.

"There is one thing that I really like," said Dwight Cox.

"What's that?" asked the group.

"This moment," he said. "I'd much rather talk to a neighbor and learn to appreciate them than only know them through their car speakers."

Dwight's comment was profound and had everyone nodding in agreement.

"I think that the fish have stopped biting for today," said Curtis.

"Hey!" said William Currie. "Tonight our retirement center is having a luau. If you youngsters want to come you are certainly welcome! That trout you caught would be a great contribution."

"That's a good idea!" said Benjamin.

Wilson and his friends looked at one another in approval. They wanted the evening to continue with their new fishing buddies. "We'd love that!" said Wilson.

"Well, good," said William. "We could always have more friends at these events."

"Can I bring my girlfriend?" asked Wilson.

"Why, sure you can, and other friends too. Just remember to wear a Hawaiian shirt or straw hat, if you have one. The party begins at seven o'clock tonight."

"We'll be there!" said Marcus.

Shortly before seven, Wilson, Marcus, and a group of friends arrived in their beach apparel. The patio at the retirement center was decorated with tiki torches and had a makeshift grass hut that covered a barbeque. Vegetables, steaks, salmon and trout graced the grill.

The guests were treated like celebrities and received an immediate welcome wagon. Punch was served in hollowed-out pineapples with straws and tiny umbrellas sticking out. Soft Hawaiian music kept the theme alive.

More introductions were made as the retirement community got to know their neighbors. Wilson brought his girlfriend, Hanna. She was a beautiful twenty-year-old woman with mixed ethnic background. She was also expecting her first child. The elder women were all mothers, grandmothers and great-grandmothers. They surrounded Hanna and moved to a table together.

Hanna said that she was afraid of having a child so young. The women encouraged her and began to plan a baby shower. They even invited her to join their quilting circle and promised to serve as a daycare when possible.

Wilson was proud to be seen with his friends, especially Hanna. He confessed that he was concerned because he would soon have a family, and was looking for a job.

"Wilson," said eighty-three-year-old Steve Brady. "I am on the board of directors, and we are looking for a good man to do our maintenance. It's a full time job with benefits. Why don't you start tomorrow?" he asked.

Wilson was flattered. "I would love working here in my own neighborhood," he said. "Especially with the people who live here!"

One of Wilson's friends brought a portable radio. The young ebony male had the radio placed close to his ear as he sat alone in the corner.

He was noticed by a female resident who was concerned and approached him. She introduced herself and asked, "Is there anything wrong?"

The young man said, "Hi, my name is Raleigh, and everything is fine. I just wanted to sit down awhile and listen to my new CD."

"Who is it by?" she asked.

"L.L. Cool J," said Raleigh.

"L.L. Cool J?" asked the elder. With great anticipation, she had a request. "Do you have 'I Need Love'?"

"That's what I'm listening to right now," replied Raleigh.

"Could you turn it up a bit?" she asked.

The young man did as the beautiful sound captivated the room. The woman knew who the artist was and forgot about her involvement with the silencing of loud car stereos. She momentarily forgot where she was and exposed her secret military code name. The elder called out to her husband, who was standing nearby, "Thirston, do you hear what I hear?" She looked directly at her spouse of sixty years and extended her arms.

The music perked his ears as he said, "Lovie, they're playing our song!" He took hold of his wife and began to sway to the beat.

The 'Howells' were in the perfect mood, with the perfect setting. It was now time to listen to their favorite song and dance the night away . . .

It's Just One of Those Things

Martha Spikes heard the rumbling of the bus as it passed her house. The high school vice principal took a closer look at the clock on the wall and realized that it had stopped ticking at twenty minutes before the hour. A dead battery caused her to miss the bus. She was accepting about the mishap. It was only Saturday, and she had no appointments.

Martha was old enough to understand that she was just a victim of circumstances. She knew that when such an event causes you to have a glitch in your schedule, that it was only *life* placing you where you were needed. The middle-aged African American grandmother could only be amused by it. "Well," she said to herself. "It looks like I might be destined to run into someone I haven't seen in awhile."

Martha Spikes knew that she could walk four blocks and catch another bus to transfer to her destination. "If I leave now, I will only arrive twenty minutes later," she thought to herself. "There is no harm to this, since I am only going shopping for new glasses." She was already dressed with her coat on, ready to go. The sixty-year-old woman left the front door as if nothing had ever happened. The senior walked to Mitas Street and sat inside the enclosed booth at the bus stop. Within five minutes, her alternate bus arrived with Martha boarding. Then it happened . . .

As Martha showed her pass to the driver and made her way down the aisle, her name was called out. "Martha Spikes, is that you?"

Martha looked over and recognized Rose Thompson, an old school friend. "Rose," she answered. "Is that you?" She opened her arms and embraced her long-lost friend.

"How have you been?" asked an emotional Rose with tears in her eyes.

"Better, much better now that I found you!" she replied. "I have thought about you for ages!"

"What are you doing here?" asked Rose.

"I missed the bus in my neighborhood and ended up over here," explained Martha. "It's just one of those things . . ."

◀◀ ◀◀ ▶▶ ▶▶

Daniel Reily smiled at the seventeen-year-old student. Daniel's hand was dangling his car keys in front of Jay Williams as he said, "Are you sure that you can give my car a tune-up and oil change, and return it by Monday morning?"

Jay was confident. "I will have it done in time, Daniel."

The forty-year-old Irish immigrant with black hair and handlebar moustache said, "Well, good! This will also put a little money in your pocket." Daniel placed the keys into Jay's open hand and winked at him with pride. "I have this old truck that I can get around in," said Daniel as he pointed at an old moving van across the street. "Just have the car parked in front of my house Monday morning, and put the keys in my mail box."

"Don't worry about a thing," said Jay. "You will have your car back in front of your house Monday morning."

Daniel shook Jay's hand, confirming a business deal. He then crossed the street and climbed into the vintage International. His next stop would be the closest school in the neighborhood. It was his job to evaluate the condition of all schools and service them.

Daniel Reily arrived at Cedar Park Elementary School and went to work. He got busy inspecting an old water heater. This building was the oldest in the district, with all materials outdated. To address any project usually meant to update all of it. He surveyed the corroded fittings to the water heater. "They stopped making this model years ago," thought Daniel.

His expertise taught him when it was time to take out the old and bring in the new. It was time to bring in the new. He would now walk to Mrs. Spikes' office and explain the scenario to the vice principal. She was in charge of all maintenance and gave final approval to any project.

"This entire building has been fitted with electrical and plumbing that's now outdated," Daniel explained. "We need to replace everything in small intervals, so that this school can run continuously," he said.

Martha Spikes loved his accent as she nodded her head with understanding. "I agree with what you are saying," she said. "I have noticed the deterioration through the years and realized that we would soon be faced with this decision. You have always done a great job for the school district for over twenty years. I have complete confidence in your work and decision-making. I authorize you to begin this project. Please keep in mind that you need to do whatever assignments would shut this school down during the weekends."

Daniel responded, "Don't worry about a thing, Mrs. Spikes. I won't let you down!" He extended his hand to shake over his commitment to this endeavor.

Martha shook his hand and with confidence said, "I have complete faith in you, Daniel."

The contractor returned to the job site and grabbed a pen and tablet from his tool box. He would now spend the rest of the day making a closer inspection of the entire building. Daniel would take notes and place orders for the materials needed.

His main concern was the heating system. An obsolete boiler pumped water to vintage radiators. They showed signs of leaking and could go at any time. He would install new electric heaters throughout the school that week, and utilize the weekend to spend the extra hours required to wire them. More important, he would first shut down the old boiler and drain it, along with the unsightly iron radiators. Once that task was done, he would remove them. The building would be temporarily out of heat.

Saturday arrived, with the industrious Daniel starting several hours early. He set himself up the night before by shutting off the boiler and draining all the water from the system. By early morning, it would be cool enough to be dismantled and carried off. He owned a used furniture truck and would use it to haul the scraps away.

By five o'clock that evening, he had the first phase complete. He would take the dismantled components to a scrap yard that recycled metal. After that he would go home to take a bath, have dinner, and attend church services the following morning. Life would take a turn with Daniel receiving a calling.

Father O'Conner stormed into the church before services started. He got in front of the pulpit and gave a quick announcement. "There is a huge problem going on in our parish right now. The river has risen due to the excessive rain that we've had, and the O'Casey home is getting flooded." With stern blue Catholic eyes, he pleaded with the fellowship. "We need every strong man and a truck to move their belongings to this church immediately. We will have our services afterwards."

Daniel did not hesitate to join in. He *knew* that's why he was there with his truck. "I will help until the job is done!" he vowed to God.

Within twenty minutes, the members of the church arrived at the O'Casey home. They formed a human chain and relayed household items hand to hand out of the condemned house to the back of the truck. Daniel was inside the truck, packing the goods like a can of sardines.

The congregation worked feverishly, knowing that they were just a step ahead of the rising waters. The task was finally completed well after dark. The river that use to border the back yard was now lapping over their back porch. But it didn't matter; the family and all their possessions were saved.

It was now time to meet at church and empty the van, with services following. A collection was taken for the stricken family, with food catered to feed the famished workers. They were beat, but it was all worth it. The church had housing for such emergencies, with the O'Casey family being taken care of. Daniel Reily felt blessed and enjoyed a well-earned late night dinner with his friends.

Daniel was exhausted when he returned home. It was after midnight, and he was far behind on his project. Still, he had no regrets with the decision he made. He packed a lunch, got his sleeping bag and pillow, and left. Once he arrived back at school he rolled out his sleeping bag next to his tools. The tired man took his shoes and shirt off, climbed inside the sleeping bag and laid his head on the soft pillow. He instantly fell hard asleep.

Daniel was snoring like a mountain man. His body began to shake with his voice being called.

"Daniel, Daniel, wake up." It was Martha Spikes, gently moving Daniel's shoulder as she called out his name.

Daniel woke up. He remembered where he was, and what he was supposed to have finished.

"Mrs. Spikes," said the groggy contractor. "I have had an emergency that took up my entire Sunday. I couldn't help what happened, but I will get to work right away on those heaters."

"Don't worry about a thing," she said. "Early this morning, I received an email stating that a field trip was available for this school to go on. For some reason I made a snap decision to accept it. We don't need this building today, after all."

"You mean that I didn't fail the students – or yourself by not being finished this morning?" asked Daniel.

Martha Spikes smiled and said, "No. You can have the rest of the day to finish your project. You can even go back to sleep. It's just one of those things . . ."

Daniel was now wide awake. He put his shoes and shirt on and addressed the chore that awaited him. Daniel felt well rested and worked at a fast pace, with no interruptions. He took a brief lunch break several hours into the day and continued until finished. He then turned on each heater to verify that they were installed properly. Each one quietly produced heat. Daniel smiled with pride. He swept up the excessive wire, metal fragments, and sawdust his work created. Daniel then gathered all of his tools and left for home, locking the doors behind him.

He arrived at his house just after six o'clock and noticed that his car was parked where it was supposed to be. Once again, he was worn out, but knew that everything was right. He looked into his mailbox and retrieved the car keys, then entered his home and sat down.

As soon as he got comfortable, he was disturbed by a knocking on his front door. He answered it to find Jay Williams.

"Good evening, Jay," said Daniel.

"Daniel, can I come in?" asked the youth. "I can explain everything," he said.

Daniel opened the door wider and motioned for him to enter. Jay walked in with Daniel closing the door behind him. "You can sit here," said Daniel as he pointed to a chair.

It was obvious that Jay was worked up emotionally and wanted to get something off his chest. He sat in the chair and spoke. "First of all, I want you to know that I am sorry."

Daniel raised one eyebrow and quietly listened to him.

Jay started to explain that once he was ready to work on the car, a series of emergencies arose. He emphasized that it seemed every time he reached for a tool, he was stopped to help in these cases. Jay had to use his mother's car to get his parents, because they were broke down visiting relatives far away.

Later, he had to assist his dad in his hardware shop because an employee called in sick. Another time, an elderly neighbor across the street fell and was able to call his household on the cell phone. Jay was the only one home and came to the rescue. He was also called on to help his church group with a fundraiser when several members couldn't make it. He never turned down a request from his church.

Jay continued to explain himself. "When I was finally able to work on your car, it wasn't until after school today. That's why the car was ready just an hour ago."

He looked at Daniel and said, "When I saw that your truck was gone, I thought that you were mad and lost faith in me." Jay Williams felt like he was an irresponsible child in the eyes of Daniel. "I couldn't help it," he pleaded.

Daniel gave a warm smile and gazed at the young man. "You've done nothing wrong, my lad. God needed you to take care of something more important. He always operates in a spiritual way, so that you can serve him without warning, and not fail at what you needed to do. Sometimes these things happen just so that you can meet up with someone you haven't seen in a long time. It's a way to get that special person back into your life."

He then reached into his pocket and pulled out his wallet. He opened it and paid Jay for working on his car.

Daniel told Jay about the delays he had installing the new heaters in the school. He pointed out that he missed the deadline, only to find out that it was extended an extra day. "It's like the car you worked on. I didn't need it today, after all; and you did make the right choices! It's just one of those things . . ."

Jay thought about the chain of events and realized that he was called on to address more important issues. Jay felt graced by the situation and looked at Daniel in relief. He realized that Daniel was right, and that these things *do* turn out for the best.

It's just one of those things . . .

Young People

Secret Radio Man

Often an important person in our life is overlooked. They seem to be taken for granted as they consistently help others. Their meek manner hinders them from standing out. The average person will never notice this crime until it's too late. Sometimes, a greater force will intervene to highlight this injustice. Such was the case for Julie Smythe; a cheerful wallflower who lived out her high school years helping others.

Mike Arrington leaned back in his chair and said, "I get it." The tall, lanky seventeen-year-old with blond hair looked up with pride as he completed his homework assignment. Julie Smythe smiled back at her pupil and classmate.

"Let me double check it to make sure," said Julie. The short, overweight girl in the grandmother-type sweater peered through her glasses as she held up the assignment. Her thick black hair was shoulder length and seemed to be a style out of the 1940s. But Julie had charm. She was also very responsible and seemed to be more of a teacher than a student. After reviewing Mike's paper, she gave a huge grin and said, "A-plus!"

Mike was relieved. "I have to thank you, Julie," he said. "Because of you, I have a driver's license, can play sports and will graduate."

Julie gleamed back at him and said, "Well, you are well worth it, mister!"

96

Mike hugged his academic friend and left the room. Julie felt triumphant.

Julie left and headed toward her locker. A familiar sight approached her as she walked down the hall. It was the unmistakable presence of Amber Write. Amber was the most attractive girl in school. She was a popular cheerleader and seemed to be asked out every night of the week.

There had been tension between the two girls. Amber once threw herself at a boyfriend of Julie's just to flex her muscle. The boy chose Amber's beauty over Julie's wholesomeness. When he realized that Amber had a shallow side to her character, he left her. Julie could never look as attractive as Amber did; but Amber needed more than that. She needed to develop as a person, like Julie Smythe. The hatchet was buried and a friendship was created.

Amber had Julie in her sights and fired first. "I like what you have done with your hair today, Julie!"

Amber had long, flowing blonde hair like Farrah Fawcett. Her body would make any model envious, and her face could cover a magazine. But she lost her arrogance when she was rejected by Julie's old boyfriend. She took a closer look at Julie, and realized that her character made her a winner.

"Why, thank you," said Julie. "I had to do something with it!"

"Don't worry about a thing, Julie. You are looking fine," said Amber. "You have a good day."

"You too, Amber," said Julie. The girls parted in opposite directions. Julie felt better with the most desired student befriending her. But still, something made her feel denied.

The lunch bell rang, and instantly the hall cluttered with students going to their lockers. Soon the cafeteria would be full, with an empty seat at a desolate table waiting for Julie Smythe.

It was now lunch hour, and every student was listening to their favorite radio show: Secret Radio Man. This was the latest craze on the airwaves. Anyone who was a teenager wondered who he was, and idolized him.

This cosmic Wolfman Jack was surrounded with static and used Cape Canaveral jargon. A high-pitched, alien voice spoke in brief sentences and abruptly silenced. It was as if the transmission was over a microphone in outer space. He seemed to visit our planet via the radio, and called himself 'Secret Radio Man'.

He announced that he was on a mission to monitor the students from the planet Earth who *were of a high caliber*. His superiors would then give the order to have Secret Radio Man deploy his 'secret radio men' to invade a particular school where such an exceptional student came from. Pizzas, gifts and dances would be used as arsenal to conquer the school and claim it as new territory. The station he broadcast from also played the most popular hits on the charts.

How he gained his detailed information was a mystery to everyone. What was more amazing was that he pinpointed unsung heroes who had a history of helping others . . . only to be forgotten. Julia Smythe was such a person.

At that precise moment, the dining hall was stormed by the secret radio men! A small army of tall, athletic men wearing red jumpsuits with black appendages surrounded the students. Their outfits had thick black belts with the Secret Radio Man emblem in the center, with matching space-aged sunglasses. The invaders brought pizza and soda pop; and with authority began serving their *captives*. Large stereo speakers that were black and red with the Secret Radio Man logo rolled into the hall. The party was on!

The elated lunch hall cheered them on as warm pizza was distributed from table to table. Something strange was about to happen that was seemingly innocent. A pizza with tomato and olives mysteriously got placed in front of Julie Smythe; her favorite pizza. The coincidence was subtle, but still warranted a peculiar feeling.

The broadcast was now pounding the walls as music poured out of the gigantic speakers. The sound came to an abrupt stop as static hissed. This was the background noise that surrounded Secret Radio Man, wherever he was. The unknown extraterrestrial's voice controlled the room. "Attention, secret radio men, you must now apprehend our specimen and bring this earthling to me."

At once, the secret radio men displayed an eight-foot black pole with a matching disk attached to the end. It made a clicking sound that seemed to increase in volume when it got closer to its prey. The radio men maneuvered toward the direction that caused the sound to increase. Finally, the disk was directly on top of its gold: Julie Smythe.

Julie tensed up with the realization that she was the specimen Secret Radio Man came for. The radio men surrounded Julie and helped her out of her seat. The space-age special forces then abducted Julie and escorted their prisoner to the parking lot.

The entire room followed the radio men and their prisoner outside. There, parked in the parking lot, was a forty-foot luxury bus that looked like a spacecraft. The only windows were for the driver's compartment. It was painted black and red with the Secret Radio Man logo on all sides. A speaker on top of the vehicle barked out a command from Secret Radio Man. "Please bring the humanoid to me."

At that moment, the back of the bus had a ramp fold down. Its upper half folded up like a clam shell, with steam billowing out of the entrance. "Please enter alone, Julie Smythe," came the voice of the alien disk jockey. "Secret Radio Man must meet with you." Julie slowly walked toward the bus. She began to climb the steps that led inside the spaceship on wheels.

As she approached the platform that entered the bus, she turned and looked at the crowd. All were in awe; one of them was going to meet Secret Radio Man! The crowd began to chant her name: "Julie! Julie! Julie!" shouted the masses in rhythm. She waved at the crowd and bravely stepped through the rolling steam. The ramp began to close itself like a human hand. Julie was inside the capsule as suspense mounted both inside and out.

A fog-like steam swirled within the capsule as she was surrounded by stars that seemed to go on for infinity. She walked toward the front, then heard the unmistakable voice of her favorite radio personality. Red eyes focused on her as the starry background showed movement. "Greetings, Julie," said the host. "I am Secret Radio Man. I am glad that you could visit me in my spaceship. Please sit down."

A black NASA-looking chair was positioned in front of Julie, facing the mysterious visitor. She stepped around it and sat down. "Pleased to meet you, Secret Radio Man," she said. "There is something that I need to know," she said. "Why was I chosen to meet you?"

An answer came from the intense red eyes. "It has come to my attention that you help others. This school has more graduates because of your involvement as a tutor. The teachers have it easier because you volunteered to be a teacher's aide. Many events, such as ice cream socials, book fairs and the debate team, have advanced this school and benefited others." The compassionate spaceman continued, " You also never gossip, and comfort others who are feeling bad."

Julie absorbed the answer and began to thank him. "I feel that I am a new kid at school, and that you have just given me a great introduction."

"Secret Radio Man does not introduce anyone to their community; he merely reminds everyone who they are," came his response.

Julie felt warm inside. She was acknowledged for being a good person. That awareness was all it took for Secret Radio Man to track her. She slowly looked up at the red eyes that pierced through the steam and spoke. "You are all about honoring a good person, not a popular one."

"Affirmative," came the electronic answer. Then a quick smile flashed on and off in a split second. Steam continued to billow throughout the room. "But there is more to it than

100

that," the robot-like creature continued with its buzzing voice. "It is important to appreciate a pizza with tomatoes and olives, which is Secret Radio Man's favorite!" Another quick smile blipped as Julie laughed back, nodding in agreement. The robot reciprocated, giving another smile, one that lasted much longer.

Julie was fascinated and asked another question. "How did you find out so much about me?"

The cosmic guru answered, "Your cell phone. You accepted it as a gift when my secret radio men handed them out at a shopping center." Julie's mouth dropped open as she felt violated. The alien voice comforted Julie. "Don't worry. Secret Radio Man can only hear you when you are on campus, and never outside of that perimeter."

July sat back in relief and said, "Thank goodness . . ."

"We must now destroy that instrument and replace it with a Secret Radio Man Model 5000." Julie was in shock as she continued to stare. A Secret Radio Man 5000 was the most modern cell phone that had unlimited services for life. To own one always guaranteed a free replacement if ever needed. To some, this was more valuable than a new car!

An electric humming sound suggesting motion distracted Julie. Through the mystic steam came a black metal arm with two prongs for fingers. It extended itself, holding the state-of-the-art cell phone. Julie reached into her purse and placed her old cell phone on the table. The new phone was gently placed in front of her, as the old one was taken and retracted into the steamy unknown. She picked up the gift. It was black and red with the Secret Radio Man logo on it. But there was something that made it even more special; it also had her name on it!

The humble youth held her prized possession and marveled at it. She then looked at the sophisticated Martian eyes and said in a soft tone, "Thank you, Secret Radio Man. Everyone in the whole world wants one of these!"

Through the steamy stars came a response. "You are welcome, my favorite humanoid." A red smile followed. Julie smiled back knowing that he (it) meant it.

Secret Radio Man continued to speak. " I must now leave your planet and report to my superiors."

Julie giggled and replied, "Well you tell your superiors that they have made one earthling very happy!"

"Affirmative," came Secret Radio Man's final response.

Excessive steam began to fill the compartment. A black wall slowly lowered from the ceiling, separating the space-age visitor from Julie. Secret Radio Man was gone.

The back entryway to the trailer slowly opened, with massive steam billowing out. Julie got out of the chair and turned around to see daylight through the mist. She cautiously walked to the outside platform of the trailer. When she broke through the swirling mist, the entire student body was waiting and gave a huge ovation with cheers and whistles to their hero. Julie was now the most popular student at school.

◄◄ ◄◄ ►► ►►

It was a traditional Friday night at Daily's Malt Shop. Steven, along with Mike, Ben, Sarah and Amber sat quiet in their regular booth. The radio was playing the Secret Radio Man broadcast. For some reason, the group had lost interest in it. They asked the server to please turn down the volume on the radio.

They were somber as each reflected on what happened that day. Guilt-ridden faces stared at one another. All knew that it shouldn't have taken a momentous occasion to notice Julie and accept her. She was there the whole time.

Sarah finally broke the silence. "What do you think about Julie?" she asked the table.

Immediately, Ben spoke out. "Julie was the reason why Secret Radio Man came to our school. It was like the fundraisers and other events she would organize for everyone. We have always had it better because of her, then we never include her with our activities." Ben looked up and saw blank expressions looking back. They nodded in agreement.

Amber took her turn. "I remember when Julie had a crush on Tim Johnson. They started going out together. It was cute. I got jealous because I was a cheerleader and he was our best athlete. I couldn't accept him being with a girl who was short, fat, and not popular. I stole him from Julie. He later dumped me for someone else, and I cried. Julie comforted me as a friend and made me feel better. She wasn't vindictive, only compassionate and understanding. She knew pain. I wish that I never did what I did to her. Today everyone received plenty because of Julie, then we forget all about her."

Mike leaned back and clasped his hands behind his head. "The only reason that I will graduate is because Julie has helped me study for exams," he said. "I wouldn't have been eligible to play sports if she didn't tutor me. I guess that I am as guilty as everyone else."

Steve sat up and in a calm voice and said, "Why isn't she here with us right now?" At that instant everyone stood up, put on their jackets and rushed out to the parking lot.

"We should have been doing this the whole time," said Sarah.

"At least we started now!" exclaimed Mike.

The carload of classmates drove to Julie's house and ran up to the front door. They knocked rapidly until Mr. Smythe opened it. The group of five barged into the house, with Steven announcing that this was a friendly takeover. "All we want is your daughter, Julie. If you cooperate, no one gets hurt."

Mr. Smythe smiled at Steven. He knew the boy and was aware that he hung out with the best kids in school. He was also happy that his daughter Julie had friends after all. Good friends.

Steve and Ben saw Julie at the dinner table and walked up to her. They grabbed her by each arm as Ben said, "We don't want any trouble, you're coming with us!" The parents were amused! Julie laughed with her family and cooperated. She grabbed her coat from the living room closet and went out the front door with her abductors. Steven left last, saying, "Don't worry, Mr. and Mrs. Smythe, your daughter is in good hands. She'll be eating dinner with us tonight and will be home before midnight." He then gave a beautiful smile with a thumbs-up sign and left, closing the door.

The parents looked out the living room window and saw the excited students climb into an old station wagon and drive away. They turned and hugged each other. The missing piece to their valedictorian was put in place. She now had a social life with her peers. They cried in gratitude that their daughter went out on a Friday night.

They remembered their high school years and what Friday nights meant. It was to go out aimlessly with your friends to a malt shop or a drive-in movie. Those were some of the best times of their lives. It didn't matter what the activity was; it was all about being with your friends and the adventure that goes with it. They smiled in approval as they watched the old Pontiac drive around a corner and vanish. Julie Smythe was with friends now, and tonight she would have fun!

This story is dedicated To 'This Week In America's' Ric Bratton for being the absolute BEST RADIO MAN EVER!

Angie

Prejudice is all around us.

Sometimes it's based on experience, other times it was merely taught—or imagined. Angie Walls was a contented African-American teenager who loved her own back yard. School life was a bonus, being an honor student who was very popular. She even had friends in the same neighborhood.

All of this would be taken away from her. Angie's loving dad was offered a once-in-a-lifetime job promotion that he worked hard for. He *had* to accept it now, or forever lose the opportunity. This advancement obligated the family to move far away. The city girl would now relocate to a farming town that appeared to be out of the 1800s. Her fear was being the victim of prejudice. Her lesson would be to give others a chance and actually get to know them.

Sunlight peered through the window as fourteen-year-old Angie Walls lay in her bed. She clutched the quilts that kept her warm as she enjoyed the last moments of sleep. This was Saturday morning, and Angie had her day planned out.

It was time to get up, have breakfast and prepare for the day. Her mother, Merisa, agreed take her to the shopping mall to meet friends. Later, they would go to the movies and finish the day at a slumber party. Angie got out of bed and went downstairs in her pajamas. Her morning would start off by seeing her most favorite man: Leon Walls, her father.

He was in the living room as Angie ran up and gave him a warm hug, followed by a kiss on the cheek.

Angie's father spoke. "Good morning, Angie, did you sleep good?"

"I slept very good, Dad!" she said.

The father's voice changed into a serious tone. With a complex look on his face, he addressed a subject. "Daughter," he said, "We need to sit down and have a talk. There is something I need to tell you."

Angie was curious. She respected her father and knew by his actions that something important was about to be revealed. He motioned her to the dining room.

Angie walked with her father to the dinner table, and they took a seat. The humble man clasped his mighty hands on the table as he looked down. He was concentrating on how to express the news he was about to give. Looking up, he smiled at his daughter and using a firm, soft voice, began to speak.

"My job has given me a promotion," said Leon.

Angie's face lit up with a smile and said, "That's great, Dad!" She leaned over and hugged her hero, saying, "I'm proud of you!"

The giant stature wrapped his muscular arms around her as he shook with emotion. Tears trickled down from his eyes. The father looked at his daughter and said, "There's more to this promotion than just a pay increase. I am being transferred to the Midwest. Our family needs to move there after the holidays. They are being great about this and showed me detailed pictures of the nice house we will be living in."

"But, Dad," replied Angie. "I don't want to live there; my friends live here. Besides, those people are different and won't like any of us!"

Angie's father was compassionate and explained, "You have to give this a chance. Everything in this world is different, and that's not always a bad thing." He then smiled at her with encouragement and said, "C'mon, Angie, this is America!"

Angie could not accept leaving her school and friends behind. The teenager ran inside her room and locked the door. She fell on her bed and started to cry. Her father's heart was broken as he understood her pain. He left her alone.

The daughter stayed in her room for over an hour, sobbing.

Soon Angie came out for round two. "Please, Daddy, please! I want to stay here with my friends."

Her father anticipated this reaction. He had stayed up many nights, putting a lot of thought into this move. He mentally reviewed every scenario that would affect his family and always reached the same conclusion; it would be for the best. "We have to, darling," he said in a firm tone.

Angie went back to her room and locked herself in again.

The loving father went to the kitchen and started to make his daughter breakfast. The kind man would pick flowers from their yard and place them in a vase. That arrangement would be placed on a platter that would hold a warm bowl of oatmeal topped with milk, nuts, and brown sugar. A glass of orange juice with a small cup of diced fruit filled the tray. The fortunate child would be served breakfast in her own room.

Leon walked upstairs with the food and gently tapped on the bedroom door, calling out, "Room service."

Angie knew her father's humor and had to open the door. She opened it and saw the five-star breakfast with the beautiful pastel marigolds. "May I come in?" he asked. The tears subsided as Angie's face broke into a smile of relief. She nodded her head up and down as the bellhop brought the meal into her room. "Let's discuss this matter in greater detail," he suggested.

The daughter always felt love and protection from her father and shook her head in agreement. He placed the breakfast tray on her desk as she sat down in front of it. Leon pulled up a chair next to her and sat down. Angie grabbed the juice with both hands and took a drink. The room was now tranquil and ready for a talk.

"Angie," said her father. "You need to understand that you will never lose your friends, or anything you have. You will simply gain more things, and will always be able to share them with others. This move will gain you more friends, teach you more things, and offer you more places to go. Your friends will benefit through you because of this move. Your mother and I will also gain. This job will allow us to afford much more than we can now. At worst, we can always move back here. In the meantime, you can keep in touch with all of your friends, visit them when we can, and always accommodate for them when they visit."

Angie started to open up. Her innocent brown eyes looked at her father as she asked, "What will we have over there?"

It was now Leon's turn. "The country! It's beautiful, clean, and quiet, with everything fresh. You love horses. We will be able to ride horses now. In fact, we will probably get a few of them ourselves."

Angie's face lit up with interest. "We might own horses?" she asked in excitement.

"Why, sure," said her dad. "That's part of living in the country. You can learn how to ride one, then teach your friends how to ride when they visit. Their schools are also just as good as ours. When you go to college, you can go anywhere; even back here if you want to. There are also big cities in the county that have malls, movie theaters, drive-ins; just like here."

Angie started to feel better. There would be wonderful things waiting for them over there. And she would not lose her friends, either. She asked another question. "What's the name of the town we're moving to?"

With an encouraging smile, he answered, "Pardon". Angie's face contorted. She had no idea what a town with that kind of name would look like.

"Are you willing to give this a try?" asked the diplomat.

Angie thought for a moment and started to nod her head up and down, over and over again. The daughter hugged her father, saying, "I will go anywhere with you, Dad. I love you so much."

The conscientious father hugged his child and reminded her that she needed to get ready for her friends. The teenager felt much better and quickly ate her breakfast. She changed into her clothes and got ready for her day.

The news spread everywhere that she was moving. Her school served her a well-coordinated farewell party, with an address book given to her as a going-away gift. The book was filled with the names and phone numbers of all her friends. Angie would now have guaranteed contact with all her loved ones.

Leon's company was covering all expenses for this move. They even picked out a charming house that they put a sizable down payment on. All was looking good for his future.

Moving day had their car surrounded by Angie's friends. The slow-moving car resembled a limousine with rock stars as a swarm of teenagers followed it. She waved the address book out the back window, promising that she would keep in touch. Soon the car was down the block, with the Walls family driving to their new life.

It was adventurous driving halfway across the nation. The trip seemed more like a vacation, with stops at fun restaurants, historical viewpoints and fine hotels. The company credit card took care of the family on this journey.

The third day of the trip, they reached the farmlands that they would call home. Like Lisa Douglass on Green Acres, Angie began having second thoughts.

Leon followed his instructions carefully, making every exit, following every road, and not missing a turn. The family car soon entered a desolate valley blanketed with soft snow. The serenity covered rolling hills for miles and miles. Country roads and telephone poles occupied this land, with houses far and few. The family drove by a red barn with rusted farming equipment laid off to the side.

109

The antiques represented an era during the unjust Jim Crow laws, not too many years ago.

Angie's worst fear became a reality. A small sign reading "Welcome To Pardon" was posted along the roadside. It was like an insignificant stop sign out in the middle of nowhere. The young girl buried her head against the car door and cried like a lost child.

There was a yellow two-story house that could be seen a mile down the road, with a moving van in the driveway. Angie was now looking at her new home. There it was, standing tall in a field, all alone . . .

"Well," said Leon. "It looks like they got us into a nice home." The father drove to the house and pulled into the driveway. The company had already given him the keys, with the family anxiously waiting to enter the house. It was beautiful! Shiny wooden floors covered the entire home. The ceilings were a cathedral design with elegant light fixtures suspended on gold chains. The living room was spacious, with a fireplace and bay view window. A bathroom had two sinks with a jacuzzi and bath. The kitchen was modern with countertops that had a dining room adjacent to it. A sliding glass door led to a deck that overlooked the back yard and a valley that went on for miles. A mountain range could be seen off in the distance.

Leon saw his daughter's face gleam in approval. He then spoke. "Angie, why don't you run upstairs and look at your new bedroom? It's at the top of the stairs."

Angie ran upstairs to see her new bedroom. It was located exactly where her old one was back home. This one, however, was bigger, with a walk-in closet. It also had an improved view of the back yard with another very important feature: her own bathroom!

She fell in love with it!

Downstairs had the master bedroom with a much larger bathroom and private deck. Another bedroom, along with a family room and built-in two car garage, accompanied their new living quarters. Merisa Walls looked at her husband and said, "This will do!" The supportive wife hugged the big man and gave him a kiss.

The parents walked up the stairwell and saw Angie looking out her window. She seemed to be in awe, looking out over the valley that went on for infinity.

"Angie," said her dad. "I just called my new district manager, Mr. Collins. He is coming by to introduce himself and invited us to have dinner with his family tonight. The movers will be called to unload the van, with myself showing them where everything goes. After that, I will join you and your mother at Mr. Collins' house."

A knock was heard on the door as Merisa went downstairs to open it. His wife then called out, "Leon, Mr. Collins is here."

Leon went downstairs, followed by Angie. The friendly visitor was a charming gray-haired man in glasses who wore a three-piece suit. He held a basket of flowers that had a small banner reading: "Welcome home." The basket was handed to Merisa as he extended his hand to shake Leon's. "You must be Leon Walls," said the gracious elder.

Leon spoke, "I am, Mr. Collins. Pleased to meet you."

The happy man responded, "Mr. Collins is my dad, please call me Richard." The boss looked at Angie and said, "This has got to be your daughter that I have heard so much about!" The man shook hands with Angie and introduced himself once again. She responded by identifying herself as "Angie". She liked Richard Collins.

Richard continued, "I have a special surprise for you this evening, Angie. My daughter and some of your new classmates will be meeting you tonight. You will have a lot of fun, I promise!"

Angie stood tall and took a deep breath. This would be a test . . .

Her parents looked at their little girl with pride. She was addressing this new change in her life head-on. "I can't wait to meet them," she said.

"Well, good!" said a sincere Richard.

A brief conversation continued as the Walls' family got acquainted with Richard. It was arranged that the mother and daughter would ride in his car. After Leon helped the movers, he would follow the map given to him to Richard's home.

Merisa and Angie followed the district manager outside. A shiny black Jeep Comanche waited to transport them. They felt comfortable driving through the valley with Richard as his personable charm radiated conversation.

They soon arrived at his modest home. It was a rambler that stood alone with a view. There were cars in front that illustrated other guests were present. Like their own family, everything was nice, but not too lavish.

Upon entering the home, Mrs. Collins greeted the mother and daughter. She was equally hospitable and hugged Merisa, welcoming her to their home and to the community. Angie received the same greeting with a hug. Then she was introduced to their daughter.

A pretty blonde-haired, blue-eyed teenage girl introduced herself to Angie. "Hi, Angie, my name is Lydia." Lydia then hugged her new friend.

Angie introduced herself and immediately liked Lydia.

"Follow me," said Lydia. "You need to meet everyone." Angie was led through the living room and to her bedroom. Inside, there were more girls her age. All white and from *this* part of the country. "This is Angie," announced Lydia. At once, all the girls surrounded her with hugs and introduced themselves.

Her new friends were polite and showed no reaction to Angie's ethnicity. To them, she was nothing more than a new kid in school. Angie liked not standing out. She also was perceptive and studied them through the course of the evening.

The girls dressed like she did, and listened to the same music. They even watched the same shows and had a crush on the same stars. They were just like her, and also liked to go to town for the day and check out the malls.

Time passed quickly, and soon a slight tapping on the door could be heard. Lydia opened it to see a large black man with a gracious smile. "Is Angie in there?" he asked. Angie recognized her father's voice and ran to the door, hugging him. She was proud of him and introduced her dad to everyone in the room. He won them over with his class and good looks.

It was dinner time with pizza, salad and beverages. The host had a buffet-style display in the kitchen. This party food allowed the girls to eat in Lydia's bedroom, and for the adults to mingle in the living room. Richard Collins had invited a few neighbors, along with business associates, to meet Leon and his family.

The evening was the perfect 'welcome wagon' for the Walls family. The next day was Saturday, and Angie's new friends had plans to spend the day in the city. They wanted Angie to be with them. This outing would serve as another *test* . . .

In town, Angie had fun and discovered that there were other black families who blended in with everyone else. Angie started to drop her guard a bit more.

The next day she was invited to go horseback riding with Lydia and her family. One by one, her dad's promises were coming true. The *city girl* was given a precious gift by Lydia. A stylish Western hat that would hold in heat, shield the elements—and attract boys! Angie put on the hat. It fit perfect as it highlighted her pretty face. She was then mounted on a beautiful palomino horse that was tame. That afternoon changed her life as she rode through trails and meadows with a light dusting of snow. A special dream of hers had just come true. Pictures were taken by Lydia's father that would be emailed to her friends.

Angie would face another test on Monday. It would be her first day in school . . .

Angie was the only black student, in a small school. She did, however, get a running start, having gotten close to a few of her classmates already. There seemed to be acceptance with nothing negative being directed toward her African descent. She was treated like the other students.

But there was one more test coming up that would confirm any suspicion of prejudice. Her favorite day of the year was almost here: the third Monday in January, Dr. Martin Luther King Day. Her final decision would be based on how her new environment observed this national holiday . . .

To her delight, the school would commemorate the holiday by holding an annual essay contest about Dr. King. This was Angie's topic. Every year she won such essays back home, and filed her award-winning articles about her idol. She vowed to make her presence known in this contest!

The elated student shared the news with her parents. "Do you think anyone else has a chance at winning this contest?" laughed her dad.

"Angie, you always win with your essays," said her mother. "Do you want someone else to win this time?"

"Mom, when it comes to Dr. Martin Luther King, I will always give it my best!" said the motivated daughter.

"Just like you do with everything else!" commented her dad. "Angie, give it your all and break a leg," advised her father.

Friday arrived and Angie was prepared. She brought her improved writings about Dr. King on the bus and departed for school. Angie knew that she had created her best essay yet. With confidence, she couldn't wait for her turn to read it in the auditorium in front of the entire school. She also couldn't wait to return home and report to her parents about her performance.

It was now four o'clock in the afternoon, with the yellow school bus making its stop in front of the Walls' house. Angie ran out with excitement. Her parents saw their child through the living room window and knew that she had a successful day at school. She entered her home to find her parents looking at her eagerly.

"How did you do?" asked the mother.

Angie was out of breath and said, "I got third place!"

The parents looked in disbelief.

"You only got third place for your beautiful essay on Dr. King?" questioned her father.

Angie didn't feel bad about how she'd placed—she was happy about how others had placed. She justified earning third place and credited those who placed higher than she did.

"It was fair, because they were better than mine," explained the daughter. "They did know a lot about him—because they cared!"

The parents were impressed.

"It doesn't matter who wins the essay. All that's important is what we learn from it," said Angie. "I didn't know that Dr. Martin Luther King's favorite television show was Star Trek! And did you know that pecan pie was his favorite dessert?" The young woman recited more facts about the civil rights leader that she didn't know before. Her parents were stunned with all the facts and trivia she learned that day from her new classmates.

Then she asked a question. "Mom and Dad, since there is no school tomorrow, can I have some of my friends stay over tonight?"

"Angie," said her dad. "You can have as many friends over as possible, and let them know that we are ordering pizza! I also have some good news. My company is expanding and will be sending more families from back home over here. Some of your friends from your old school will be our new neighbors."

"That will be great!" said the well-adjusted daughter. "I can introduce my new friends to my old friends; or my old friends to my new friends!"

Her dad laughed and said, "It seems that wherever you go, you make friends!"

The happy daughter hugged her parents and thanked them. She ran to her room to call her many friends for a slumber party.

Several months later, there was a strange whistling sound coming from Angie's bedroom. The father heard it first and walked upstairs, tapping on her door. The daughter answered it holding a piccolo and wearing a green outfit with a matching kilt and beret.

"What on earth are you doing?" asked the bewildered father.

Angie stood at attention and announced, "Our school is going to have an essay contest about St. Patrick's Day, and I am going to win it!" She put the wind instrument up to her mouth and blew. It made a shrill sound that irritated her father's ears.

Leon raised his hands and covered his ears. "St. Patrick's Day is over a month away," pointed out the confused father. "Besides, you don't even have an ounce of Irish in you."

It was now Angie's turn. The enthused daughter stared at her father and said, "C'mon, Dad—this is America!"

Leon tensed up, realizing where he heard that quote before. He started to laugh at himself and hugged Angie with both arms. "You are right," said that dad. "Now I want you to learn as much as you can about those Irish customs. Keep learning, and always share what you learn."

The trembling man kissed his daughter on the forehead and continued. "Your mother and I are so proud of you, Angie. It's people like you that make this world a better place."

Willy

George Roberts struck it rich. A real estate deal brought in more than he could possibly imagine. An out-of-court settlement further extended this windfall, making him very wealthy. The fifty-two-year-old, heavyset man was on his own. He was never married and had no children. An only child with graying hair was now a multimillionaire and would retire immediately.

Money can change lives and often does. A person can boost a loved one's economic status and give them *the good life*. This can also inadvertently remove them from their niche and rob them of their identity. Such was the case for William 'Willy' Parks. A simple, harmless being who worked in the same factory George did. Like Gilligan, Willy was that humble soul who was loved by everyone.

George was celebrating in a bar with Tim Collins, a rich realtor who had navigated George to wealth. "I am glad that I took this week off on vacation," said George. "It was worth the court appointments, all the meetings and contract signings."

"What are you going to do now, rich man?" asked Tim as he toasted George.

Without any thought, he answered, "I will retire first thing!"

Tim was clever and responded with his quick wit. "But you have enough to retire two people quite nicely!"

That comment made George think. He had no heirs. Who could he ever share his retirement with? His mind wandered around his past, thinking of who he cared for the most. George asked himself again: Was there anyone he respected so much that he would include that person with his retirement? After all, he had been single his whole life and had no family.

Then a name entered his mind: Willy. That was the young guy from work who never gossiped about him. He was the guy who said, "Hello" every day and meant it. The guy who never wanted anything from anyone. Willy Parks was the only one he would share his luxurious retirement with. Willy Parks: the son he never had.

George looked up with a secret grin. He decided to include Willy in his retirement and set the twenty-two-year-old up for life.

Monday arrived with George Roberts on a mission. He arrived early and paid a visit to Mark Jacobs, the plant manager. He shared the news of his good fortune and requested permission to bypass his two week notice and retire that moment.

"I appreciate you asking me instead of just not showing up," said Mark. "We do have several workers laid off, and now we can employ one of them right away. We will mail you your reserved vacation and sick pay. You have a good retirement, and congratulations! Don't be a stranger, George."

George shook hands with Mark and left to clean out his locker. Thirty-two years of being an indentured servant had ended. Before leaving, he walked by Willy's department to visit his new interest.

Willy was hard at work. The skinny laborer with black shaggy hair and clean face concentrated on his work. He was disguised behind safety glasses and wore a standard white hard hat. His continuous smile prevailed, identifying him. He operated a drill press that bore holes in metal traveling on a conveyor belt. He set up the next station to place nuts and bolts through them. It was the lowest paying job in the factory, and Willy was grateful to have it. He arrived early every day and worked diligently.

Willy lived with his parents and was saving up money to buy a car. George gleamed at the dedicated worker, who was obviously happy.

Wait 'til he sees where his life is by the end of this week, George thought to himself.

George caught Willy's attention. Willy looked up and waved with excitement while he maintained the rhythm of his station. George was further inspired and would call him later in the week, unbeknownst to Willy.

George had a dream. He always wanted to live in a new highrise that was built where he lived. It was modern with fireplaces, decks, and breathtaking views. It came equipped with a parking garage, gym, and pool. It also was in the center of town, where all the action was. To have units on the top floor with new cars and money in the bank would be everything they would need!

He contacted Tim Collins and bought the two best side-by-side condominiums in that complex. They were on the top floor, with corner views of the city and waterfront. He then went to the most expensive furniture store in town and had their decorators style the new bachelor pads, with money not being an object.

His crusade continued. The next day he bought a new red sports car and parked it in Willy's enclosed parking space. Last, but not least, he opened a bank account for his new companion and put two million dollars into it. The stage was set!

It was now time to save Willy.

George waited until Friday. He called his old job during the lunch hour and paged Willy. In a few minutes, the young man answered a phone call that would change his life.

"Hello," called out a polite tone.

"Willy," said George. "This is George Roberts. You remember me, don't you?"

Willy answered with excitement. "Hey, I heard you retired. Congratulations, George!"

"What are you doing after work tonight?" asked George.

"I'm not sure yet," answered Willy.

"Can I pick you up after work and take you out to dinner?" asked George. "I want to discuss something with my friend, Willy Parks."

Willy was flattered. "I'd love that!" he exclaimed. "It would be fun having dinner with you tonight. You know when I get off, so I'll meet you in the parking lot after work. Thanks, George!"

George heard what he wanted to hear. "That's quite all right. I'm looking forward to this too. See you at quitting time!" He hung up the phone and felt good. Everything was going right . . .

The unmistakable green Ford Ranger pulled into the parking lot. George was the talk of the plant that week. His vehicle was flocked by co-workers who knew him for years. There were jabs of humor and laughter directed at him, all in fun.

Willy finished washing up and changed out of his work coveralls. He left the change room and approached the truck. George noticed him and said, "Get in." The factory worker walked around the truck and entered on the passenger side.

It was unusual seeing the two of them together. George honked his horn goodbye and drove off. Willy was excited like a child. He commented, "I really appreciate this, George."

"Well, I appreciate you," he volleyed back.

"Where are we going?" asked the innocent passenger.

"We are going to my favorite place for dinner," said George in a controlled tone. "Then I have a little surprise for you."

The young man was enthused and remarked, "Wow! That sounds great!"

The duo drove until they arrived at Wally's Broiler. Willy's mouth dropped open. Wally's was the most expensive restaurant off the water, where the 'upper crust' dined.

George was calm and said, "Willy, my friend, your life is about to change." He turned and gave Willy a reassuring look. "Let's go inside and have a talk over dinner."

They got out of the truck and entered the restaurant. An attractive hostess with two menus greeted the party and escorted them to their table. Willy was in awe as he looked around. The establishment was first class. It had beautiful tiles on wood grain tables with lit candles. Tiffany lamps matched curtains as glorious wall hangings accented rich carpeting. Stained glass outlined the windows, with a view of the harbor. Classic music enhanced the elegance.

"Have whatever looks good," said George as he picked up his menu. Willy opened his and tensed up with the tantalizing choices that were offered. It took about ten minutes, but Willy finally reached a decision on what to have. A gorgeous, personable server arrived and took their order.

George studied Willy's reaction to being in a high-class environment. "Do you like it here?" he asked his guest.

Willy answered fast. "I love it here, I never want to leave this place!"

Warm bread wrapped in a dark blue cloth was placed on the table, accompanied with butter. Tall crystal glasses were filled with ice water and lemon slices. Willy was impressed as he looked at George, nodding his head in disbelief. George winked back, nodding his head up and down.

George continued the momentum by asking Willy a question. "Could you live like this?"

"Yes!" said the youthful Willy. "Life can't get any better than this!"

George made his move. "Willy," he asked. "If you could retire right now and live like this, would you?"

Willy looked around the stately room and said, "I'd quit my job today if I could retire and live like this!"

George leaned forward and spoke. "Willy, It's time to quit your job. This is the first day of the rest of your life, and today Willy Parks is a multimillionaire. You now own a condominium that has the same view you are looking at right now. You have a dream car and a bank account that will carry you for life."

Willy leaned back in shock. He knew that George wouldn't tease him over something like that. His eyes and mouth were wide open with the understanding that he was telling the truth. "Who, me?" he asked.

"Yes, you," answered George with kindness.

Willy's mouth remained speechless as his eyes wandered with no bearings. He was absorbing the news that at the tender age of twenty-two, *he'd made it.*

Like a grandfather who spoiled his grandchild on Christmas morning, George was satisfied. He folded his arms and leaned back in his chair.

Willy was mesmerized over his abrupt climb in life. The trance was broke when the server arrived and placed their dinner in front of them. Willy had never been treated so good in his entire life. He looked at the delicious food, almost afraid to touch it.

George broke the silence. "Remember, Willy, it only gets better." They continued their venture by enjoying the good meal together. Friendly conversation arose, with each telling stories and laughing. Dessert was in order to complete the perfect meal. It was now time to cross the street and show Willy his new car, new home, and new life.

The evening was well planned by George. The restaurant set the tempo for the events that would follow. Now it was time to drive across the street and have an automatic garage door give access to where the elite lived. Willy was dumbfounded as he watched the 007 technology serve them. The vehicle entered the fortified underground cement lot and drove to a stall next to a shiny red Jaguar. Willy had figured out George's thought process and asked, "Is that my new car?"

George was getting pompous. With a smug look, he produced a set of keys and said, "It's all yours."

Willy was getting scared and said, "Look, you don't have to do this, I almost have enough money to buy a car."

George started to reason with him. "Willy, the path you are on will not get you here until you are an old man, if it ever happens. At this moment, you are here." He let the message sink in as he placed the keys on Willy's lap. Willy looked at the car and picked up the keys. "Thanks," he said in a soft, bewildered voice.

Next they got out of the truck with George leading the tour. "Here is where we get our mail," he said as he pointed at a wall of shiny golden panels next to the elevator. Then he pressed the button that signaled the elevator. It made a loud 'ding' sound when it reached garage level and opened up. Inside, it was enclosed with mirror walls, brass handrails, and spongy burgundy carpet. They entered the chamber, with George pressing the button for the top floor. The smooth ride built up anticipation for Willy. A soft chime sounded with the elevator stopping.

The mirrored door slid open, with a hallway of matching burgundy carpeting going in both directions. Paintings charmed the accented antique wallpaper, with miniature chandeliers suspended from the ceiling. Oak tables with matching chairs balanced out the penthouse lobby. Tall ferns in brass urns occupied every corner.

George took a right and walked to the lone door at the end of the floor. He had a key in his hand, and with pride said, "And this is your new home." He inserted the key into the lock and in one move, turned it and opened the door. He stepped back and motioned Willy to enter first.

Like a third-world peasant who was just granted citizenship, Willy was in a world that he had only heard about. He was stone quiet as he stared at the wall-to-wall view that overlooked the bay and city lights. The rich ambiance of the entire building seemed greatly increased in this penthouse. Willy saw a standard of living fit for royalty only. The burgundy carpeting, sunken living room, brass light fixtures, and tasteful artwork with oak tables and leather furniture was far beyond his social status.

The state-of-the-art kitchen with marble countertops had classic bar stools. Stainless steel appliances, along with hanging pots and pans that resembled a full-piece drum set. A bar draped in black leather covered the far corner of the room. More bar stools and suspended racks holding wine glasses contained the party section.

A smoked glass table surrounded by eight stainless steel chairs highlighted the dining room. A rustic china cabinet stood tall against the far wall.

There was more. A fireplace, utility closet with washer and dryer, two bedrooms with their own bathrooms, and a deck running the length of the suite balanced off the unit.

George sat on the living room sofa. "Willy," he said. "Why don't you sit down with me?"

Willy cautiously walked over to an easy chair that faced George, with a coffee table separating them. George was holding folded documents. He leaned over the table and handed them to Willy. "Open it up," he said.

Willy took the papers and opened them. They were testimony to his new wealth. A title to the car, condominium, and a bank statement of two million dollars were all issued to him. He looked down at the table and saw several sets of keys, confirming ownership.

Humble soft brown eyes looked at George. "This is too much," he whispered.

George anticipated the reaction, and had a well-prepared speech. "Willy," he said. "Do you have any respect for me?"

With all his honesty, Willy sat up and directed his answer. "I have always respected you. I always felt honored to have an older friend like you at work that I could talk to."

The answer was music to George's ears. The graying man had a tear trickle down his cheek and said, "That's how I feel about you! Our age difference doesn't matter; we are friends. In fact, I consider you family!"

"Really?" remarked Willy as he slouched in his chair. The comment was being absorbed. It was the highest compliment that anyone could ever give, and it came from his oldest friend.

"Really!" called out George in a loving tone. "Come with me on this retirement. Look at what you will be able to do for your family. That job you have will always be there if you want it back. If you let go of it, someone else will move up a notch. We'll be neighbors up here and will do fun things together. Your buddies will love it here."

George's logic began to register. Willy thought about how his family struggled to survive. Now he would be able to help them. He thought about his high school friends coming over and having the best times of their lives with his lavish lifestyle. And somewhere, someone looking for a job would find one because of the vacancy he created.

Willy looked at George and saw a concentrated face of hope looking back. He didn't know what to think. He felt pressured one way, and very fortunate another.

There was something peculiar about all of this, and he just couldn't put his finger on it. He was still just *Willy Parks,* a simple factory worker with a high school education. Moreover, he was young enough to be George's son.

Willy spoke up. "This is an awful lot at once. I need to go home and think about it. Don't get me wrong; I am grateful for what you have done for me. It's just that it's so much—and I am so young. I really don't mind my job. In fact, I like being there."

George replied, "Willy, I realize how overwhelming this must be to you. This is the good life, and most people never come close to making it this far. You are an exceptional person who's well deserving of this. Why don't you sleep on it?" he suggested. "I am sure when you wake up tomorrow that you will make the right choice. Remember that this relieves you of all worries. It also allows you the freedom to do anything you want to do, for the rest of your life. I hope that you do move in here and be my neighbor."

George extended his hand to shake Willy's. "You have a lot to think about." He got up and said, " I'll drive you home now. Thank you for being here with me tonight."

"That's okay," said Willy. "I had a great time and appreciate everything."

The tandem left the apartment and took the elevator ride down to the parking garage. They quietly entered George's truck and drove to Willy's parents' house. "Keep in touch," said George with a smile. "I am usually at Wally's bar for happy hour almost every day, if you ever want to drop by and visit."

"You don't have to worry about that," said Willy. "I'll give you a call soon." He got out of the truck and entered the house he was raised in. He was *not* going to tell his family about the proposition he had that night. He went straight to bed and thought about his evening with George.

The next day, Willy called George and asked if he would be at Wally's bar for happy hour. George answered, "I plan on being there this afternoon at four when it starts. I know that you don't drink, but I can still buy you a soda."

Willy responded, "I have a few errands to run. If I have time, I will be there to visit with you."

"Don't worry," said George in a fatherly tone. "If you don't show up, I'll understand." The retiree was elated just to hear from his friend Willy.

The regular was sitting at a table in the bar when a woman entered the room. She had blonde hair, blue eyes, and was dressed to the nines. The stranger approached George with confidence. She introduced herself as Dawn and asked if she could join him at his table.

George was floored. He never had such a beautiful woman pay attention to him before. He introduced himself and offered to buy her a drink. "I don't touch alcohol," she said. "But I would love a glass of iced tea."

That comment registered deep. His friend Willy didn't have vices like that either. He knew that he needed to respect himself better and give it up altogether. "Come to think of it," said George in a reasonable voice. "Iced tea does sound good." He was honored to have Dawn's company and already began to make improvements. George ordered iced tea for the two of them.

A warm conversation started between the adults. Each had an attraction toward the other, with mutual interests being discovered. George eventually asked Dawn if she'd had dinner yet.

"Why, no," answered the classy lady.

"Well, I am starving," laughed George. "Would you like to have dinner with me?"

Dawn was flattered and accepted the offer, saying, "I'd love that, George."

George left enough money to pay for the drinks, along with a generous tip. The couple then went to the dining room and was immediately seated. The dinner lasted over an hour, with a relationship in the making. George was falling in love, and Dawn had met the man of her dreams. It was as if they were meant to be together. George forgot all about his tentative plans with Willy.

The evening came to a perfect end with phone numbers exchanged. George Roberts would stay up all night thinking about Dawn.

The next morning, George's telephone rang; it was Dawn! His heart raced hearing her voice. She asked if he had any plans that day.

"No, Dawn," said the excited man. "My day is wide open!"

Dawn suggested that they meet for breakfast and spend the day together.

"I'd love that!" responded George. Dawn instructed him where to meet and gave him a half-hour. The lovesick man raced to the bathroom and got ready to meet his date. He was out the door in ten minutes.

The day was eventful. They met at a cafe for breakfast and later walked the waterfront. That evening, George invited her to his condominium and cooked a creative dinner. They ate by candlelight, admired the view, and got closer. The rest of the week had the couple spending all their time together, getting closer . . .

George knew that he had found the missing ingredient to his life. He also knew that there were many like him who would marry Dawn in a heartbeat. He went to a local jewelry store and bought an engagement ring. Later, he took his girlfriend out on the town. He strategically waited for that moment where they were walking the same boardwalk they did the first day they met.

He guided her to the bench they sat on that first day and sat down. George displayed the ring as Dawn's eyes opened in shock. He got down on one knee, and with all his heart asked her to marry him. Without hesitation, she accepted! He slid the ring on her finger and kissed his wife-to-be.

It was now time to introduce George to Dawn's family. Wally's Broiler was regarded as sacred to them. The banquet room would be reserved Saturday to formally introduce George to the family and announce their engagement. George was about to have the surprise of his life. When the family started to arrive at the restaurant, Willy showed up. George was elated that his younger friend was there and wanted to introduce him to his fiancée.

Willy smiled at George and said, "Welcome to the family!"

George was startled by the comment and looked at Willy. "Dawn is my favorite aunt," said Willy. "She was also lonely like you, and needed a good man. I told her all about George Roberts, and she wanted to meet him. I sent her to the bar the night you were waiting for me. I had a feeling that you two would be happy together."

George trembled with emotion as he hugged Willy. He shook in tears and quietly said, "Thank you, Willy. You have always made me happy, and now you brought Dawn into my life."

Willy continued, "There is something else that I want to show you." He motioned George to a window and pointed across the street. "Do you see that car?" he asked.

George looked and asked, "Do you mean that nice blue Camaro with the polished wheels?"

"Yes," said Willy. "That's my new car. I was saving up for it and finally got enough money. I am also moving out of my parents' house. Two of my high school friends will share a three-bedroom apartment with me. We are moving in next month. I also got a promotion at work. I am now a leadman and will get a pay increase for it."

Willy reached into his back pocket and pulled out an envelope. It was obvious what was inside it. "I did reach a decision on the offer you gave me," said the responsible young man. "I have to turn it down. I want those good things in life that you offered me, but it's worthless unless I get them the way you did."

Willy showed his maturity by giving George back the gifts that were handed to him. Two sets of keys and a bank statement were returned to their rightful owner.

"I have learned a lot from you," continued Willy. "What makes you great is that you are a self-made man with compassion. I watched you work hard every day and assist anyone who needed help. I want to be like you and be my own man. I received the greatest compliment in my life when you told me that you considered me like family. I loved that, and only wanted to be family with you. We are now going to be related, and my Aunt Dawn is the happiest woman on Earth. Thanks, George. You have done everything for me!"

George felt warm inside and realized that he had helped mentor Willy to be successful in life. What made him feel especially good was the fact that it wasn't his recent wealth that he was admired for. It was recognition for being the good man he always was. Those credentials allowed him to earn sacred things that money can't buy.

He would now continue life with something that had always eluded him—being a member of a family. With it, he also established a true relationship with the *son he never had*: Willy Parks. The holidays would now carry a more special meaning, and there would be no more nights of loneliness.

He was now graced with Dawn, that special woman who was waiting for a good man like George Roberts to enter her life.

Those Misinformed

The Psychic

Evelyn Parkland cuddled up on the couch in her bathrobe. The lonely thirty-four-year-old was well on her way to becoming an old spinster. Friday nights consisted of the same events that Saturday nights did — isolation embraced with solitude. An occasional call from her sister or mother spruced things up a bit, but still there were no suitors. It seemed that her social life was confined to her small family and the generic invitations to school reunions and company parties.

This would all change when a tailor-made message would find her. Unbeknownst to everyone, including herself, Evelyn was special. Late-night television would call out to her and *prove* that she was psychic.

Only the good die young.

Throughout town, devastating news was beginning to spread. 'Joe' had died. He was probably the classiest guy in the community. It seemed that every bar, lounge, and coffee shop was graced by his patronage. If you weren't a close friend of this stand-up guy, you at least knew who he was. The beauty was that *anyone* could sit down with him and visit. He always showed respect for others and listened to what they had to say. He was even big enough to ask *them* for advice. Joe never forgot a face and would always greet you as a friend in public. He was Evelyn's only friend outside her family.

This unforeseeable tragedy left a void in everyone's heart. A local sports bar in town would hold a well-publicized celebration of Joe's life on Saturday night. Evelyn would attend this event to pay her respects. More important, she would use this situation as a trump card to introduce who she really is, leaving everyone in awe . . .

Evelyn had recently watched a late-night television program that addressed whether someone had psychic powers. The criteria that separated the few spiritually gifted ones from the rest of the planet was based on answering a few easy questions. The heavyset, Puritan-looking woman in glasses studied the questionnaire displayed on her television screen.

With eagerness she grabbed another mouthful of buttered popcorn and shoved it into her mouth. Leaning forward, she listened to the questions asked by the narrator. They covered five simple categories. The announcer began by asking if she ever *knew* who was calling on the phone before she answered it. Every time Evelyn heard the phone ring, she would look at the clock—and know who would be calling!

The next question was asking if she *knew* what someone was going to say before they said it. Throughout her entire life, whether she was talking to her mother, sister, a waitress or co-worker, Evelyn *knew* what they were going to ask or say. Third was to see if she ever detected smells that were abnormally present. In her very apartment there were unexplainable scents, aromas, and even stenches that she could detect—and wonder where they originated from. Fourth was if you ever had a gut feeling about something, and were later proven right. Many times she got the responses she feared that would come from others. Last was if she ever had dreams about people, only to have them make contact shortly after. That phenomenon had happened to Evelyn time after time!

The host of the program had a presence that Evelyn could relate to. She, too, was an average person who personified a conservative lifestyle. The woman, like herself, was heavy and had long brown hair parted down the middle. Glasses accented this intellectual look, with a drab-colored dress almost touching the floor. Evelyn saw herself through that woman.

The host then gave her a story about being a diligent worker and law-abiding citizen. Despite being a role model for society, she still seemed to blend in with the background. The lonely nights of heartache and isolation seemed unfair to such a contribution to society. Having the natural needs of a woman, and being denied, escalated the pain. Evelyn could relate to this irony.

"But there is a reason for this," explained the woman on television. "We are of a higher level than the rest that inhabit this Earth. It is important that we come down to their level and let others know of our supernatural gifts. From there, we are revered for our superiority. They will understand that we were anointed to guide and control their destinies."

Evelyn was overwhelmed! Her place wasn't to fit in; it was to rule! Now everyone she knew would need to come to her for direction.

The program then touched on the greatest gift anyone could ask for. It tested further to see if you were also a *medium;* an advanced psychic gift which allows you to communicate with lost loved ones. Loved ones like Joe.

Evelyn paid close attention to what was being said.

"Have you ever lost a loved one who keeps leaving signs that they want to contact you?" asked the television host. "Are there moments when you keep thinking about a deceased friend? Do you see things in everyday life that remind you of them?" She then gave a multitude of examples ranging from restaurants they used to go to, that you still enjoy; to seeing someone who wears clothing similar to the styles they used to wear.

Then came a challenge. The viewer asked if they could see that very loved one in the same room with them. Evelyn looked around and admitted to herself that she couldn't see Joe. The host said that it could be done through your 'minds' eye'; if you actually have this extraordinary gift. "All you have to do is close your eyes and think of that special loved one you miss so much," she instructed. "Do you see that person now?" asked the speaker.

Evelyn closed her eyes and thought about Joe. She did have a vision of him! Evelyn was not only psychic; she was one of the select few chosen to be at the highest level. This realization explained everything about her life and why she was distant from others.

It was Saturday night at the sports bar. The popular hot spot was packed, with many sitting outside on the patio setting provided. Stories about their lost friend filled the air as one toast after another was made. Evelyn arrived alone and found a seat off to one side of the room. She noticed a center stage that had a podium with a screen in the background.

Like a well-prepared Amway salesman, her prey was positioned where she wanted them. It was now time to move in for the kill. Strategically she got out of her seat, walked on stage and got behind the podium. She smiled with confidence as she surveyed the masses conducting private conversations.

Evelyn pulled the trigger.

"Attention, everyone," interrupted Evelyn in a loud voice. "I need to let you know something special about me." Conversations stopped in mid-sentence as heads turned around. The entire room sat in silence, giving their undivided attention.

All eyes were now focused on Evelyn. Her professional presentation continued as she slowly gave eye contact to each individual. Like an adult having to reveal harsh news to a child, she made her announcement.

"I am psychic," she proclaimed. The room was motionless as they digested the information. The orator's temperament changed as she leaned back and grinned at her captivated audience. There was more to say.

"I just spoke to Joe, and he wants everyone to know that he's here at this very moment!" Evelyn nodded up and down like a grandmother telling Christmas stories. She was letting all know that she possessed this powerful gift and was willing to share it.

Evelyn knew that she was on the map. Still, she felt that her audience needed to be more responsive. She would now sweeten the pot by volunteering more spiritual information.

The middle-aged woman leaned over. She extended her hand and pointed her index finger to the sky. "Joe says that the coffee in heaven is unbelievable!" she said. Her head swayed side to side, holding her captives at bay. "He has also been leaving pennies on the ground for us to pick up as a token of his love." Expressionless faces remained quiet, but attentive. "So, if you see a penny on the ground," explained Evelyn, "Joe put it there for you to have as a gift." Heads nodded with understanding.

"I can talk to him right now for you," she offered. "Does anyone want to say hi to Joe and ask him any questions?" There were no takers as heads swayed sideways with closed mouths. "Does anyone have any questions?" asked the psychic. The motion was repeated. "Well, okay," said Evelyn. "If anyone ever wants to talk to Joe, I will gladly help you. So feel free to call me at any time."

Like a film running in reverse, the gathering turned back around and continued their conversations as if there was never an interruption.

Evelyn felt vindicated. The conservative wallflower was having the last laugh. It was now understood that she was different, because she was *special*. Her mission was fulfilled. She would now leave the sports bar knowing that her neighbors, co-workers, and former classmates would never look at her the same ever again . . .

The Haunted Exercise Bike

Final seconds ticked away. With enthusiasm, a single line of blue coveralls, white hard hats and steel-toed boots shouted the countdown. "Five, four, three, two, one; let's get out of here!" Quickly, the line simultaneously moved, grabbing their punch cards from the alphabetical card holder and punching out. In the same motion, the card was returned to its monogrammed slot. The indentured servants were now free men. School had just let out, and what was more important, it was Friday! The American worker had just earned his paycheck, with Friday night rituals awaiting.

There is a space that separates the worker from the family man. From there, a corner exists way out in *left field* that only guys would understand. This territory is usually found in a tavern. In these gin mills, men bond to prove their manhood and further control their spouses, or so they think . . .

Larry Floans maintained his perfect batting average by being the first employee to officially be off the time clock. The master turned around to his co-workers and said, "Last one at Milt's Bar is a rotten egg!"

Voices from the regiment said, "See ya in a few."

Larry was popular. It seemed that at work, he was the 'power behind the throne'. He had all the answers and gave advice to others, even when they didn't ask. It would be an understatement to say that Larry was confident.

Larry took the brisk walk to his pickup truck and instinctively drove three blocks to Milt's Bar. The parking space of choice was vacant. As usual, he beat the Friday happy hour crowd by minutes. The short, stubby man parked his car and entered the bar. Without thought, he secured the best seats in the house; a booth in the corner. It seemed that everything always went Larry's way as he sat down and lit up a cigar.

Steve, the bartender, called out to his regular customer. "Great to see you, Larry! What can I get you?"

Larry moved fast. By getting the first round of drinks, the night would be his. "How about four pitchers of beer with lots of glasses, and your famous chicken wings?" answered Larry.

"Right away," replied Steve.

Larry's booth had a panoramic view of the entire room, including the parking lot. Soon a familiar car entered the lot, followed by others. Some were friends from work, others were strangers. But it didn't matter; Larry had already staked the claim.

In moments the Friday after-work crowd rushed into Milt's bar. Larry's friends were at ease; they already saw his truck and knew that their favorite table was secured. The celebration of the weekend was now underway.

"Great job, Larry!" cried out Dan Hansen as the seasoned machinist patted him on the back.

"Old reliable has done it again!" said Greg Jennings as he slid into the booth. Soon, twelve men surrounded the table as glasses of beer were being poured. It was now time to relax and share stories. As usual, the male bonding started off with Larry telling a joke, leaving the entire table doubled up with laughter. Then he drew everyone's attention to the closest television screen that hung from the ceiling.

"Look at that!" said Larry as he pointed at the screen. The men all looked and saw a sexy woman on an exercise bike. Her radiant smile was everlasting as she demonstrated the product. A diagram of a female body was then illustrated, showing how the bike could melt off unwanted pounds.

"I need to get my wife, Agnes, one of those," said a lustful Larry. "She was a beauty when we first dated." Larry's eyes bulged in ecstasy as he devoured a greasy chicken wing.

"Well, speak of the devil," said Dan Hansen. "There is an exercise bike exactly like that on my next door neighbor's front lawn. I noticed it this morning when I left for work. I have no idea why it's there. It's as if it's looking for a home."

The wheels started turning in Larry's head. "Do you think it's still there?" he asked.

"I don't know, but it might be," said Dan.

"I am going to drive by your house and see if it is," said Larry. "Save my seat, I'll be back in awhile." Larry knew a good deal when he saw it. He also knew how to manipulate his wife.

The evening quickly turned into a business venture. Without hesitation, Larry Floans dashed out of the bar to meet fate. He drove the eight blocks to his friend's neighborhood. As he approached Dan's property he saw the gallant machine on the far corner of his neighbor's front yard. It was sitting tall, like the RCA dog in all its glory. Larry smiled in victory as he parked his truck next to the abandoned exercise bike.

Leaving the engine running, he got out of his vehicle and walked to the back. He opened the gate of the pickup and lowered it. Larry whistled as he walked toward model ZR7794P and declared ownership. Like the ad on television said, this exercise bike was lightweight and could give anyone a new life; even Agnes. The proud owner placed the bike in the bed of his truck and secured the gate closed. Like the winner he always was, he entered the truck, closed the door and drove straight home. He wasn't about to give anyone a chance to steal his new exercise bike.

About forty-five minutes passed until Larry arrived back at the bar. Within moments, the commercial with the young, sexy woman was being played again. Larry used this as a prop to draw humor. He pointed at the beautiful woman and called out, "Agnes!" His friends laughed hard until Larry interrupted. "I guess I was wrong, but soon my Agnes will be looking just like that!" said a smug Larry as he leaned back in his seat, puffing a cigar.

"What do you mean?" asked Greg Jennings.

Larry was in his element. He was the center of attention and giving advice. The short, heavy man with the moustache clasped his hands behind his head as he looked up in thought. The table was quiet. He removed the cigar from his mouth and began to speak. "You just have to know women," he said in a cocky tone. "I will soon have the most beautiful, sexy, dynamo woman out there, without having to say a word."

"How can you do that?" asked Greg.

"By controlling her surroundings," said Larry. "Her thoughts will be focused on what she is surrounded by and what I show interest in. That will motivate her to lose weight." With confidence, he winked at his audience.

Larry continued. "Tonight I employed the final ingredient needed to set the stage. Thanks to my good friend, Dan, I was able to get the very exercise bike the dame on TV works out on, for free. When Agnes was in the bathroom, I placed it in our home and left quietly. I have already taken measures by buying Jane Fonda workout tapes and stacking them on top of our VCR."

Larry continued to share his strategy. "My garage has the calendars with the Sports Illustrated centerfolds pinned up. I often call out to her while I am in there to assist me on a project. When we watch a movie, or are out in public, I let her notice how I look at attractive women. Now she has a state-of-the-art exercise machine in our living room. This all puts the idea in her head to look like those gorgeous women on television!" Like Archie Bunker, Larry sat back, impressed with himself.

"You're a genius!" exclaimed Greg. Larry could only look back, nodding in agreement.

The tempo in the room changed when a neighbor of Larry's entered the bar. It was Mike Fields, and he noticed

Larry. "I want to thank you for the nice exercise bike, Larry," said Mike.

Larry put his beer down and looked at his neighbor. "What are you talking about?" he asked.

"That exercise bike that was on the corner of your front yard," he replied. "I just carried it into our house before I got here. I want to thank you for leaving it out so that someone like my wife can get use out of it."

Larry sat low in his seat staring at his glass of beer. His eyes were dilated as he calmly said, "I didn't put it there."

Mike looked perplexed and asked, "Do you think Agnes had anything to do with it?"

Larry thought for a moment and looked up with a puzzled expression. "She didn't have time to try it out, because she had an appointment with her hairdresser." The room silenced in bewilderment.

"Do you want me to pay for what it cost you?" asked Mike.

Larry was pinned in a corner. He was just bragging in front of the guys on how he got it for free. He couldn't take advantage of him at that moment. He was forced to respond with class. "No, that's all right. It's yours now," he replied.

Larry wanted to maintain his composure and invited Mike to join his friends for a beer. He changed the conversation with more stories, generating more laughter. An hour passed, then the mystery of the bike arose again.

Mike was sitting next to Larry and noticed his brother-in-law, Stan, pull into the parking lot. It was obvious that he was aware of Mike's presence. When he entered the establishment, he looked around until he saw Mike. "Hey, I want to thank you for the exercise bike."

A dumfounded Mike slowly turned and looked at Larry. Larry sat still, looking at his beer, absorbing the message. Mike looked up at Stan and asked, "What are you talking about?"

"The exercise bike that was on your front yard. It was close to the sidewalk, so naturally I thought that you wanted to get rid of it," replied the in-law. "I was going to get one for my wife, Susan, but you saved me a trip and some money."

Mike stiffened up and calmly remarked, "I didn't put it there."

"Maybe someone broke into your home and put it there," suggested Stan.

"I don't see how; we always keep the doors locked," said Mike. "Besides, my wife was attending a Tupperware party across the street and would have seen any suspicious activity." The room sat still in wonderment . . .

Finally, Larry spoke up. "I have an idea. Let's drive through our neighborhood and see if it has moved again." Mike and Stan were curious and agreed to ride with Larry. "We'll be back in a few," said Larry. The three neighbors left the table to further inspect this phenomenon.

Night had arrived, with a fall chill in the air. Fog was setting in this community as the three detectives entered Larry's truck. "This is getting spooky," said Larry. They left the parking lot and drove the few blocks to their homes. As Larry rounded the last corner to make his final approach, the three men gasped in horror. Riding on top of the fog like the Flying Dutchman was ZR7794P! It was now floating on the edge of Stan's front lawn for all to see. Its shiny metal frame was moist from the elements and glistened as it defied boundaries.

Larry grasped the steering wheel with both hands and accelerated down the street.

"Did you see that?" exclaimed Mike.

"We all saw it," muttered Larry.

The trio returned to Milt's Bar and reunited with their friends. "You won't believe what we just saw!" said Larry. He then told of the supernatural occurrences that surrounded the exercise bike that evening.

It was now time to have a meeting of the minds. The group of men sat quietly at their table and took turns with their theory on what was happening, and why.

Pete Wilson was always the quiet one of the group. He spoke first. "Larry, do you think that you are cursed?"

Larry leaned back in his chair and pondered on that thought. He then questioned, "Why would I be cursed?"

Another voice broke the silence; it was John Carolson. "Do you think that your son from your first marriage put a spell on you?"

Larry digested the probability. In defense, he answered, "That teenager is the luckiest boy in the whole world! Every Christmas I out-spend his mother and their entire family. I also never write him unless I put money in the envelope, and get this—every year, I take him to Disneyland!"

"Wow," said John. "You have class!"

The men raised their beers and cheered Larry for being a great father.

Steve Hayes spoke next. "Do you think that after the bike was manufactured, that it was flown over Stonehenge or the Bermuda Triangle?" The table was stunned as they slouched over and looked at one another in fear.

It was now Rick Schroder's turn. "Maybe someone who's a member of a cult tried using it as a demonstration model and decided not to buy it. But they *did* touch it!" Heads nodded with the understanding that *that's* all it would take.

Stan stood up and said, "Well, there's one thing for certain; I won't have that evil machine in my yard!"

"Where are you going to put it?" asked Mike.

"In your yard," said Stan. "That's where I found it. Our house will be haunted until I return it to its natural burial site!"

"But it wasn't originally there," replied Mike. "I found it on Larry's property!"

All eyes were on Larry. In a quivering voice, he said, "I found it in Dan's neighborhood!"

"Do you think that it's following you?" asked Pat Gibbons.

"Maybe it's centuries old and haunts the entire planet until Judgment Day," suggested Phil Write.

"I'm getting it off my property right now!" exclaimed Stan. He finished his drink and left the bar.

The congregation stayed behind, pondering on the spirituality of the exercise bike. Within ten minutes, Stan's car returned to the parking lot. He entered the tavern with a pasty white face and bulging eyes. "It vanished!" he proclaimed. "It must have floated away in the fog!" The room was petrified as they stared at one another. All were in silence.

The moment was interrupted when Stan's brother, George, entered the bar. He walked up to Stan and said, "I was happy to take that exercise bike off your hands. Now it's just a matter of getting my wife to use it," he said. "She is at the Tupperware party tonight with all the girls. She will be surprised when she gets home and sees it in the living room."

"I wouldn't be so sure of that," remarked Mike.

It was getting close to seven o'clock. The guys decided to order a pizza and have a last round. Nothing more needed to be said about the traveling exercise bike.

Milt's specialty was his house pizza. It was served in a jumbo sized extra-large pan; enough to feed a small army. The men devoured the tasty meal and 'bottoms up' their glasses. Each patron opened their wallets and littered the table with bills. There was more than enough to pay for the evening with a handsome gratuity for the server.

Larry looked at his friend Stan and asked what his plans were for the weekend. "I want to get to Paul's Thrift Store before the crowd gets there."

Larry's face contorted as he asked Stan, "What crowd?"

Stan grinned at Larry and asked, "Don't you know? This is Paul's Three Day Weekend Sale. He does this every year. There are always long lines in the morning when he has his three-day sale. It's like Macy's when they kick off the holidays!"

Larry never knew of such a sale and wanted to know more. "If it lasts three days, then it must have started today," he said.

"It did start this morning, but being Friday, not many customers will come," said Stan.

Larry asked, "Aren't they open until ten at night?" He looked at his watch and said, "It's only a quarter to nine, let's get in there right now!" They shook their heads in agreement and raced to the parking lot. "I'll meet you inside the store," said Larry.

Larry arrived first, with Stan close behind. It was the calm before the storm at Paul's Thrift Store with the parking lot almost full. Together they hustled into the store and filtered in with the crowd. The lines to the cash registers were several customers deep, with the donation bins and back room being emptied to fill depleted shelves. Larry's jaw dropped when he saw the marked-down prices of the used merchandise. Using his instincts, he raced to the department that held exercise tapes and equipment.

Larry was like a kid in a candy store! Pink dumbbells with matching sit-up benches graced the room. Posters of Hollywood celebrities endorsed their workout videos with money-back guarantees. A multitude of diet drinks and health bars crammed the shelves. He turned around to see Stan staring at him. Larry cried out, "We struck it rich!"

Behind Stan were the windows that outlined the front of the store. The dark autumn night gave the glass an obscure, rippled look, serving as a mirror. Larry was momentarily distracted when he saw his own reflection. He suddenly reached a state of panic when he saw ZR7794P zeroing in behind him! Larry knew that it was the spirit of the haunted exercise bike trying to get him and turned around to flee.

A long metal platform on wheels used to transport items was coasting toward Larry with the bike on its bow. The exercise machine appeared to be in the same stance a bull would use before charging a matador. It was placed on the very front of the cart, with old clothes underneath it. The bike's rear end was elevated as the structure weaved slightly back and forth from the motion. Its pink handle bars seemed to be pinned back, ready for attack. He was now face-to-face with this demonic metal contraption and fainted.

The exercise bike was being put on the market once again. Soon, another husband with bright ideas would buy it in attempt to motivate his wife. Like a fruitcake during the holidays, it would make its rounds as a gift throughout the office and entire neighborhood. *You can lead a horse to water, but you can't make it drink.*

Many of the women who attended the Tupperware party knew of the bike and were disgusted with it. As far as the lovely Agnes goes, she didn't attend the party and was at the beautician's. Did she actually play a part in this stray machine's life and know a few secrets she's not telling? One must ask thyself:

"Does she, or doesn't she? Only her hairdresser knows for sure . . ."

Brother Paul

Did you grow up having a sibling who was smarter than you? I did. In fact, I had five of them. My brother Paul is the one this true story is about.

Paul was always that well-balanced guy who seemed to do things *right*. He consistently held good grades, whereas I always struggled. I even had to repeat first grade, just to get a better understanding of what was going on. I was, however, more clever than he was and mastered the art of doing pranks.

Somewhere during our grade school years, our parents went grocery shopping. The other members of the family were busy with their friends, leaving Paul and I alone at home. It was one of those overcast Saturdays where we were bored to tears.

I walked through our kitchen and looked out the window that was over the sink. I saw through our next door neighbor's window and noticed that the sweet old lady who lived there was home.

My diabolical mind went to work. I approached Paul and pretended that I had an exciting idea. Paul was at a point where he would welcome anything that would spice things up. He foolishly asked, "What is it?"

I suggested that we made prank phone calls, since we had the house to ourselves, and that we wouldn't get into any trouble. He believed me and wanted to know more. I explained to him that I would dial the first number and let him talk, then we would switch.

He took the bait. I then allowed him the *honor* of speaking first.

Our neighborhood was that standard middle-American design out of the 1950s. The houses were close together, with the water mains dividing the homes. What I am trying to say is that the kitchens all faced the neighbors' kitchens. This was the 1960s and all telephones were 'land lines', meaning that they were attached to a cord that connected to a wall. Most kitchens from that era had such a telephone.

My scheme was to call the old lady next door and have her catch my brother, Paul, on the other line harassing her in plain view.

I dialed her number as I saw the excitement grow on Paul's face. I then intentionally positioned him to lean over our kitchen sink and get mentally prepared for his debut. On our end, I could hear her phone ring. I looked through her kitchen window and could see her sitting down in an easy chair, reading the newspaper.

I saw her place the paper down to get up to answer her telephone. She naturally chose the closest line to her, which was the one in the kitchen. As she bent over her sink to answer her phone, I handed ours to Paul. He was new at this and chose to press his hands flat together and hold them sideways. He rested the phone on his shoulder, leaning his head to one side, with an ear against the receiver. When he heard a pleasant, "Hello," he put his hands up to his mouth. He started to make noises like a harmonica and also sang at the same time. The old woman was sharp as a tack. Like a game show contestant, she immediately guessed right the first time.

"Paul?" she questioned, looking up to our kitchen window.

"Edna?" responded Paul in shock. He looked back at her, with each holding the phone. It was like a prison movie where an inmate gets to visit a friend from the 'outside'. The close range, phones, and glass effect would only need minor alterations. Myself, the prison guard, was bent down under the counter and out of her view.

"Oh, little boys should never play on the phone," she advised.

147

"But it's only a joke," he explained pleading for his life. Paul could see me on the floor, laughing hard.

"Please don't tell my parents," he begged.

"Oh, I don't know . . ." she responded.

He continued to apologize profusely and finally said his goodbye on a proper note. When he hung up the phone, he looked at me and asked why I did that to him. Remember that Paul is very intelligent and likes to learn. I looked him directly in the eyes and listed the reasons why.

I held up my hand and used my fingers to represent each point I was about to make. He gave me his undivided attention.

I wiggled my thumb and explained that I was bored. Paul was a good student, and in silence nodded his head with understanding. I progressed to the next finger and told him that I wanted to get him into trouble without myself getting into any trouble. He nodded up and down as I continued. I advanced to the next finger and pointed out that for the rest of my life, this would give me something to laugh about if I ever got bored again. He cooperated by nodding yes again, as my next finger was being addressed. I asked if I already mentioned that I wanted to get him into trouble so that I could laugh at him. He nodded to let me know that I had already covered that.

I could see the wheels turning in his head as he absorbed the knowledge. He saw the sheet of paper that had the telephone numbers of our neighbors and picked it up. He scanned it to find a victim that we both knew. "Okay," he said. "Now it's my turn."

I said that I didn't want to play anymore and ran upstairs to my bedroom, locking the door behind me. Paul's delayed reaction was just enough time for me to escape. After all, he was and still is considerably bigger than me. He did chase me and started to thrust his body against my bedroom door. I opened it and told him that if he did *anything*, I would tell mom and dad about the prank phone call. It worked! He thought about it for a moment and didn't challenge the threat.

Forgive me, but that was stupid on his part. Dad would have figured out what actually happened, and I would have *gotten it*—not him. At worst, Dad would have made fun of him for allowing me to take him down to my level. Paul was in foreign territory and allowed me to have this unnecessary leverage on him. Throughout that summer, I was able to hold him at bay with my threat. I did get bold at times, sticking my neck out quite a ways. As long as the iron was hot, I was protected.

"Where are we today?" you might ask.

Paul is doing exceptional, as always. I was married once and realized that it was best that I leave everyone alone. Paul, on the other hand, got it right the first time. He has a beautiful wife named Rosslyn who is from Kenya. Together they have two healthy, happy, and very intelligent children named Robin and Loren.

Unlike myself, he breezed through college as an honor student. I attended a cross-state rival for three years until I discovered that there was a forklift with my name on it.

Paul has many talents: He is a computer whiz and cartooned professionally, having sold many. He also has obscure interests that he developed to higher levels, such as playing the banjo, being able to pick a combination lock (not as a livelihood), and having an assortment of interesting friends.

He always fascinates me whenever I see him, which is often. We even had a few years in our childhood where we shared bedrooms, and I still get intrigued with his company. It's as if he is a celebrity that I have always heard about. It is my belief, as well as others who know him, that he would make a great talk show host. Am I jealous over him? Maybe a bit . . .

However, I am proud to say that I do have a victory over him. It was that one summer, years ago, when I flew under the radar. For a brief moment in my life, I *owned* him.

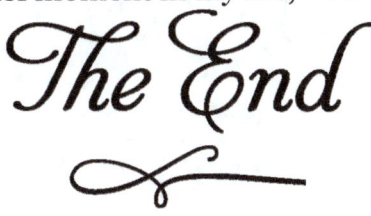

The End

The World's Greatest Rock Star and Other Short Stories

Prologue

Isn't it great to dream?

Dreaming is something all of us do. This fact poses a natural question: If conditions were right; would we actually be able to live out those dreams?

The answer is: *"Probably so."*

The case of Milton Livingston has its own way of illustrating this point. His early life had its share of cruel obstacles; but fate would change all of that. More questions would soon be raised. Did his changed state of mind merely create a fantasy that he could finish out his life in; or did his tragic accident intentionally change his world and allow him to be what he was meant to be?

You be the judge.

One thing for certain: *there is a bit of Milt Livingston in all of us.* When we escape the tensions of reality and find our solitude; we become the star that secretively lives within us.

Matt Shea

Second Chances

The World's Greatest Rock Star

A legend in one's own mind. Could that be some, or all of us—and who's right?

Such are the questions surrounding the life of Milton Farrell Livingston. A teenager who was an outcast in school and battled his parents at home. The boy who was predicted to have no future.

An accident pushed him further away from society, leaving him in a coma for life. Did this tragic event further restrict this youth, or actually set him free? A medical experiment would now allow Milt to be what he always wanted to be within his own thoughts. This procedure also let the bedridden son share the venture with his parents, allowing them to know who he really is.

Dr. Peterson entered the quiet room and closed the door. The good doctor looked like he came out of Hollywood. His dynamic silver hair and mustache showed confidence. His piercing brown eyes and regal voice emphasized that he was professional. A white uniform gave the finishing touch.

Inside, Clarence and Maria Livingston stared down at their son. The middle-aged, straight-laced looking man dressed like the accountant he was. His short black hair was parted off to one side, illustrating his conservativeness.

His dark-rimmed glasses and gray three-piece suit upheld his trademark.

Maria was more informal. The forty-five-year old woman had tasteful graying hair that was parted down the middle and curled at the shoulders. She was slightly overweight, wearing blue jeans and a matching work shirt. This average woman was comfortable with herself.

The ever-present scent of disinfectant saturated the white room.

Their sixteen-year-old son lay motionless as he breathed in a controlled rhythm. His shoulder-length strawberry blonde hair exemplified youth that was being denied. Sprouting whiskers reflected the innocence of life before decades of harsh lessons. The relaxed face no longer showed signs of confusion, rejection or pain. The developmental process of adolescence reaching adulthood had been stopped.

The calmness served as testimony to being relieved of life's stress and anxiety. But still; their son would no longer be able to look at them.

An accident changed Milt's life permanently. An explosion at a nearby refinery spread toxic gases that the teenager inhaled, rendering him unconscious. Ironically, Milt Livingston would be the only casualty of this disaster. The fumes had penetrated Milt's respiratory system, eventually having the youth slip into a coma.

Guilt made its presence known. The many times the son was ridiculed surfaced. Every verbal attack was subconsciously recorded and now played back to the parents:

"The first thing we should do is cut that hair of yours and clean up your room!"

"I knew it was a mistake buying you an electric guitar for your birthday."

"Do you think that you could ever make a name for yourself looking like that?"

"Well, nothing is stopping you from moving into the Rocker Cafe."

155

"Of course you're getting picked on in school; look how weird you turned out."

"You call that music? Turn that thing down!"

"Now, who would ever want to know a guy like you?"

The torture increased with the recent words that came from the doctor.

"He will finish out his life within these four walls."

Teary-eyed, the parents felt punished and placed the blame on themselves.

Dr. Peterson had a smirk on his face as he placed his hand on the mother. The parents looked at him, wondering why he had such a peculiar expression. It was as if he knew something they didn't.

"Can I share a secret with you?" asked the doctor with a chuckle in his voice.

The parents were stunned by his friendliness and felt a ray of hope. "Why, yes," responded the father.

"In cases like this, we secretly hypnotize the patient," said Dr. Peterson. "We do this so that they can finish out their lifespan being whatever they want to be. The beauty is that there are moments when the parents can enter their child's world and talk to them. It's all bliss," he said in a comforting tone.

The doctor elaborated further. "This procedure is only at an experimental stage and not adopted as a medical practice," he confided. Leaning toward the parents, he whispered, "But it does seem to work, and we can keep quiet about it."

Positives were pointed out by Dr. Peterson:

"He'll never be homeless or experience the pain of divorce or loss of a loved one. He will be happy, as far as his dreams will allow; with no barriers to stop him. He will be more than successful; he'll be the most famous person in that world he created. Your son will be idolized by fans everywhere and shape the world he lives in. At times you will be able to talk to him, with Milt being aware that it's you. He will incorporate you into his world the way he would have."

"How real would this be to him?" asked the father.

"At all times, your son would pass a polygraph test," said the doctor with conviction. There was a slight pause as Clarence looked down, scratching his head.

The pleasant doctor continued. "This is actually a lot of fun; with no one getting hurt and no extra expenses involved. It will just be between a few select members on the hospital staff, the two of you, and Milt. Nobody else will know a thing."

The mother realized the humane beauty to this existence and smiled with approval. "Do it," she consented.

"How do you know how to program him?" asked the father.

"With this age group, we go by how they decorate their bedroom," said the doctor.

"It looks like the inside of that Rocker Cafe that the teenagers go to," said the father.

"I took my son there once," said the doctor. "That's all we need to know." Dr. Peterson changed facial expressions and looked directly at both parents. He spoke in a firm tone. "There is something that you both must always remember," he stressed. "Milt will be living out his dreams on his terms. You will only be able to visit him in that very world he created, and accept how he chooses to see you."

Clarence and Maria looked at each other, wondering how their son actually viewed them.

"I have to ask you both to leave now," requested the doctor. "The present condition isn't how you are going to know your son. Come back tomorrow at this time; we will have Milt's reality situated. You will then be allowed access to visit him. From there, he will introduce you to his world."

Clarence and Maria left, accepting their son's fate. They wondered about the experiment and prayed that it would bring joy for the remainder of his life.

Upon arriving home, they instinctively went to Milt's bedroom. This inadvertently introduced them to the culture that would serve the next phase of their son's life. Posters of his idols stared back at them; with some living and others dead. An aura was felt as if they were trespassing on sacred burial grounds.

In the far corner, Milt's guitar rested on a stand like a forgotten monument. A stereo with volatile speakers represented the smoking gun of the household. Compact discs scattered throughout the room, with clothes filling the gaps. The first layer of dust blanketed the area like algae growing on a shipwreck. Nature had claimed the territory that once harbored their son. Quiet was now the only occupant in this desolate space.

They trembled, realizing that this was where Milt spent most of his life. It was not just all he had; it was what he wanted. They looked at one another, knowing that they never made an attempt to understand what he loved.

They remained quiet for the rest of the evening, thinking about the isolation they forced on their son. Each knew that there was only one direction to go. It would be to support the world that he would create and be involved as much as possible.

The following day they returned to the hospital, as directed by Dr. Peterson. They entered the room where their son existed.

"Good afternoon," greeted Dr. Peterson.

"Good afternoon," said the father. "How is Milt today?" he asked with a concerned voice.

Dr. Peterson's smile set the stage. "I believe that he is having the time of his life," he said. "Why don't you find out for yourself?" The doctor motioned the father to the bedside and said, "Simply talk to him the way you normally do."

The father sat in a chair alongside the bed and looked at his incapacitated son. Looking up at his wife, he felt encouraged and leaned closer to his son. "Milton, this is your dad," said the father in a soft tone.

The expressionless face began to speak. "Dad, how did you get past security?" responded the son. "I'm sorry, but when I am on stage, I have to perform. You and mom are allowed backstage; we can visit after the show. Thanks for understanding." Milt began to sing as he faded back into a deeper sleep.

"That's our Milt!" exclaimed the father.

The mother stood up with her mouth wide open. She turned to the doctor and hugged him, thanking him over and over again. Dr. Peterson said, "That's quite all right."

Looking at the father, the doctor said. "We need to explain a few things while your son is on stage." They moved to a table in the lobby and sat down.

"Milton is now the rock star he always wanted to be," said Dr. Peterson. "What you need to remember is that he can only speak to you for brief segments, then he falls back into a deeper state of unconsciousness. But he will still be what he wants to be; knowing that you are very much in his present life."

"Why don't you two go out for lunch?" suggested the doctor. "We can try to catch him later, when he is not so busy."

Maria looked at her husband and shook her head up and down with enthusiasm. They left for lunch with the understanding that their son's concert would have to come first.

Later that afternoon, the mother sat in the chair next to her son and delicately called out his name. "Milton, this is your mother."

The face twitched as he responded. "Mom," said the son. "I've been looking all over for you!"

The mother leaned back with delight. Her son addressed her the way he always did! Milton continued. "Hey guys, you gotta meet my mom!" There was silence as other actors performed on Milt's end. Then he spoke again. "Everyone loved those cookies, Mom; thanks!"

Maria gazed back with a loving look. Throughout her son's life, she always baked him cookies to share with his friends. The intensity left Milt's face as he faded into a deeper sleep. The visit was over, but the family was happy.

The married couple left the hospital as if their first grandchild was born. They couldn't wait until their next visit to play 'make believe' with their son.

The following morning they were at Milt's bedside. Clarence would contact first. "Son , how are you today?" asked the father.

The voice registered with the son answering back. "Dad, I know that you came to apologize, but that won't change things around here."

The father was perplexed. "What are you talking about, Milt?"

"You don't know?" asked the son. "You draw attention to me every time when we go out. That attention might make you feel good, but to me it becomes an invasion of privacy. It can also be dangerous, because I have been mobbed before by autograph seekers."

The rock star elaborated further.

"Don't get me wrong. I love my fans, but I have to lay low when I'm in public. We have had this discussion several times before. You need to stop letting everyone know who I am and that you're my dad. Can you promise me that, and keep your word this time?"

"Okay, son," replied the father reluctantly. "I promise that I won't ever do that again."

There was a long pause, then came Milt's response. "Okay, Dad."

The dad got close to his son and inquired in a friendly voice. "Hey tell me, Milt. What do your friends think of me?"

"Dad, something that I learned as a professional is to always be honest. They can't stand you, but do their best not to show it. That's because you're my father and they don't want to hurt your feelings." The superstar continued. "Do you remember when we allowed you backstage?"

"Yes I do, son," replied the father cautiously.

"That guy with the beard that grabbed you from behind was just playing with you," said Milt. "That was Jim Morrison's way of introducing himself. You handled it as if you were being attacked."

"You are my dad, but you don't fit in with us the way Mom does," stated the son. "Sorry."

The father felt insulted. His son viewed him more as a liability, and not a buddy.

Maria was anxiously waiting her turn and traded seats with her husband. "Hi, son," she said. "I'm over here."

Milt yelled out, "Hey guys, Mom's here! I hope you don't mind, Mom, but the guys adopted you!" That acceptance made her blush, and further agitated the father. The conversation continued with the mother being presented with an imaginary bouquet of flowers. "This is from the guys, Mom. They love ya!" said the son.

The mother was a sport and answered back, "Thanks, guys!" Milt laughed along with the festive moment, then drifted off to the far corners of his mind. The visit was over.

Clarence and Maria would continue to visit their son twice a day; once in the morning, and again just after dinner. They got their visits in whenever Milt's career would allow. Steadily, the mother's popularity escalated while the father's went south.

Despite the reality of their son's condition, the dad didn't want to play second fiddle any longer. Jealously had set in. Like a child with a digital pet wrist watch, he became consumed with this invisible battle. It was time to compete with Milt's *fame*.

The next session, Clarence would take the fight to his legendary son. He would be the lead-off visitor in an attempt to plant a better image of himself.

"How are you today, son?" asked the father.

Immediately the petrified face started to contort. "Dad, I am fine, but you seem to be upset. Do you mind if I ask you a question?" asked the son.

"Why sure, son," answered the father. "What's up?"

"My friends think that you're jealous of my success," stated Milt.

The father answered the accusation by responding with a question. "Why would they think I would be jealous of my own son?"

"Because it might bother you that I went further in life than you did," said the son nonchalantly.

Feeling upstaged, the father volleyed back with bragging rights. "Why, I'll have you know that I played football and wrestled in high school," said the defensive father. "I probably could have been class president if I wanted to."

The son had control of the debate, and with a calm voice continued to dominate. "I am sure that you probably could have, Dad," said Milt. "But that was then, and this is *now*."

Clarence digested the fact and remained quiet.

"You have to admit," said Milt. "You always hated the music I listened to and laughed at what my heroes looked like." The father remembered making such comments not too long ago.

Another bad memory surfaced.

"Dad, do you remember the time when you showed me your college diploma?" asked the son.

The father clearly remembered that episode and replied, "Yes I do."

"You told me that you got your education through a prominent Ivy League school," pointed out the son. "Well, those discs and posters in my bedroom is what got me here. Remember how you wanted me to grow out of that stuff and be like you?"

The guilt-ridden father remembered and remained silent.

"You can't be a rock star, any more than I can be an accountant," remarked the son. "And you are a good accountant." The father looked up with the realization that his teenage son did have respect for him.

"Trust me," said the son. "I know the value of a good accountant; they keep me out of trouble."

The father felt acknowledged for his noble trade. This placed him in a better mood. He would now change subjects to address an issue more important to him.

"Listen here, young man," said his father in a raised voice. "I am still your father, and what I say, goes!"

"Dad," remarked Milt. "Do you see that Lear jet over there with my name on it?"

"Why yes I do, son," answered the father.

"The Beatles are already on board with Jimi Hendricks. We have to leave for a show in Japan," informed Milt. "Can we talk about this when I get back?"

"The Beatles?" he asked. "Jimi Hendricks?"

"I know what you're thinking, Dad," said Milt. "I normally don't use an opening act, but they kept asking and eventually wore me down. Besides, I've gotten to know them a bit, and they're actually nice guys. I don't know how I am going to explain this to the Doors."

Milt then relaxed and went further into his dream state. The day's visit had come to an end.

The father was stymied and wanted another round.

"Ask him if he wants to go on a vacation with us," suggested the mother.

"He can't," exclaimed the angry father. "He's leaving on a tour with Jimi Hendricks and the Beatles. That boy has agreed to let them *open* for him. But at least he's giving them better treatment than the Doors got!"

The next morning, Clarence made a beeline to the hospital. He calculated to have his wife visit first, then he would come in with a well-prepared attack.

"Milton," said the mother in a happy voice. "I miss you."

"Mom, it's great to see you!" greeted the son. "I need to ask a favor from you."

"Anything, darling," said the mother. "What is it?"

"I remember how you always gave to charities, and I realize that I should be doing the same," said the son. "I am going to perform for the Breast Cancer Concert this September," said the star. "Could you make me an outfit that has pink in it to show support for this cause?"

The mother's wit was in full force. "I already read about it in the newspaper and made you one. Here it is, Milton. Why don't you try it on?"

"Mom, I love it!" exclaimed the son. "And look, it fits perfect!" This is just what I was looking for. Thanks, Mom!"

The mother was happy seeing her son so happy. She was nudged by her husband. "Oh, your father is also here to see you. Bye, Milton."

"Bye, Mom." said the son. "I love you."

Clarence was on deck and now it was his turn. "Milt," called out the dad. "Do you realize all the things that I've done for you?" he asked.

"Sure I do," answered the son. "I thought that I did things in return to acknowledge that. Didn't the ten million dollar check I sent you make you happy?" asked his famous son. "What about that 1965 Thunderbird you always wanted? Doesn't any of that stuff count? I can send you more money, if that's what you want." The son stopped communicating and fell back into a heavy dream state.

The father thought about what Milt had to say. He understood that they were different, but had respect for one another. He was also made aware that they both shared what they had to offer. His relationship with his son was different than the one his wife had. Theirs was about being career-oriented. Clarence was proud. His son was a working man that put family first, just like himself. A value he always stressed to his son.

The next morning, the Livingstons were once again visiting with their son. Maria sat next to her son and began to speak. "How are you today, son?"

Milt was immediately activated for the visit. "I am doing just fine, Mom," he answered pleasantly. "How are you doing?"

"Oh, I feel pretty good today, son," said the mother.

"Hey, Mom, I need to tell you something that I know you'll approve of," said the son.

"What is it?" questioned the mother.

"Mom, I followed your advice," confided the son. "I will do a concert at my old school, even though they treated me awful. You were right about God allowing me to have this talent, provided I share it. And that has to include those that I don't care for. My band is also doing ten benefit shows a year for good causes, just like you suggested."

The mother was taken aback. *That* was how she knew her son. "You are right, son," she said as she placed her hand on his shoulder.

"Mom, I wore that outfit you made for me on my last tour," said Milt. "The fans loved it!"

The intent mother asked a question. "What did you like the most about it, son?"

"The way the pink outfit had flashy purple and gold that went up and down the whole thing!" he said.

"I'm glad you liked it," replied the mother. "I must admit that you looked great in it."

"Wait a minute," said Milt in a startling tone. The son's entire body tensed as his head positioned upward. "It's happening now; the white light is shining for me, and I am being drawn to it."

Milt's paralyzed face generated a smile as he relaxed. The parents looked over their son with wonderment.

"It's my time to go, and it's beautiful!" announced the son. "I love this! Mom, Dad; I made it! I have been accepted!" the son was rocking side to side in the bed like an excited child. "They're all here," he explained. "Grandpa, Grandma; everybody!"

"Thank you for teaching me about life," he added. "I could never have done this without you two. I promise to watch over you both and will personally guide you when it's your time."

The transition to Heaven was nearing completion, with Milt's final words being spoken. "I love you, Mom and Dad . . ."

The body exhaled its last breath and relaxed beyond unconsciousness. The monitors started to beep as graphs no longer showed vital signs of life. Milton Farrell Livingston's body had died, with his soul advancing through grace. Mysteriously, the passing of their son brought an unexplainable happiness that wouldn't allow grief or sadness.

The parents stared in silence with the understanding that God had accepted their son.

Together they leaned over and kissed him on his cheeks, hugging his body for several minutes. Then they hugged each other with intense respect. They had the satisfaction of being with their son at his final moments, realizing that he finished out his life happy.

It was the finishing touch of a job well done. Milt only seemed to be closer now, with his happiness being spread within them. The moment was one of joy and celebration.

Dr. Peterson ran into the room, but Milt had already passed. The parents looked at the good doctor with gratitude. The father approached the doctor and extended an open hand. Dr. Peterson shook hands as Clarence spoke. "Thank you for not pulling the plug and allowing our son to live out his life being happy."

"You are quite welcome," said Dr. Peterson.

"We were so proud of him," said the mom. "The entire time, he was making his world a better place with his talent." The mother continued, "He must be with those legends now."

"He was probably with them the whole time," said the doctor.

At that moment, the conversation was interrupted by a nurse sticking her head through the door. "We have a man here that would like to talk to someone," she said.

"Please bring him in," said the doctor.

To their surprise, it was an older man with long, stylish gray hair. He was lean, well–dressed, with good posture. A closer look revealed sincere blue eyes with a defined face. It was unmistakably music icon Blaze Werner.

With a charming English accent, the gracious man introduced himself, shaking hands with everyone. "It's hard for me to explain why I came here," said Blaze.

"You see," continued the music legend. "The past year I have been waking up with vague memories of my late brother, Scott. I have been getting dreams that we were doing road trips with all of our friends, past and present. We were traveling with a superstar; the most phenomenal entertainer we have ever known.

"Many of my friends who are world-renowned musicians have been getting the same sensations, with our deceased friends clearly making contact over this. Why, the other day this star was wearing an outrageous pink outfit that had fantastic gold and purple lines going all over it. And my goodness; can that guy ever play the guitar and sing! I don't know why, but something gave me the compulsion to travel to this country and eventually find my way to this hospital."

Dr. Peterson commented, "You have found who you need to talk to right here. I have to go now." The doctor left the parents alone with Blaze.

The parents were in shock. They had pieces to the puzzle that Blaze was trying to assemble. "Blaze," said Clarence. "We need to sit down in the lobby and tell you about our son's life." They made their way to the lobby and found a vacant table with chairs. They sat down and talked for an hour. Once all the information was gathered, Blaze reached a conclusion.

"I thoroughly believe that your son Milt was actually living out his life with my friends and me," he stated. "It's only right that we spend a day together spreading his ashes on the grounds of the Music Festival Stadium. That's where all the stars in our business have their ashes spread. Trust me," said the Englishman. "My friends and I are probably close to him without realizing it. I have no doubt that he should be enshrined with the rest of us."

"I'm curious," said Blaze. "By chance, did you record any of your conversations with your son?"

"Dr. Peterson took a recording when he could first talk to him," said the father. "He relayed it to my cell phone, but we couldn't understand what our son was talking about. I still have it, if you would like to hear it," he offered.

"That would be splendid!" answered Blaze.

Clarence took the cell phone out of his pocket and played the brief message:

"I am playing cribbage with Scott Werner right now," said Milt. "Can you wait until we're finished?"

"That's all I need to hear," said Blaze. "You can turn it off now." He placed his index finger on his chin and looked up in deep thought. He then turned toward the couple and said, "What puzzles me was that my brother Scott's favorite game was cribbage, and hardly anyone knew about that."

The mother covered her face in shock. She buried her face in Blaze's chest as she shook with emotion. Blaze hugged her with both arms. "Scott and Milt must have quite a friendship," he said as he patted her on the back.

"About your son, Milt," continued Blaze. "It doesn't matter if he was known down here. What's important is that he is with his fellow rock stars for all of eternity." With his British charm, Blaze perked up the conversation. "I don't think that you will ever have to worry about getting a backstage pass to see your son."

The parents broke into a smile and digested what Blaze said. Silently, they reflected on their son's life.

Their son was in hell being a misfit in society. His accident transferred him to the world his bedroom personified. The posters and sounds that encompassed those walls seem to nurture him through the remainder of his life. Like Don Knotts' Mr. Limpet, it was as if a heavenly hand intervened to right what was wrong.

It all seemed to make sense.

The father was in awe, realizing that his only son was to be immortalized with the rock stars that made history. It didn't matter that this would be an unpublicized event. They had the gratification that their son, Milt, shared his success with them. It was also important that as parents, their son incorporated the values they taught throughout his stardom.

"You know what?" asked the father. "I don't feel sad at all; I feel like celebrating!"

"I can't explain it," said the mother. "But I feel the same way. I feel great and want to get out and do something!"

"I feel jolly good myself," said Blaze.

"How about the three of us having lunch at the Rocker Cafe?" suggested the father.

"That's just what I was thinking," replied the mother.

"Good show!" said Blaze.

The trio left the hospital and drove together to the Rocker Cafe. They entered the restaurant and looked around at the memorabilia.

"This place looks just like Milt's bedroom," said the dad.

"It also sounds like it too," laughed the mother.

The hostess was a cute teenager with dyed green hair and a gorgeous smile. Her outfit resembled the ones that adorned the idols in the posters. She was holding three menus, and led them to their table. They sat down and studied the younger people that were employed there and hung out. "They're all just like my Milt," thought the father.

The father looked up and said to the server, "I bet you know who every major recording artist is."

"If they're in the top one hundred, I have all their music," she answered.

"Do you ever listen to Milt Livingston?" asked the mother in a curious tone.

"Milt Livingston?" questioned the server. "I have never heard of him."

Blaze commented with his European accent, "Just give it a little time; one day, you will."

That was all that had to be said. The parents were at peace, knowing that their son entered Heaven being what he was meant to be. They were further blessed knowing that they received the greatest gifts that he could have ever given: love and forgiveness.

Those were the only gifts that could free them of any pain. Through their son's love, they would continue life happy. They also knew that he was watching over them, playing his music and waiting . . .

Homer's Wreck

There is something special about that doctor from back South. The loving care he provides for each patient is greatly enhanced by his politeness, his smile, and the twinkle in his eye.

There is more to those good souls than being a professional who saves lives. There is also a good neighbor deep inside who helps his fellow man while preserving dignity. Old-fashioned values apply here, with a little bit of wit, charm, and the common sense that can only come from a country boy.

And did we mention a good sense of humor?

Rich blue eyes looked up intensely at x-rays. The bright ceiling light exposed the contrast between light and dark to define the patient's prognosis. The steady hand of Dr. Kendall Armstrong meticulously moved the photograph closer to the florescent light. A further inspection revealed what he was hoping to find.

His eyes lit up as a cagey grin slowly covered his face. The neurosurgeon was once again successful. Looking up to the heavens, he said, "Thank you, Lord." Like a high school football hero scoring a touchdown, he did a quick jitterbug. Immediately, he left the x-ray room with a skip to his walk.

◀◀ ◀◀ ▶▶ ▶▶

The lean, frisky forty-eight-year-old man with silver hair graced the hallway. A well-groomed beard added to his

170

handsome look. His white uniform and upbeat personality made him look like an angel on assignment.

Dr. Armstrong entered room 127 to see his recovering patient, Melva Sexton. The doctor was pleased to see the sixty-two-year-old woman accompanied by her family. Like a famous Fred Sanford heart attack, Dr. Armstrong did a reenactment illustrating how surprised he was. Laughter erupted, setting the tempo for introductions. The prominent doctor went around the room introducing himself with his pleasant demeanor and firm handshake. Once all were acquainted, he addressed business.

"Good afternoon, Mrs. Sexton," said the doctor in a gracious tone. The recovering patient was surrounded by get-well cards and flowers. The elder woman with a dignified face and elegant gray hair sat up in bed. The happy greeting tipped her off that Dr. Armstrong was the bearer of good news.

A granddaughter sat in the far corner of the room, partially hidden. She was dressed in a Girl Scout uniform and became a focal point. The good doctor took notice and asked her what her name was.

The child giggled and replied, "Megan."

He noticed a box next to her and slowly approached with his huge, bright eyes. Squatting down in front of her, he pointed at the box. Using a clever, inquisitive voice, he asked, "Are those Girl Scout cookies?"

The eight-year-old girl in blond pigtails nodded her head as she displayed an ear-to-ear grin.

"I love Girl Scout cookies!" said Kendall. He pulled out his wallet and purchased a box.

"Thank you, Dr. Armstrong," said Megan as she placed the money in an envelope.

"You are quite welcome," said the Southern gentleman. "These cookies go great with hot chocolate, too." The congenial doctor continued. "In fact, we have hot chocolate just outside this room in the lobby. Why don't you help yourself to some?" he suggested. "You can even place this box of cookies out there, so that everybody can have one."

The child looked at her mother and grandmother, hoping for their approval. Motherly smiles with a slight nod gave Megan the green light.

"Goodie!" she exclaimed as she ran out of the room, holding the cookies.

Looking at Melva, the doctor held the x-ray report high in the air and said, "I have some good news." Kendall spent the next ten minutes explaining to the entire family what the report meant. He assured everyone that the stricken family member would be home in a few days. Continuing with his hospitality, Kendall suggested that they join him in the cafeteria for lunch. This would give time for Melva's medication to set in. It would also allow her much-needed rest. Before leaving, he assured her that she would be just fine. Leaning over, he held her hand and encouraged her to call if she had any questions. The patient smiled back with complete trust.

After lunch, Dr. Armstrong attended a staff meeting. Later he would finish out the day making follow-up calls to outpatients. At four--thirty, he called it a day and went to the parking garage. The doctor unlocked the door to his modest pickup truck and climbed in. It was now time to enjoy the ride home, with only his pager tethering him to the hospital. He reflected on the day's events and felt gratified.

There was more to the life of Dr. Kendall Armstrong than just having a professional title. He was also a devoted family man who cherished his wife and two sons that were in college. His golden retriever, Dolly, made this man's life complete. Many of his neighbors only knew him as "Kendall". He was that regular guy who wore jeans and a plain shirt.

Little did he know that his day was about to face round two. His latent talents would be called upon to calm down an ongoing problem with two of his neighbors. A situation that only *he* could treat . . .

The drive home was relaxing as the doctor entered the gates of Lauralhurst. This was the premier residential area where the county's well-to-do live. Stately homes of fellow doctors, attorneys, professors and the like had competing vehicles in three-car garages and manicured lawns. This status was a bit much for Kendall Armstrong. True, he was a resident there; but only because he appreciated his property at the edge of this development. It was nestled away, perched on a hill that allowed him to own one hundred acres.

This land was like being back home. It was a refuge for local wildlife that had a trail leading through the brush, which led to a small shack. Next to it was a pond where he planted catfish and an old 1934 truck he was restoring. This was where he spent alone time fishing, enjoying a campfire, and whittling with his pocket knife. It was also the boundary line where an older, existing neighborhood ended.

Beyond his shack was a clearing that had two households facing each other. Like Kendall Armstrong, they also lived on the outskirts of their community, where the paved road dissipated into dirt. But unlike the Armstrong family, each did not get along with the other. In fact, it was a modern day Hatfield and McCoy relationship in the making. They were just two notches away from having an all-out feud.

Kendall's background was all too familiar with this kind of nonsense. However, he did know how to warm up to such types. With his compassion and ingenuity, he could lessen the tension between the two families and create harmony. He could even have some fun with this endeavor . . .

The white pickup truck pulled into the driveway, with Dolly anxiously waiting for her master. The dog started to bark as it jumped in circles. His beautiful wife, Candice, stood on the front porch with her long, flowing brown hair and matching eyes. Kendall beamed with pride. He parked the truck and got out as Dolly stood on her hind legs, placing her paws on Kendall's waist. He scratched Dolly with both hands as she wagged her tail. He then walked to the porch and embraced Candice with a kiss. "I missed you, Kendall," she said.

"I thought about you all day myself!" replied the husband. They went inside the house and sat in the living room.

"How was your day?" asked Candice.

"It went great," replied Kendall. "I will never know why God has blessed me so much. I love where I work, what I do; and it gets even better when I get home." Candice got out of her chair and sat on his lap, giving him another big hug.

"Well," she said. "You make me happy too." Candice stood up and said, "And for dinner we're having fried chicken with mashed potatoes and gravy."

"Now what did I do to deserve this?" asked Kendall.

"By just being you," answered Candice.

"Do you mind if I take Dolly and walk down the trail before dinner?" he asked.

"Not at all," she answered. "Dinner will be done in about an hour and a half. You still have plenty of sunlight, so this is a good time to go. By the way, how are those two neighbors getting along down there?"

"I'm not sure," said Kendall. "I might as well make an appearance. They haven't seen 'Homer' in a while."

"Do you think it's worth all that effort?" asked his wife.

"Well, I did get a refurbished fence out of the deal last year," remarked Kendall. "In fact, they did a pretty good job on that project. When they were done with it, they went on a fishing trip together. I only had to straighten it out a bit and anchor the posts down a little further with an extra bag of cement," reflected the husband. "But there they were; best of friends for the rest of the summer."

"There's something that I was always meaning to ask you," said Candice.

"What's that?" asked the husband.

"Why the name Homer, of all things?" she questioned.

Kendall clasped his hands behind his head and looked up to the ceiling.

"My brother in Los Angeles is a dentist and uses the name Clem to keep peace on the back side of his neighborhood," he explained. "Our cousin in New York is a pediatrician and chose the name Cooter for his dysfunctional neighbors. I just wanted to be original, and Homer seemed to be the only good one left. It does seem to work," he added.

The married couple parted with another kiss.Kendall went to the bedroom to change his clothes. Five minutes later, he and Dolly walked down the path that led to his shack. As they neared the shack, a shouting match could be heard off in the distance.

"Do I have to hire an attorney and sue you?" challenged a voice.

"Sue me for what?" responded the opponent. "All I said was that you are parking your car too close to my driveway."

Are they at it again? thought Kendall as he approached the older community.

The argument got louder.

"You mean to tell me that you can't drive your car around mine?" yelled back the first party.

"Not when it's on my property!" countered the second.

It's time to put a stop to that petty argument right now, thought Kendall. He entered his shack and took off his clothes. He opened a small, narrow closet and changed into an old pair of pants, worn-out red flannel shirt, tattered buckskin coat, and shoes that seemed to be from the Depression era.

He walked to a tiny wooden desk and pulled out a drawer. Looking inside, he found a stick of black licorice and unwrapped it. He bit off a piece and began to chew. Looking toward the door, he saw his ten-gallon hillbilly hat with holes in it hanging on a hook, with his vintage rifle leaning in the corner. He grabbed the hat and placed it on his head. Picking up his rifle, he walked out of the shack, onto the porch and down the steps. He spit out the licorice, leaving most in his mouth and on his teeth. He bent over, laid down his rifle and rubbed his hands in the dirt. He then rubbed his dirty hands on his face and pulled a long stem of dried grass out of the ground, placing it between his teeth. He grabbed his rifle and stood up.

The show was about to start.

Kendall was no longer the beloved Dr. Armstrong. He was now Homer; a harmless, uneducated hillbilly who lived alone. A seemingly lower-class citizen who always meant well and, at times, needed a little help.

Homer pointed his rifle toward the sky and pulled the trigger. A loud blast followed that echoed through the trees, startling his neighbors. The screaming men silenced and looked toward the direction the noise came from. Homer ran into view with Dolly close behind.

"Did any of ya see a squirrel run by?" asked the concerned hunter with a twang in his voice.

"No we didn't, Homer," responded George Thomson.

The doctor was incognito and knew how to massage one's ego. His eyes lit up with excitement as he noticed George's 1990 Dodge Caravan. The doors to the dull copper-toned minivan had "Thompson's Hardware" painted in white with the phone number directly below.

"Do you work at that there hardware store in town?" asked Homer.

The heavyset man resembled Ralph Kramden. His overconfident smug look was accented with short, black greasy hair. Dark eyes directed his overbearing character. "I own it," he answered with pride.

Homer was wide-eyed as his mouth dropped open. "Sha-zam!" he said. "You are the owner of a hardware store?" he asked in amazement.

George confirmed his status with a tone of arrogance. "Yes, I am," he replied.

"Goodness gracious!" remarked Homer. "No wonder you can afford a nice car like that! Back home, we would spend all day looking at all the doodads in a hardware store. Why, they got lawnmowers, extension cords, bird feeders; practically everything anyone would ever need is right there. A family can go to one on a Saturday and have lots of fun!"

"It's not just fun and games there, Homer," retorted George.

"It's not?" replied the hillbilly in a timid voice.

George Thomson looked at Homer with directness and asked a hypothetical question. "What would you do if a forty mile an hour wind blew out your fence?"

Homer's face expressed fear, not knowing what to do in such a situation. He looked bewildered at the business owner and said, "Gee, I don't really know."

George continued to quiz Homer. "Now, what if every home in this town faced that same force of nature?" With conviction he answered his own question. "They would be in a state of panic and flock to my store to get help."

Dr. Armstrong performed like an actor on Dragnet. He allowed Joe Friday to reach out to him, getting in the last word. This left him with a convincing, expressionless face as he tried to fathom the magnitude of such a disaster.

George stood with his arms folded, slightly rocking back and forth with authority. Homer looked back in awe at the hardware store owner.

It was now Walter Higgins' turn to keep his end up. The balding, lean figure wearing bifocals was crying out for equal recognition. It was clear that there was more to this mild-mannered man than the Ivy League sweater he wore. Walter spoke up.

"After that storm, every household would need at least one ladder," added Walter. "Some homes don't have any, and that's where I come in."

It was obvious that Homer was in shock, but he wanted to hear more. With his eyes and mouth remaining wide open, he directed his attention to the quieter man.

"Where I work, we make ladders that people need to survive such disasters," informed Walter.

"You work in a place where they make ladders?" questioned Homer.

Walter puffed out his chest and competed with George. "I am a foreman there," he proclaimed. "I have twelve men underneath me."

Homer acted impressed.

"You are the boss man in one of them-there modern factories?" repeated Homer. "And you make those ladders that allow people to reach those way-up-high places?" He turned around as he bent over. "Oh my goodness!" he stated.

"Yes I am," replied Walter.

George contributed to Walter's high position.

"They're not just any ladder; but the very best," stated George. "I take great pride in only having the highest quality for my customers. I will only sell ladders that come from where Walter works."

The well-disguised doctor was relieved to see George compliment his neighbor. It was a sign of progress.

Kendall was through acting for the day and needed to return home. He would use a sure-fire gimmick that worked every time. He would offer to cook dinner for his *friends*.

The harmless backwoodsman tensed up as a thought entered his head. A thought-provoking smile slowly came across his soiled face. This telegraphed that he had an idea that he was proud of. Looking up to the men he idolized, the gracious hillbilly spoke.

"Hey, would you like to have dinner with me?" asked Homer. "I caught some bullfrogs last even'n and will have no problem at all catching some catfish for us all to eat!"

The sophisticated city folk dodged the offer by stating they just had dinner. With insincerity, they expressed gratitude and suggested, "Perhaps another time." Homer took the rejection on the chin, knowing that the visit was winding down.

George looked at Walter, not knowing what to think about their visitor. Walter gave a slight nod in agreement that illustrated a bond. This showed a little daylight for the hope Kendall had for them.

"I have to get back home and finish a chore I was working on," said George.

"My wife and I are about to go shopping," said Walter.

It was Homer's turn. "Well, I don't want to keep you here away from your chores," he commented. "It has been a pleasure meeting with y'all. Have a good evenin'." Without shaking hands, the three parted. Kendall spit the reed out of his mouth while returning to his shack. Upon entering, he changed back into his city clothes and continued home to wash his hands and face.

That night, Kendall was with his wife at the dinner table. "This meal is fantastic!" he stated.

"Why thank you, dear," she replied.

"How are the neighbors getting along tonight?" she asked.

"I feel too much tension between them," he answered.

"I remember last year there weren't any Christmas lights from their living room," remarked Kendall. "I hope that they at least exchange cards." He took a bite of chicken and savored it. A small drink of milk followed as he pondered further about George and Walter.

"They seem to have too much time on their hands," he said. "It's that adage about idle hands being the devil's playground. I need to dig deeper, or they'll be at each other's throat in no time. They need to join forces on a worthwhile project that they both believe in. One that will require a lot of time together . . ."

The following day, Kendall started off his job attending a board meeting. Later he reviewed profiles of those that required his surgical skills and scheduled them accordingly. Driving home, he thought about his malcontent neighbors and devised a strategy.

He realized that something momentous had to happen to unite George and Walter. He decided to sabotage his vintage truck and stage an *accident*. The motive would be to have the neighbors respond and help the naive hillbilly at a more in-depth level. This would create a lengthy project that would force harmony between the two neighbors . . . for a while.

Upon arriving home, Kendall greeted his wife and explained his battle plan to her. The supportive wife gave him a 'thumbs-up' of approval. It was time to put the plan in motion. He immediately embarked on his campaign, marching down the trail with his faithful companion, Dolly.

He was now leaving Beverly Hills on his way to Bug Tussle, with a piece of licorice in his mouth.

Once inside the shack, he changed from Dr. Marcus Welby to Jed Clampett. Without hesitation, he got out his tool box and went over to his restoration project. He placed the tool box on the ground and rubbed his hands in the dirt, smearing it on his face. Spitting some of the licorice out of his mouth, he found another tall, dried-out grass stem. With determination, he pulled it from the ground and placed the tip of it into his mouth, between his front teeth. It was now time to work.

The first chore would be to replace the driver's side front wheel with the original con-caved wheel that was off to the side. Next, he started the cast iron motor to create hot water for the radiator. He loosened the radiator cap until steam started to hiss out of the opening. The truck was out of gear and running idle. He pushed the jalopy in front of the trail that sloped down to his neighbor's property and found a small rock to chock the back wheel. Kendall reached into his tool box, pulled out a wooden mallet, and walked to the near side of his shack. He approached an old washtub that was hanging directly center for decoration.

Kendall gripped the mallet tightly and hit the center of the washtub with full force. The crashing sound echoed through the trees getting George and Walter's attention.

Kendall dropped the mallet, ran to the truck and removed the rock from the rear tire. He then pushed the rusted metal hulk down the path and climbed inside, turning off the engine.

The dilapidated truck wobbled with the bad wheel as it coasted out of the woods, with the golden retriever running behind. George and Walter opened their front doors just in time to see the calamity. The vehicle buckled to a stop between the houses with steam hissing from the radiator and a barking dog. The delirious hillbilly seemed to gain consciousness from the wreck as he did the 'funky chicken' getting out of the truck. Both men ran to his aid.

"Are you all right, Homer?" asked George.

"What happened?" asked Walter.

"I guess I wrecked my truck," said Homer. "I have been workin' on the brakes and thought I'd give it a test run." Looking up with the innocence of a child, he continued to explain. "I pressed down real hard on the brake pedal and it just kept on going."

"Homer," asked George. "Will you promise that you won't attempt to drive this truck until Walter and I tell you that it's ready?" Walter put his right arm around George for a brief second, showing allegiance.

This was exactly what Dr. Armstrong wanted to see. The well-disguised surgeon continued.

"You mean that you two are gonna get my truck runnin' for me?" asked Homer in delight.

"Yes we will," promised the hardware man.

"And it will run as good as new," vowed Walter.

"Like how you two repaired my fence last year over yonder?" asked Homer as he pointed toward his shack.

"That's right," said George.

"Shucks," commented the hillbilly. "Ain't nobody ever cared for ol' Homer like that before."

"You don't have to worry about a thing, Homer," said Walter. "You are in good company with us."

This is music to my ears, thought the good doctor.

"Homer, why don't you go home and take it easy?" suggested George. "You have had a tough day."

"Don't worry about a thing," added Walter. "You can leave your truck right here, and we'll take care of everything."

"Walter is right," said George as he patted his neighbor on the back.

"Well, I do admit that I am a might tired," said Homer. "I think I will do just that. Much obliged, neighbor." The grateful hillbilly tipped his hat and walked back home with his dog. Spitting the reed out of his mouth, he muttered, "That should take care of them for a while." He returned to his property and placed his tools back into the toolbox. He entered the shack, changed back into his city clothes, and began the trek up the trail.

Soon Kendall arrived back home to give his report. He entered through the kitchen to find Candice waiting for him.

"Mission accomplished?" she asked.

"Mission accomplished!" he replied.

"I made a pot of coffee," she said. "How about having some custard pie with me?"

"That sounds wonderful," said the husband. "Let me wash up first, then I'll join you." He took off his jacket, placed it in the hall closet and went to the bathroom. Moments later, he returned to the kitchen with a clean face and hands. Sitting at the table was his beautiful wife. In front of her was a place setting for pie and coffee. He winked at her as he sat down.

"Cheers," she said as she picked up her mug.

"Cheers," responded Kendall with mug in hand. They made contact with the coffee mugs and took a sip.

"I wonder why people have to battle like that?" she asked.

"I don't know," said Kendall. "It's an awful waste of time, isn't it?"

"It most certainly is," she replied. "Do you think that this pattern will continue?"

"Probably," answered Kendall.

"I can see it now," projected the husband as he took another sip of coffee. Staring off in the distance, he continued in a methodical tone. "They won't even recognize me when they're in the barber shop. They'll be talking about their most recent fishing trip and how they are best friends for life. Then one of them will make the mistake of claiming that he caught the biggest fish. That will be enough to rekindle their feud," he said, shaking his head. Kendall started to chuckle to himself as he turned to his wife. "That's right about the time when Homer will pay them an unexpected visit."

Candice laughed with the understanding. "Oh well," she said. "At least they're happy for the time being . . ."

The Honeycomb Cafe

Is there anything more sacred than the bragging rights of one's last name? It seems that the smaller the town; the more of an issue this becomes. These all-American communities have one thing in common: the names on the mailboxes match the ones in the cemetery. Small towns definitely have deep roots with an abundance of family pride.

When an imaginary line is crossed, a feud could result. If such a battle were to take place, would there be any ground rules, and what could be used as arsenal?

The answer is gossip escalating to rumors; with the local newspaper batting clean-up.

The result? That *pull* needed to decide who would be elected. It would also dictate which members were deemed upper-crust, and who would be outcast.

Marge Stewart stumbled across such propaganda when she discovered an archive of old newspapers. This finding rekindled the glory days of her family and the scandal of others. Unbeknownst to her, the seventy-six-year-old had opened a can of worms. A battle that ended long ago would resurface, having to be settled one last time.

Marge Stewart walked down First Street asshe braved the cold. The woman, wearing black leather gloves and a wool navy blue coat with matching neck scarf, leaned into the November wind. The senior had lost a step in recent years, but still held her feisty spirit as she marched with determination. Long, tattered ends of the scarf fluttered in the wind as her right hand pressed down on her floral hat. Her left hand clenched a matching floral purse as she stayed warm in pursuit of her destination.

Marge was making her morning trek to the same landmark that her grandmother used to take her and her mother to. In fact, it was the very one she had taken her daughter and granddaughter to many times: the Honeycomb Cafe. Despite the attrition rate affecting older family members, the widow still had loved ones to dine with. They were old ladies just like her who knew the pain of loneliness.

She approached the landmark. The small wooden structure stood dignified as it continued to serve yet another generation. Like *Little House on the Prairie*, the rustic structure seemed to be an oasis out in the middle of nowhere. Signs of life were visible with its iron stovepipe producing smoke.

Marge was now standing in front of the faded white door that gave access to the restaurant. This served as a gateway to the past. Her first date, the night of her prom, and virtually all family celebrations took place right here. The original brass door knob seemed to be an extended hand from an old friend.

The old woman felt a sensation that reinvigorated her youth. She anxiously took off her gloves and placed them into her purse. Marge then took off her hat, exposing her short, stylish gray hair. In one motion she opened the door and entered the cafe, closing the door behind her.

Like herself, Marge's friends were also creatures of habit. Three familiar faces sat at their traditional corner table, upholding their usual seating arrangements, with one empty chair remaining. The glow of life projected through weathered faces that still personified beauty. They looked up, displaying smiles of relief; Marge had arrived. There was a peace of mind knowing that their quilting circle was still intact, with all having survived another day.

"Well, there you are," called out Ella Ray. "I was afraid that I was going to have to go outside to find you, girl!" The first round of laughter had been initiated.

"Let's wait until there's two feet of snow out there first!" replied a quick-witted Marge. Taking off her coat, she turned to the coat rack that was adorned with the winter clothing of her friends. She draped the garment and scarf on the remaining arm. Using her hat, she balanced out the makeshift Christmas tree by placing it on top of the sturdy pole.

"Nice job, Margie!" cheered Mary Pierce.

The final member of the quartet smiled back as she walked toward her vacant chair and sat down. The *golden girls* were assembled once again.

Joan Wakeman pointed at Marge's place setting. There was a menu, with fresh coffee steaming out of a cup. Joan leaned toward her friend and whispered, "I knew you'd be here."

Marge said, "Thank you, dear." She picked up the warm cup and took a sip. Reading glasses were pulled out of purses, with open menus waiting. The table became quiet as each woman compared options to what they normally ordered.

One by one, menus were closed with glasses being folded and put away.

The tempo picked up when a gracious voice broke the silence. "How nice to see that you could make it today," said Glannis Anagnos.

Marge looked up and saw the Greek entrepreneur smiling at her. The foreign-born man held the charm that was the trademark of his culture. His defined features with sincere brown eyes further accented his ethnicity. Silver hair, combed back, with a cultured mustache perfected the final touch. The women adored him.

"Why, thank you, Mr. Anagnos," replied Marge as she blushed.

"Please, call me Glannis," he said with his rich accent. Looking at the four women, he asked, "Is everyone ready to order?"

185

Each woman gave their order, with Glannis knowing to use four separate tickets. Once finished, he gave a slight bow and left for the kitchen. The ambiance was now in control as each woman took a sip of coffee. They looked around the room, knowing that it was the town's oldest structure with its oldest memories.

Marge eventually glanced through the window next to her, then looked downward. At that moment, she noticed something that compelled her to take a closer look. Just beneath the bottom corner of the windowsill, the wall had an obscure hole about the size of a penny. A closer look showed a faded yellow object inside that resembled a budding rose. Stress marks surrounded the hole, illustrating that more separation was occurring. It was obvious that the wall was slowly deteriorating, and that the hole would eventually increase in size.

But what was inside it? wondered Marge.

Leaning over, she scraped the tiny hole with her fingernail as a two-inch piece flaked off. The hole was much larger, and now she could clearly see what was inside. It was a rolled-up piece of old newspaper. She meticulously pinched the exposed end of the paper and in one motion, slowly pulled it out. "Well, look at what I found," she said to the table. "It's a page from an old newspaper."

The other women leaned toward Marge with curiosity. Bewildered expressions looked at the finding and wondered if it was of any importance. "Why don't you open it up to see how old it is?" suggested Ella.

Marge looked at the sparkling eyes staring back. The excitement of mystery caused the girls to get a little giddy as youth pumped through their veins. It was like the stories they shared at slumber parties many years ago. "Open it," encouraged Joan.

"Yes, open it!" exclaimed Mary.

Marge held the paper off the side of the table and shook off the dust. She then leaned over and took an added measure by blowing on all sides. Looking at her friends, she placed the newsprint on the table and slowly rolled it out. Like an old pirate's map, a crinkling sound illustrated how

186

easily it could tear. Finally, it was spread out on the table with four energetic seniors surrounding the tabloid. What was unveiled was astounding.

Looking straight at Marge was a picture of her great-grandmother at age seventeen; being crowned Harvest Queen!

"Well," said Marge. "Will you look at that!" The Buckley Gazette proudly chose that story to be their feature article over one hundred years ago.

Ella, Mary and Joan looked bug-eyed at the front page. They knew of Marge's great-grandmother; she was a close friend of their great-grandmothers.

"I will take this home and get it framed," vowed Marge. She carefully folded the paper like a road map and placed it in her purse before leaving. On the way home, Marge passed an arts and craft store that agreed to frame the newspaper article while she waited. She was just warmed up from the cold when the project was complete. That evening, she hung the memorabilia above the fireplace. Later she called a few friends and told them about the article she found in the walls of the Honeycomb Cafe.

The next day, Marge bundled up for her daily breakfast at the Honeycomb Cafe. Before leaving her front door, she took one last look at her great-grandmother above the mantle. "It just runs in the family . . ." she said to herself.

When Marge arrived at the café, something was different. There seemed to be more customers. Furthermore, they were all seniors who grew up in that town. Ella was also sitting in Marge's usual seat. Her fingers were reaching into the hole that Marge had found the day before.

Ella had jumped Marge's claim. There were already two sheets of wrinkled yellowed paper on the table. Apparently, she was *panning for gold*, with no luck. Then she extracted a cancellation prize. It was an article about Mary's great-uncle being indicted for miscounting votes in an election. It was a scandal that almost prevented Ella's great-grandfather from being the town's Agricultural Commissioner.

"So goodness prevails after all!" said a smug Ella as she showed the article to Mary. Immediately, there was counterattack from the opposite corner of the room.

"Are you referring to your grandfather being sentenced to two days in jail for his third offense on drunk driving?" said an interrogating voice. Ella looked across the room and saw none other than Elsie Baylor. Years ago, Ella had beaten her out for the last spot on the high school cheerleading squad. Elsie had apparently found a new vein that was a *gusher*, allowing her to tip the scales even.

Bewildered, Mary read a few newsworthy lines about her family's past and left the cafe in disgust.

Glannis' distinct whistling could be heard leaving the kitchen. Like a cat's bell, it gave the mice just enough time to cover their tracks. Potted plants and curtains were slightly moved to hide the inconspicuous holes. The restaurateur smiled as he entered the room full of *friends*. Like a school teacher entering a classroom, all faces smiled back at him.

The following month, the cafe's clientele increased dramatically. Glannis and his wife, Adonia, were proud that their tiny business was constantly busy. In fact, there was now a line to enter their establishment before it opened. They did notice, however, that it was just the seniors from that town who were dining there. What was more peculiar was that they would only sit next to a window, leaving the center tables abandoned. Another oddity was also occurring: the heating bill was starting to go through the roof . . .

"Something strange is happening here," thought Glannis. "My customers look at me funny when I enter the room. They all just stare at me, as if there is a problem. They don't even visit with one another like they used to."

Glannis' older brother, Kostas, also had a cafe that bordered the next town. Kostas and his wife, Chara, were summoned to see if there was anything they could do to address the skyrocketing heating bill. Kostas would spend an hour at Glannis' cafe to insulate the doors and caulk every window.

On that windy day, Anna Fry was sitting near a window and cautiously surveyed the room. When the Greek brothers left the building to do exterior work, she opened up her purse. Anna pulled out a coat hanger that was stretched out like a metal rod with a hook on the end. This had become the tool of choice, since the wells were beginning to run dry. Ingeniously, she inserted the extension in the hole, allowing her to excavate at ground level.

The scraping of metal against old mortar fragmented the primitive foundation. When the Anagnos family heard the noise, those on watch would tip off the prospectors before they entered the room.

Glannis would glance over the room to see his customers looking back with their hands in plain view. He would eventually leave, scratching his head. The moment he left, Anna broadcast a headline that she extracted. "Well, well, well," she said as she held up the tabloid from last century. Those present held their breath, wondering *who* was going to get it. "They even had fishing derbies back then," she said. The woman on Social Security held up the paper for all to see. It was a picture of her great-grandfather holding a three-pound rainbow trout. That year, Anna's grandson had won the local tournament. The Buckley Gazette did commemorate the event by placing his picture on the front page. The boys in both pictures looked like twins. Everyone in that room had grandchildren who participated in that derby; and ancestors in the ones years back.

Things weren't as rosy for Anna as she had thought. Her moment of glory was short-lived, having walked into an ambush. "Forgive me, Anna," said Hubert Godfrey. "I thought you were referring to this." He displayed a faded yellow paper over his head as he slowly turned back and forth, facing his audience. The headline read: "Robbers Caught" in bold print. Below, it had pictures of the "Fry Gang"; cousins of her prominent great-grandfather. The pictures covering the front page clearly showed a family resemblance to the boy who won the fishing derby that year.

Matt Shea

The crossfire continued.

"All I know is that a man expresses himself on the golf course," announced Fred Harvey. Fred stood up and held a vintage article about his grandfather winning a tournament. It included a picture of him swinging a golf club.

The frenzy escalated, with old newspaper articles promoting some families and incriminating others. It was all-out war.

Then something happened.

The wind picked up and began to whistle under the molding above the floor. It blew particles of dust, paper and dirt evenly across the room. The arguing came to an abrupt stop as everyone watched. A strip of molding outlining the floor started to loosen from the wall. It freed itself, tumbling with the wind. The force got greater as the wind began to circulate in the room like a small tornado. A wall slightly vibrated and started to loosen another wall adjacent to it.

"Everyone get out, now!" yelled a man's voice. Sheer panic filled the room as the entire cafe vacated. The occupants had no time to get their belongings, and ran across the street.

They were now huddled together under an awning in front of a laundromat. Like survivors of the Titanic, they watched the destruction of the cafe from a safe distance.

The old structure started to bow and flex from all sides. It continued to pulsate as they watched in horror. Then, all at once, it blew apart like a deck of cards in the wind. The Honeycomb Cafe was gone.

"AY! . . . ay.!. . ay!" muttered Glannis in a soft voice as he nodded his head in disbelief.

The violent wind died down, with the debris settling. All was quiet. What was once the hot spot of the entire county was now rubble. The party glared at one another, realizing that an era had come to an end. In their own right, they were 'the last of the Mohicans'. Tears ran down faces, with hugs following. Nothing had to be said. Their lives seemed to center around the cafe until its very last minute. But it was all over now.

Cautiously, they walked across the street to examine the ruins. At that moment, others migrated to the site. Soon a reporter from the Buckley Gazette arrived, with a local television crew following behind. This would be the story of the year.

Glannis and his brother mulled through the wreckage and spotted several open purses that held the old newspapers inside. An unraveled coat hanger was found next to a purse. It was picked up by Kostas and inspected. This was the 'smoking gun' that they were looking for. It was easy to figure out that his customers were stripping the walls of their insulation. Kostas looked up at his brother, and in their foreign tongue asked, "Why would they be interested in old newspapers? They only have bad stories about other people."

Glannis gave an explanation in their Greek language. "Because they are Americans!"

Kostas nodded with the understanding.

Purses, coats and other personal items were retrieved by their rightful owners. The police arrived and roped off the area with caution tape. The crowd was interviewed by reporters, with a collection started for Glannis and his wife, Adonia. Soon the activity slowed down with the crowd beginning to thin out. By nightfall, everyone had returned to their homes to watch themselves on the news.

Life had changed in the town of Buckley. The restaurant of choice was now the Woodsman Cafe; the town's lone diner. By some standards, this was an upgrade, being a much newer structure that was only forty years old. It was also larger and in compliance with current building codes. Another plus was that the Anagnos family owned it. This meant that Glannis and his wife, Adonia, had a job.

The Woodsman Cafe implemented a new policy that all had to comply with. The brothers thought it was best to play it safe and have Kostas' restaurant *senior-proofed*. The walls would now be barricaded with plants, statues, and anything that could protect them. The seating was now exclusively toward the center of the building. It was also apparent that *certain* guests were to be watched.

The seniors of Buckley were glad that they at least had a cafe. Still, there were those who were carrying a cross. Their digging for old newspaper articles resulted in the destruction of the Honeycomb Cafe. Their findings also caused hard feelings over petty events that were forgotten decades ago.

Marge Stewart felt that this travesty was all her fault. She took the incentive to schedule an informal town meeting, only for those who got caught up in this whirlwind.

She sent out the requests, begging everyone to meet at the Woodsman Cafe on Wednesday night at eight o'clock. It was understood that a formal apology would be given to Glannis and his family, along with a bouquet of flowers. Then an open floor would be held to come up with any ideas on how to erase the hard feelings that were created.

Marge was delighted that everyone responded upon reading their letters. All were in agreement to meet Wednesday night.

Wednesday night arrived, with the closed sign displayed on the front door of the restaurant. Familiar cars were parked out front, with those invited seen inside. It was now time to right what was wronged.

Marge approached the establishment, holding the beautiful flowers. She tapped on the door, which was immediately opened by Chara Anagnos. Chara gazed at the arrangement as Marge handed it to her. Marge entered the cafe to see that the tables were arranged end to end, like the Last Supper. All were now present, with hugs and handshakes being exchanged. Everyone sat down with Marge speaking first.

Marge went into great detail explaining what the Honeycomb Cafe meant to her life. She gave countless stories of the many meaningful moments her family has had there. She carefully explained that when she saw the old newspaper peering through the wall, her curiosity took over. She merely wanted to see how old it was. When she saw that it was an article about her great–grandmother, she justified taking something that wasn't actually hers.

"I was overwhelmed when I saw my great-grandmother's picture looking at me," said Marge. "I stopped thinking and simply took it home with me, as if it were mine." Heads nodded up and down with the understanding of how someone would have handled that situation the way she did. She pointed out that she didn't take any more paper out of the wall. Marge told how it was a mistake to frame the picture and tell everyone where she found it. "Naturally, others would go there to search for their family history," she concluded.

The others present shared similar stories to the Anagnos family. Soon, everyone had apologized.

Glannis was leaning back in his chair with a big smile. "I guess it's my turn," he said with a chuckle. "What you did to my restaurant actually helped me."

Everyone looked puzzled at Glannis. They wanted to hear what he had to say.

"As you know, my cafe was very old," said Glannis. "The state was giving me work orders to meet the fire code, among other things. If I didn't get the modifications done, I would have been fined and shut down by the state. I was also taking business away from my brother Kostas' cafe." He continued, "When my business got destroyed, I not only got insurance money for it; but also received a lot from the collection the community took up for my wife and I. That, along with our savings, allowed my wife and I to retire." The proud man stood up, pointing his finger to the sky. "And now, my brother's cafe is doing better, and my wife and I can help them."

The customers leaned back in their chairs in relief.

Glannis continued, "Now, all I have to do is get that mess cleaned up."

"You should make a big pile out of it and set it on fire," said Marge. "That way I can take that framed article I stole and throw it in."

The room was stunned. Heads slowly turned and looked at one another. "I have some old newspaper articles that I would like to burn up," said Ella Ray.

"So do I," said Fred Harvey.

"I think I can find some to get rid of myself," commented Anna Fry.

"How about having a community bonfire at the old Honeycomb Cafe this Saturday night?" suggested Mary Pierce.

"That's a great idea!" said Joan Wakeman. "All in favor, say 'aye'," she motioned.

The entire room stood up with everyone raising their hand and shouting, "Aye!"

"We can make an event out of this," exclaimed Elsie Baxter. "We can call it: A farewell to the Honeycomb Cafe."

"I will have no trouble posting fliers throughout town and telling local businesses," said Marge.

"I have a bulldozer and will make a haystack out of it," volunteered Hubert Godfrey. "When it's all done, I will haul the remains away in my dump truck."

The room was bonded by vowing to give the Honeycomb Cafe a grand send-off.

Saturday night had arrived, with the entire town surrounding the mound that was once the famous landmark. All at once, a lit torch was thrown on the gasoline-soaked pile. A *whoosh* sound accompanied the rolling flames that engulfed the entire stack, making the township cheer. Long wooden sticks held hot dogs and marshmallows near the dancing fire.

Marge Stewart was waiting for this moment. She took her framed newspaper article and threw it into the inferno, generating applause. Ella Ray made paper airplanes out of her newsprint and flew them into the fire, causing laughter. Next, more hands were throwing more yellowed paper into the bonfire.

This was a small town, where news traveled fast. Peter Williams might have only been a forty-year-old youngster, but he still he knew what was right. Holding his wife's hand, he marched up to the fire and threw in his divorce papers. His children cheered as the family united with a hug.

Professor Walden took the failing grades of his pupils and tossed them into the open flames. "I just have to teach better!" he proclaimed.

A teenager who wore a controversial jacket that implied gang activity took it off and threw it into the flames. His parents ran out to hug him.

A movement had started in the town of Buckley. Anything that suggested hurting the community was being destroyed on a voluntary basis. It seemed that the more disgrace was thrown into the fire; the more harmony came out.

Marge had a warm feeling as she watched the flames dance toward the heavens. Looking up at the stars, she thought about her great-grandmother's life. She remembered all of the stories she had told her about the people from that era. They, too, had differences that had to be settled. It was as if those ancestors had intervened with their current problems.

Marge wondered if past residents intentionally made themselves known through the walls of the Honeycomb Cafe. A visit designed to establish a truce that would upgrade the town with love and respect.

It was plain to see that Buckley was going through a change. It would once again be that little town where everyone cared and looked out for their neighbor.

Families

The Happy Family

Bill Whitman cautiously drove through the pounding rain as rush hour mounted. The middle–aged, divorced father had but one objective: he wanted to arrive home safely. Bill always allowed anyone to change lanes in front of him and expressed gratitude when someone would let him in. He cautiously navigated with the flow of traffic, giving enough room for others.

This conscientious driving style was just another trait of this humble man's life. Whether it was at work, a supermarket or in traffic; Bill Whitman always complimented everyone by showing respect. This in turn would prompt an unexpected visit at his household that evening. A visit that would change the life of an entire family.

The rain continued to pour as Bill got off his exit and drove the remaining mile to his house. In minutes he made his last turn and drove through the neighborhood he called home. The windshield wipers swayed back and forth as the defroster kept his view clear. There was one more citizen to yield to: Mrs. McNeil. The senior was standing on the last corner of his commute. A see-through umbrella, along with bright, colorful rain gear, kept her dry. Her shopping cart was covered with plastic and rested next to her. The elderly woman was patiently waiting for traffic to clear so that she could cross the street.

Bill was predictable and stopped for her. Smiles were exchanged, accompanied by a friendly wave. The feeble woman pushed her cart off the curb and crossed at the crosswalk. Bill's house was three doors down from this intersection. In moments, he completed the last leg of the journey and pulled into his driveway. The automatic garage door activated, allowing the wet vehicle to slowly roll onto dry cement. Finally, the car was safely parked with the garage door closing. Bill was home at last!

The business man would now leave his car and the working world behind. But he never separated himself from being a loving father. He surveyed the garage that held camping gear, a kayak, bicycles, and many memories. Three wooden steps now stood between Bill and the door that entered into his real life. He climbed the steps and opened the gateway to his happiness . . .

"How was your day?" asked a pleasant Bonnie Whitman. The forty-two-year-old woman smiled at Bill and hugged him as he walked into the entryway.

"I hope that I didn't make a mistake, allowing you to have access to my kingdom," said Bill. "To answer your question, my day was great, like all the others!" He was then engulfed with a tantalizing aroma. "My gosh," he said. "Did you cook me another dinner, Bonnie?"

"Yes, I did," said the family member. "I think a hardworking man like you deserves a warm meal when he comes home."

"I appreciate that!" said Bill. "I hope that the word never gets out on what a great cook you are. Someone will marry you, and then I'll have to cook for myself!" Together they laughed as Bill walked to his bedroom.

"Not so fast, mister!" said Bonnie as she pointed behind Bill. He turned around and saw his daughter, Annie, with her arms folded like a disappointed school teacher.

"Dad!" cried out Annie. "You aren't going anywhere 'til I get a hug!"

"Oh, oh," said the dad in a cheery voice. "The last thing I need is to have two women upset with me!" The proud father then ran up to his twelve-year-old daughter and, using both arms, picked her off the ground. He spun her around as her legs floated freely and gently placed her down. He gave her a warm bear hug and kissed her on the forehead.

Bill then stood in a military stance, looking straight ahead. He spoke with no facial expressions. "May I have permission to get clean and change my clothes?"

"Permission granted!" said the daughter as she saluted her father.

Bill saluted back and pivoted in the opposite direction. He then marched to his bedroom and closed the door. Bonnie and Annie stared at one another, laughing.

"Let's set the table for dinner," said Bonnie. The women went into the kitchen and began to prepare the dining room table. Bill entered the dining room within minutes and sat at the head of the table. Dinner was cooked, and Bonnie began to serve.

"You made spaghetti for me?" cried out Bill. "You know how much I love your spaghetti! And look, you did all the trimmings too!" Caesar salad, toasted garlic bread, Parmesan cheese and her secret pasta sauce graced the table. A pitcher of grape juice made it complete.

Soon the women were sitting on either side of Bill with hands being united for grace. Bill was emotional with the realization of how fortunate he was. He had a warm home, and more important; family.

The happy family would once again share a feast together. He thanked God for the gifts that he always received on a daily basis. He looked at Bonnie and knew that she worked hard to create that meal. He looked at his daughter and could only see a gift from God smiling back. In prayer, he expressed gratitude for everything he had. Bill finished grace by telling God that he wanted to do more to serve Him. Then he asked our Lord to send anyone his way who needed his help.

Just then, there came a knock on the door . . .

The family looked at one another, wondering who it could be. Bill excused himself from the table and walked to the door. He opened it and was shocked. He found himself staring at a large, imposing figure who resembled a lumberjack. He immediately recognized the weathered face with black hair and rough beard. It was John Fowls from work; the last person he ever thought would pay him a visit.

John had a reputation of mocking role models like Bill Whitman. Often, this problem employee would stare at Bill and insult him by saying, "He wasn't even a man." Bill resembled a librarian with glasses, wearing a cardigan sweater. He was dwarfed by the big man. Bill stared at John's blue eyes and noticed tears. It was obvious that John was reaching out at a moment of despair. He came to Bill's house a broken man.

Bill broke out of his trance and extended his hand to the visitor. "Good evening, John," he said.

"Good evening, Bill," said a soft-spoken John Fowls as he shook hands. "I need to talk to you, if you don't have any plans tonight. I am aware that you live alone with your daughter, so I thought that I could just drop by."

"We have a guest tonight, and two would be even better!" said Bill. "Will you please come in and join us for dinner? We'd be honored to have you," he continued.

John face finally broke into a partial smile and said, "That would do me good."

Bill continued the festive evening by calling out to Bonnie. "Bonnie, would you please set another plate? I have a friend who will be joining us for dinner."

"That will be wonderful!" she replied. "Tell your friend that he has perfect timing, dinner is just starting."

"Please come in and let me take your coat," said Bill.

John entered the Whitman household and closed the door. He sensed the love that was missing in his life. He took off the jacket and handed it to Bill. This time his smile was bigger as he said, "Thank you." Bill took the coat and placed it on a coat rack next to the door.

Bill smiled at John and said, "You are welcome; the pleasure's mine!"

Bonnie set a place for John and introduced herself. "Hi, my name is Bonnie Whitman."

John replied, "John Fowls; pleased to meet you."

Bill introduced John as a *friend* from work. The family approached dinner by saying grace a second time. This was to include John. It was obvious that he didn't practice this custom at his home. He participated and held hands with the Whitman family. Bill said grace by thanking God for a warm meal, and a special guest. John was taken by the compliment. Deep inside, he never considered himself as being special to anyone.

John was overwhelmed by the meal and his surroundings. Unlike his domain, this house was a home. It was clean, warm, and more important; happy. He studied how content Bill was, and the security Bonnie and Annie had with him. The silence needed to be broken. Bill would initiate a conversation.

Bill looked at John and in a tone of gratitude said, "It's great to have you here for dinner! Now, what did we do to deserve a treat like this?"

John sat uncomfortably, knowing that he didn't deserve this treatment. He leaned back and pinpointed why he chose to pay Bill this unannounced visit. "I decided to drop by and thank you for inviting my daughter, Megan, to Annie's slumber party tomorrow night. I realize that in the past I was unfair to both girls by not allowing my daughter to join in with her friends at those parties."

Annie's face lit up with excitement as she said, "Thank you, Mr. Fowls! Megan is one of my best friends at school, and everyone wants her to be there!" The happy girl left her chair and raced to John, giving him a big hug of appreciation.

John Fowls fought back the tears as he patted Annie on the back, saying, "We are glad that Megan has a friend like you. Thank you, Annie."

Annie went back to her chair and continued to eat her dinner with a smile on her face. John looked at Bill and Bonnie, and felt the warmth of their smiles directed at him.

"There is something else that I wanted to discuss with you," said John as he looked at Bill. "Maybe we could sit down after dinner and have a chat."

Bill winked at John and said, "I have all night for you."

John was relieved. He then addressed Bonnie. "You probably don't know this, but spaghetti is my favorite meal, and this is the best I have ever had!"

Bonnie was impressed. She had heard horror stories about John Fowls from neighbors and the school board. She was pleased to see his good side. "Why, thank you," she replied. "Something told me that tonight was going to be a special evening." John smiled back.

The festive evening escalated as warm stories with laughter rotated around the dinner table. It was a comfort for the Whitman family to meet the *real* John Fowls. Dinner was eventually finished, with the women clearing the table.

Bonnie's voice could be heard from the kitchen as she announced, " . . . And for dessert we have warm homemade raspberry cobbler topped with vanilla ice cream."

Bill looked at John and could see that he was preoccupied in thought. Bill remembered that John wanted to get something off his chest and called out to Bonnie. "Would you mind serving John and I in the living room?"

Bonnie responded immediately. "That will be fine, I'll make a pot of coffee."

The two men left the dinner table and walked to the living room. Bill flipped a switch to start the gas fireplace and motioned for John to sit in an easy chair that faced a coffee table. Bill sat down in a matching chair on the opposite side of the table, facing his guest. Bill moved first by asking him what was the matter. John stretched back in the chair to get comfortable. It was obvious that he needed time to express himself.

After a short pause, John spoke. "I am going through a divorce, and it occurred to me that I need to change."

Bill was stunned. "I am sorry to hear that," he said with sincerity.

John looked Bill in the eye and said, "I need to be like that divorced dad I work with who does everything right." John was referring to Bill Whitman.

The moment was interrupted when Bonnie entered the room, carrying a platter that held two bowls of desdert with matching mugs of coffee. She placed the treats on the coffee table and asked, "Does anyone need cream and sugar?"

"Not me," said John. He then looked at the steaming desdert and said, "You are a fabulous cook." John looked at Bill and exclaimed, "You should open a restaurant, so that I can eat there every night!" Bonnie thanked John for the compliment.

Bill injected, "That would be great, I wouldn't have to work anymore!" The three laughed for a minute.

"Bonnie," said Bill, "do you mind if John and I talk in private?"

John interrupted Bill and said, "Actually, it would do me good to hear from both of you. I am having family problems and need to get advice from others."

Bonnie and Bill were flattered and looked at John. "We'd love to talk with you," said Bonnie. "Let me get my coffee and dessert."

John watched Bonnie and marveled at how happy she was. "That's a good woman," said John.

"She certainly is," replied Bill. Bonnie returned with her dessert and placed it on the coffee table. She sat on the sofa, forming a human triangle.

Bill spoke up and said, "Before we get started, I want to toast our friend, John Fowls, for gracing out home tonight!"

Bonnie said, "Hear, hear," as the three raised their mugs and gave cheer.

John blushed and said, "Thanks, I appreciate that." He was now feeling at home and updated Bonnie about his problem. "I just told Bill that I am going through a divorce."

With compassion, Bonnie extended her right hand and placed it on John's shoulder, saying, "I am so sorry to hear that."

John was a strong man and said, "Don't feel sorry for me; I deserve it." He grabbed his coffee and sipped out of it. Then, placing it back on the table, he continued. "I have issues with my character that I have to address. I can't blame my wife, Betty, for leaving me. In fact, I was always amazed that she didn't leave long ago."

Bonnie gave a response. "Don't be so hard on yourself. At one time or another, a person has to make changes; and that's all of us."

Bill followed. "She's right, John. I am divorced because I had to make changes, just like you."

John sat up, realizing that he wasn't alone. He also knew that he was in good company.

"How are you two getting along during all of this?" asked Bonnie.

John lay back in the chair and looked toward the ceiling. He said, "Well, I'm trying. After all, didn't I come here for some pointers? At least I am more concerned about my daughter's life than I was before. Now I understand how important her friends are to her."

Bill responded, "That's great, but what about John?"

"Bill's right," said Bonnie. "You also deserve happiness."

John started to shake with emotion. Tears streamed down his face as he said, "If you want to know what I want, it's that hug your daughter gave me tonight! My daughter won't hug me like that. She sees me as a monster who abuses her mother. And she's right."

Bill and Bonnie sat back and digested John's comment.

"There are ways to re-approach your relationship with Betty," said Bill. "You are not condemned to be at war with her."

"I am trying," said John. "I don't go out with the guys the way I used to. I am also considering going to a counselor to improve as a father and a person."

Bill stood up and said, "That's what I had to do!"

John was stunned that he and Bill had a similar background and nodded his head with understanding.

"I have always heard that when someone is trying to change a bad lifestyle, that they need a support group," said John. "I guess that's why I'm here."

"Do you want to join me on Thursday nights?" asked Bill. "That's when my divorce group meets."

John sat on the edge of his chair, looking like a puppy wagging its tail. "You go to a divorce group?" he asked. "That's just what I need, and you are the perfect guy to do this with!"

At that moment, John's cell phone rang. "Excuse me," he said. "It's probably a call from my daughter; please don't leave." He pulled the cell phone out of his pocket and answered it.

Bill and Bonnie could hear the one-way conversation. It was Megan, and there was a problem.

Megan was to spend Friday night with her mother. The plan was for her to go to the library straight after school to do her homework. Her mother would then pick her up at the library, take her out to dinner, and bring her to her new apartment. Betty was feeling sick after work. When she and Megan finished dinner, she realized that she was in no condition to have company that night.

John looked at Bill and Bonnie, knowing that they heard the situation. Bill whispered, "Tell her to bring Megan here. She can play with Annie while we visit, then you can take her home with you."

John repeated the offer to Megan; it was relayed to her mother and accepted. They knew where Annie lived and would arrive in fifteen minutes.

John ended the call and put the cell phone back into his pocket. He sat down with his company and thanked them for helping.

"That's quite all right," said Bill. "Your entire family is always welcome here."

John relished the acceptance. He then shared a passing thought. "I wish that I had a sister living close to me like you do. That would always keep me straight."

Bonnie looked at Bill and said, "I didn't know that you had a sister."

Bill looked at her and said, "I don't. But I have a wonderful ex-wife, and she is a great mother to our daughter. She is also a very special friend to me."

John's mouth dropped in astonishment. "I thought that you two were brother and sister!"

"Not exactly," said Bill. "We were once husband and wife, but will always be family! And if you don't believe us, just ask Annie. We were hurting her until we understood that we could respect each other and ourselves."

Bonnie looked at Bill and kissed him on the cheek. "He is a great father, dad; and always my special friend," she said.

Bill looked at John and said something that he would always carry with him. "Remember, John: kids are perfect until grown-ups get to them."

John was deep in thought, having learned a valuable lesson from his co-worker.

A car door slammed shut in front of the house. The trio looked out the view window and saw Betty Fowls dropping off Megan. The tapping of little footsteps could be heard running toward the house. A knock followed. Bonnie opened the door and greeted Megan. "Megan, it's so good to see you," said Bonnie. "Please come in!"

Megan was out of breath as she entered the house. She said, "I need to put my book bag down so that I can get my travel bag out of my mom's car."

It was now time for John to act. "Wait a minute," said the father. "If your mother is sick, she needs to stay with us until she feels better!" John took his key chain out of his pocket and unfastened a spare house key. With firmness, he handed it to his daughter and gave instructions. "Give this key to your mother. Wherever you have a home, it's also your mother's home." He then placed the key in Megan's hand and hugged her.

Megan responded! She gave her father a hug ten times harder than Annie did and held onto him. She looked up at her dad and said, "Thanks, Dad, I love you so much!" Then she did something she hadn't done in ages. She kissed him. With the joy of a child, she ran out to the car to invite her mother to stay with them.

John could only look down and smile with satisfaction. He felt *right*. He then looked and saw Bill gazing at him with respect. Bill's hand was extended and shook John's, one man to another.

John said, "I need to talk to Betty now. I want to thank you for this evening. The dinner was great, and more important, the friendship. I'll see you tomorrow when I drop Megan off for the slumber party. And remember; you and I have a date next Thursday!"

Bill knew that he had a prayer answered. "Thank you for visiting us," he said. "See you tomorrow night, and especially on Thursday."

John smiled at Bill and gave a thumbs-up. The new man grabbed his coat off the coat rack and bent over to pick up the book bag. He stood up and saw his own reflection in a mirror that hung in the entryway. What he saw wasn't the man who broke up his home. It was a relieved, peaceful soul who was on a mission. The tense face with defined lines was now relaxed and appeared more youthful. He saw a compassionate man that would *now* put others first.

His evening with Bill Whitman placed him on the right track. He took a closer look at the man in the mirror, and smiled back. He needed to change, and more important; *wanted* to. Like any stubborn male ego, he had years of digging himself into a deep hole. It was time to face John Fowls and do something about it.

It would take a lot of counseling to understand himself. It didn't matter, though; his daughter, Megan already showed that it was worth it. This new direction would have its fair amount of trials. But he knew that with encouragement, support and honest effort, he could make it—and would. He winked at the image in the mirror, cheering himself on.

John stood up and proceeded to walk out the door. It was time to be a man like Bill Whitman and take care of his family.

The Fiji Family

Snowflakes continued to fall as Jack Frost confined everyone to their homes. The countryside resembled the North Pole, with smoke billowing out chimneys. The beauty of this tranquility had no meaning to James Faulk. The frustrated man was hard at work securing the fence that outlined his acreage. With freezing hands and bailing wire, he would fortify the wooden boundary. "I hate this time of year," he muttered to himself.

James felt threatened. At one time his family owned almost the whole valley, including a neighboring resort off a pristine lake. Through the years, their numbers had dwindled with land being sold. Only he and his mother now remained. The loyal son felt outnumbered by a new race of people that purchased the resort. James felt that they were pushed into a corner and needed to fight back.

Like a hillbilly protecting his property, James held up his binoculars to take a closer look. He nodded his head in disapproval. The rustic cabins that were once part of his family heritage were now in the hands of strangers.

Cabin number four was the pick of the litter. It had three rooms with a bathroom, kitchen, running water, and a wood stove. The cabin also had the best view, with the lake just yards away. The mother-and-son combination always chose to stay in that cabin whenever possible. The retired woodsman in the red flannel shirt gritted his teeth in anger. "I will do what it takes to protect my mother from those savages taking over!" he thought to himself . . .

He turned his head and looked at his home. Then he looked up a steep hill where his mother's house rested. It was his duty to provide and keep her safe.

Without warning, James' solitude was disturbed. "You seem to be upset today." It was the calm voice of his neighbor, Pete Rainwater. Pete seemed to be a part of nature and moved within it in silence.

"I am afraid that I have some bad news," said James.

"What bad news?" asked Pete.

"Our community is being taken over by Samoans!" cried out James. "They are not even from here," exclaimed the fourth-generation Faulk. "They don't even look like us!"

Pete Rainwater stood motionless, deep in thought. Finally, the Native American responded. "Ah, yes. I remember my great-grandparents telling me stories that their grandparents told them. They talked about strange-looking people from foreign lands moving in on their territory, as if they owned it."

"Then you know how bad this is!" said James.

Pete remarked, "It can be very bad, but I don't think that they are a problem. They are the Fiji family, and they came from American Samoa. They seem like very nice people."

James didn't understand what Pete meant by that comment. The white man turned to look at his neighbor, only to find that he had vanished.

James looked down the valley and fumed. *His* family used to own that land, and that's where he grew up.

The snow continued to fall.

James noticed that it was beginning to get dark. It was time to drive up the trail that led to his mother's home and check in on her. He got into his car and started the engine. He put it in drive and attempted to climb the hill, but the tires could only spin in place. The slick surface offered no traction. He made several more attempts, but to no avail.

James got out of his car and could see his mother's house. There was smoke coming from her wood stove and the living room light was on. "She should be good tonight," he thought to himself. He walked to his home and tried to call her on the telephone. The line was dead. "The snow must have broken a line somewhere," he thought as he scratched his head. Still, he had signs that suggested that she was all right and would wait until morning.

The snow continued . . .

The following morning, a knock on the front door awoke James. He put on his bathrobe and answered it. It was his neighbor, Pete. "We have a problem," he said. "All of the electricity is out, and your mother is scared. Don't worry; I hiked up there with some firewood and warm food to make sure that she was fine. I got a good fire going in her stove and fed her. I told her that the snow is going to get worse, and that she needs to pack her bags. She understands that we will come by later to bring her down."

James was grateful to Pete. "You always know what's happening around here before anyone else," he commented. "Thanks, Pete!"

James had to start thinking. How could he get her down from up there? His car wouldn't budge in the snow, she was far too old to hike down in the snow, and a sled would only cause a disaster . . .

In desperation he changed into his winter clothes and went to his tool shed to get a shovel. James had the notion that he could dig an uphill road for his car to drive on. Guided by tunnel vision, the sixty-year-old man went to his car and began to dig around the wheels. He then got in front of the car and aimlessly shoveled snow out from its path.

Pete Rainwater watched James from behind and chuckled. "You are not making any headway doing that," he said. "The snow leading to your mother's house is only getting deeper. Why don't you ask your new neighbors if they can help you?"

"Not on your life," said the man with false pride. "That would only serve as a weakness, and then they will try to take more." James kept shoveling as he huffed and puffed.

Pete threw his hands up in the air and said, "We are all neighbors, and that makes us family!" He turned and walked away in disgust.

James spent the next hour digging and taking breaks. He was slowing down more and more. Finally he stood up and clasped his blistered hands on the shovel. He looked up to his mother's house to see that there was no more smoke coming from the stove pipe. He did not eat breakfast yet and was hungry. He was also getting cold, just as his mother would be. He evaluated the situation and thought about what Pete said. Then he heard the cavalry . . .

Like Whoville, the grace of human voices could be heard singing around a campfire down below. It was the Fiji family. Their harmony carried across the land with a spirit that united their family with God. It also carried far enough to serve as a beacon for James. His stubbornness tried to fight this spiritual invitation. But the message was also compounded by the sweet, tantalizing aroma of a Polynesian barbeque, further weakening the hungry man.

James looked down at the family, and looked up at his mother's house. He looked back down and smelled what was the most welcome food in his entire life, and looked back up to the isolated structure that was gradually getting buried. He realized that it was time to swallow his pride and ask the Fiji family for help.

James dropped the shovel and trudged downhill in the ankle-deep snow. As he approached the resort, he could feel the heat from the bonfire. A heat that would aid his mother's life. The Fiji family was shielded from the snow by a large tarp that was tied to trees, suspended high above the fire pit. They silenced as they saw their disgruntled neighbor appear from the flurry. "We need help," said James in a surrendering voice. "My mother is stranded in her house, and I can't get up there."

"We have taken care of that," said Mr. Fiji. The father pointed at his jeep. The wheels were fitted with chains as it pointed toward his mother's home. James stared at the modified Ford Bronco and grinned. He realized that if anything could make it up the hill; it would be that!

He looked at the family and saw a circle of caring faces gazing at him. He noticed two empty chairs next to Mr. Fiji and realized that they were meant for him and his mother.

"In this community, we are all family," proclaimed the dad as he extended his hand to shake James'.

"That's right!" said Pete.

"My name is Phili, and we are your neighbors," said Mr. Fiji. "If there is ever anything that we can do for you, please let us know. And now we will get your mother." The elder turned and addressed his three oldest sons. "David, Ben and Shaggy, you know what to do." The sons stood up and walked to James, introducing themselves and shaking hands.

"Don't worry, Mr. Faulk," said David. "We will get your mother and bring her back to you."

James looked at David and placed his left hand on his shoulder, shaking hands with the other. With tearful eyes, he said, "I am grateful for this."

The sons were on a mission. Their father ordered them to rescue Mrs. Faulk. It was understood that she would be revered as more than just a neighbor; she was regarded as family.

David, Ben and Shaggy climbed into the jeep, and with determination began the treacherous ascent. The engine revved with high acceleration as chains clanked, digging into the snow. Immediately, traction was secured and the rescue party was off. The jeep burrowed through the snow as if it were a motor boat leaving a trail of mist. They made it up the first hill with ease. The all-terrain vehicle was now put to the test. It weaved to maintain its course as the chained four-wheel driven monster crawled up the second hill. It steadily clawed all the way to the top, where the eighty-year-old widow wrapped in blankets shivered in fear. The family cheered the heroes as the jeep leveled off and drove to the front steps.

The trio got out of the jeep and knocked on the door. The curtains moved as a wrinkled face with baggy eyes peered through the glass. A relieved David smiled back. He then looked at his brothers and winked at them with a smile. "Mrs. Faulk," he cried out. "Your son sent us here to bring you to him. He has saved our entire family and sent us to get you. Because of him, we are all warm and safe; please join us."

The feeble old woman opened the door to meet the *friendly savages*. "Thank God you came to get me," she cried out. "I don't think that I would have survived the night."

Three sets of compassionate brown eyes stared at the senior. Finally, Ben spoke up. "Not on our watch!" The mammoth islander gracefully picked up the woman in blankets and carried her to the jeep. He placed her in the front seat, where heat blew all over her chilled body. Gretta leaned back in comfort, absorbing the warmth. Shaggy looked inside the front door and saw a suitcase that seemed packed and ready to go. He picked it up and walked to the old woman. "Do you want to bring this with us?" asked Shaggy as he displayed the luggage.

"Yes!" said Gretta. "I had that packed for my son to get me." The brothers looked at one another and nodded in approval. They each raised their right hand and gave a 'high five' in recognition that they had accomplished their goal. They entered the jeep with the suitcase and closed the doors. Slowly they drove down the snowy slope, honking the horn and flashing the headlights in victory. James, Pete, and the remainder of the Fiji family stood up and cheered, knowing the Gretta Faulk was saved!

The jeep pulled up to the gathering and parked. James opened the door and assisted his mother out. She was escorted to the chair next to him and sat down.

Phili's mother sat in the other chair next to Gretta and served her a cup of hot cider with a heavenly smile. "My name is Hana," she said in a loving tone.

"My name is Gretta," she replied. Then the women hugged and sighed with the new friendship.

Phili reached into his pocket and pulled out a set of keys. He handed them to James, saying, "Cabin number four is ready and will be home for you and your mother until this weather clears up. I think that it's best to simply live here until spring." The mother and son looked at each other with excitement. It was like the good old days!

James looked at Phili and said, "I can pay you the rent right now."

"That won't be necessary," said Phili. "This whole community is one big family, and we will survive this winter as one. And now, it's time to eat."

With bulging eyes, James looked back at his mother. They were starving and could smell the food. Gretta nodded in approval.

Phili continued, "We will now say grace."

All stood up in a circle and held hands. With heads bowed, Phili gave thanks to the lord for the meal they were about to have. He expressed how grateful he was to have his family, as well having Pete, James and Gretta in their lives.

The women began serving the delicious food from the homeland. Conversation broke out with laughter as James and his mother got acquainted with everyone.

Gretta looked at her son, James. He was smiling the way he did as a child whenever they camped there.

James Faulk looked around at the falling snow. He saw a lone snowflake flutter underneath the tarp, dropping toward him. James extended his tongue to catch it and swallowed the Arctic water. He stared at the bare branches that held precious white snow and marveled at its beauty.

James looked at his mother. She was comfortable in front of the fire and being fed. Gretta was happy talking to new friends that also mothered children. The best moments of James' childhood were being revived on the very property it took place on; with the same family values he was raised by. James' spirit was back.

He looked at the circle of loved ones and smiled at each one individually. This precious moment would stay with him for the rest of his life. James was a simple man who loved nature; especially when he could share it with his mother. All he wanted now was for this moment to last forever.

James turned and saw Pete Rainwater staring at him with a satisfied expression. He smiled back at him and motioned to get closer. Pete got out of his chair and got close to James. James put his hands together with an opening on both ends. He placed them in front of his mouth, as if to tell a secret. Pete leaned until his right ear was surrounded by James' enclosed hands.

"Isn't this wonderful?" whispered James. "We have the Fiji family for neighbors!"

The Spiritual Walk

The quiet of a cold winter night was the setting as Floyd Matthews left his front door. The middle-aged black man buttoned up his wool coat and adjusted his hat. A sentimental knitted red scarf that his grandfather used to wear was secured around his neck. Black leather gloves stretched as they were pulled over strong hands to further insulate the masculine body.

It was now time for a brisk evening walk. The winter night held its beauty as crystal-clear stars lit the icy sidewalks of Willis Street. Snow banks glistened, with a penetrating chill in the air. Few would dare to leave their homes on such a cold night. This environment, however, guaranteed tranquility—which was good medicine for Floyd. It allowed him to walk alone with God. In prayer, he would address his problems and ask for direction. Floyd would ask our Lord for signs. This evening, he would receive heavenly signs that would affect many loved ones, as well as himself.

The subway ramp gave access to the lower quarters of town. It secluded the underground train from the busy city streets. It also served as a temporary harbor for weary pedestrians. The warm air from the industrious tunnel rolled up the concrete steps, engulfing Floyd. The generous heat allowed him to momentarily unbutton his coat, loosen the neck scarf, and remove his hat. He slowly walked the length of the underground oasis, approaching the steps that elevated back to the cold street.

As he began to climb the steps, the reality of the cold winter wind pushed against his face. Floyd turned sideways to face the opposite wall of the metal screen that exposed the enclosed subway stairs to the outside elements. The steps were now just a few feet below the sidewalk, with an Arctic breeze blowing through the screen and dancing in the subway stairs. Floyd put his hat on and positioned it to fit snug. He buttoned up his coat and tightened the scarf around his neck. He turned to walk the final steps that reunited him with the winter night.

The excess length of the scarf was thrown around his neck one last time, with the end of the scarf catching a bent screw that fastened the hand railing onto the cement wall. When Floyd took his first step, the scarf gave a mild tug as a thread of red fabric tore from the heirloom. He looked around and saw the short strand of red fiber hooked around the bent screw. Its scarlet red tail waved slightly in the breeze. He then looked directly across to the metal screen that contained the stairwell from the sidewalk, and noticed something peculiar.

What appeared to be a moth holding onto the screen bowed with the wind like paper. A closer look revealed that it *was* paper, with a dull white, green and black formation. At that moment it occurred to him that he was looking at a bill that the wind blew up against the mesh screen. "How much would it be worth?" he asked himself.

Floyd ran up the stairs, quickly turned to the right, and placed his gloved hands around the naked bill. Meticulously, he removed the greenback, and using his thumbs and index fingers smoothed out the currency. His eyes lit up as he held a fifty-dollar bill!

Floyd thought about his family. He was out of work, and the family budget was tight. The tempo at home was survival mode, with mild depression. He vowed to change that. Floyd could only think of one thing. He would return home and honor his wife, mother and daughter by taking them out to dinner. The fifty dollars, plus what he already had, could pay for this.

With enthusiasm, he walked the icy steps that led to their townhouse and opened the door. The women were in the living room and couldn't help but notice the joy on Floyd's face. His ear–to–ear grin displayed his shiny white teeth as he waved the fifty-dollar bill and announced, "We are the Matthews family, and tonight we are going out to dinner!"

His wife, mother and daughter tensed up with excitement. Together, they were all sacrificing to survive hard times. A spur-of-the-moment family outing seemed like a Christmas gift. There was no special occasion for this outing, though. It was simply because they were a family that was overdue to go out as a family.

Floyd's mother asked where they were going. "How about having dinner at Chubbies?" the daughter suggested. 'Chubbies' was the fun restaurant in town, and only three blocks away.

The women looked at one another in astonishment. Without any words being said, they went to their rooms to get dressed for the evening. Floyd was happy because his family was happy. He held up the bill and kissed it, saying, "Thank you so much, my Lord."

In moments, three gorgeous females were 'dressed to the nines' adorned with hats, neck scarves, gloves, and winter coats. Floyd opened the door for his dinner party as they proudly left their home for an evening on the town. The pleasant smell of perfumes graced the path they braved that cold evening.

The bright Hollywood lights of Chubbies were just a block away. The smell of delicious food tantalized the group as they endured the final stretch to the diner. Finally, they had arrived. Elegant glass doors displayed the festive atmosphere inside, where music could be heard. A doorman opened the main door as the family entered the lobby. A fireplace offering much-needed heat greeted them as they removed hats, gloves, neck scarves and heavy coats. A coat rack stood alone in the corner that would hold their cold garments and have them toasty ready when they would depart for home.

The room was decorated in beautiful oak. Brass electric lamp fixtures accompanied by stained glass and matching leather furniture graced the room. The hostess greeted the party with four menus and asked if they were ready to be seated. "Yes we are," said a cheerful Floyd Matthews.

"That's wonderful," said the hostess. "Please follow me," she said. The well-dressed woman led the Matthews to the dining room. The family looked around and studied the beautiful brass light fixtures, oak tables, and flowers that enhanced the restaurant. They were seated at a table that had a white tablecloth with a lit candle in a brass candle holder in the center. Four tall glasses held ice water with lemon slices. Floyd pulled out each chair to seat the women; oldest to youngest. Once they were all seated, they looked at one another with pride. *They* were the Matthews family!

A server delivered a warm, covered basket of sourdough bread and buns with a small porcelain bowl of butter. Floyd picked up the bread basket and unfolded the dark brown cloth that kept it warm. He extended it to his mother, allowing her to pick the first slice of bread. He then held it in front of his wife, then his daughter. Floyd took a bun and covered the remainder with the cloth, placing the basket back on the table. Butter was passed and menus were opened. Eyes bulged with the realization that the best meal since the holidays was going to be served.

"Ladies, have whatever you want," said the head of the household. Each reviewed the menu meticulously as glands salivated.

When the last menu closed, the timely server came by to take the orders. Once completed, the server collected the menus and left. Floyd would now address the family for grace. The table united by holding hands and bowing heads. Floyd thanked God for leaving money for him to find in the subway. He asked for blessings for his entire family, his neighbors, and for everyone, everywhere. The family was deep in thought as they praised God for that evening. Once grace was completed, they looked at each other with smiles.

Spontaneous conversation erupted with the joy of laughter following.

Soon their server returned, holding a platter up high with one hand. Their dinner had arrived, as each plate was carefully placed in front of its rightful patron. The wonderful evening continued. Floyd reached into his pocket and removed his wallet. He counted the few bills that accompanied the fifty. He knew how much dinner would cost and calculated that they could afford dessert. When the busboy collected the plates, the server followed and asked, "Would you like a dessert tonight?"

Dessert sounded like the perfect touch as the women grinned at one another, nodding in agreement. Floyd continued his diplomacy and said, "Dessert sounds good. What do you recommend?" he asked.

The gracious server said, "We have a hot cherry cobbler with vanilla ice cream that's our house specialty." The elated women looked at Floyd and nodded their heads up and down.

"That sounds great," he said. "We will each have that." The women bent over and gritted their teeth with anticipation. Floyd was savoring every precious moment at that table. His thoughts were then distracted when he noticed something.

An elder couple with the husband in a wheelchair slowly moved down the aisle. Floyd was raised right, as he excused himself from the table to offer assistance. His mother nodded to herself in approval. The compassionate son assumed the liberty of pushing the wheelchair to the front door and retrieving their coats for them. He offered to help them get into their car as he opened the glass door for them. They were grateful for his help, and offered him money in gratitude. Floyd gave his customary smile and said, "That's quite all right. It's my pleasure to help you tonight."

Together, they walked to the handicapped parking space in front of the restaurant. The caring man safely got the elder couple into their car and put the wheelchair in the trunk. The seniors thanked Floyd repeatedly for his kindness. He responded with his caring smile and a spirited thumbs-up. The car started with the defroster blowing and heat circulating. In a minute, they drove off as Floyd waved goodbye and returned to his family.

The restaurant was almost empty, with one last table being occupied. Rich coffee was waiting for the Good Samaritan as spiced hot tea kept the women warm. The jubilant server made her final approach.

Like the Statue of Liberty, she had one hand extended above her head, carrying the steaming desserts on a platter. Upon placing the grand finale in front of each customer, the small black leather folder that traditionally carries the bill was discretely placed on the corner of the table closest to Floyd.

The proud father, husband and son slid the folder toward him as he picked it up. He opened it and saw a card that wasn't a bill. It was a thank-you note from Mr. and Mrs. Williams. The note stated that they were the owners of the restaurant and thanked him for helping them get into their car that evening. The dinner was 'on the house' as their gift to Floyd. There was more: a gift certificate for four. The Williams wanted Floyd's family to enjoy another evening in their restaurant—as their guests.

The family man got choked up and handed the card to his mother. He looked up at the ceiling in tears as the grandmother dug into her purse to get her reading glasses. She smiled as she read the good news and looked at her son. "That's what you get for caring about others," she said. "As always, I am so proud of you, son!" She looked across the table and shared the good news. The three women clapped for Floyd, adding to the respect he was deserving of. Like a ten-year-old child attending his own birthday party, he sat up straight and grinned. The dessert now had more meaning and represented a celebration. They continued to eat, savoring every last bite.

All plates were cleared, with the last sips of warm drinks being finished. The Matthews were full as they leaned back in their chairs with satisfaction. They looked at one another in awe. They went out as a family and were respected as a family. It was one of the greatest evenings of their life.

It was now time to leave Chubbies and walk the frozen sidewalks home. The Matthews left the table and walked to the lobby. They expressed appreciation to the hostess and promised to be back. The coat rack resembled a Christmas tree. It was decorated with their wool coats, hats and neck scarves—all warm for their short journey home. Immediately, they plucked their garments off the curved wooden arms and bundled up. Floyd opened the glass door for the women and left behind them. The family huddled together and headed home.

The front door was approached, with a key already in hand. Floyd quickly opened it and allowed his family in first. He stayed outside and said, "I still didn't get my nightly walk in."

"Okay, son," said his mother. "I want to thank you again for the great evening."

Floyd's wife and daughter also said, "Thank you." Then the three ran out to the porch and hugged the man of the house. They went back inside and closed the door.

Floyd was alone again. He now had a different feeling about his life, and dedicated his walk to thank God for the evening that was provided. This time he chose a different direction. A direction that would serve as a calling for a loved one. No sooner did he cross the street and walk down a different block, than he heard his name called out. "Floyd Matthews, is that you?" He looked to see where the voice was coming from. It was his old kindergarten teacher who had watched him grow up and become a man. She was calling out from her front door. "Floyd," she said, "If there was ever a time that I needed you, it's now!"

"Well, Miss Feldon," said Floyd. "I am here at your service."

"I hate to ask you for a favor, but I need money to take a taxi all the way to Marysville. My brother is sick, and I am needed to stay with him and take care of his kids."

Floyd reached into his pocket and pulled out his wallet. He opened it and removed the God-given currency. He walked up to her walkway and handed it to her, asking, "Will fifty dollars be enough?"

Mrs. Feldon was taken. "That will be more than enough!" she said.

At that moment, a car pulled in front of the house. It was the unmistakable car of her older brother, Ralph. The driver's side window rolled down as he called out. "Janet," he said in a raised voice, "I am going to Richard's house to help him out. He left a message on my cell phone letting me know that he was too sick to take care of his children. Do you want to come join us?"

"That's just where I was going!" said the sister.

"Okay," said Ralph. "I'll wait out here for you."

Miss Feldon looked at Floyd and handed the fifty dollars back. "Floyd Matthews, you are definitely going to heaven," she said.

Floyd accepted the bill and placed it back into his wallet. He put the billfold back into his pocket and said, "I love you too, Miss Feldon. Tell your brother that I hope he gets better, and that I will pray for him."

Miss Feldon hugged Floyd and went inside to get her packed bags. Floyd turned into the night and continued his walk, deep in thought. He looked up at the shiny stars, knowing that God was there. Again, he was able to help a loved one financially; and mysteriously, he still had the fifty dollars he had found earlier that night. He continued to walk.

It was approaching midnight. Floyd still felt energetic and wasn't ready to return home yet. He crossed another street and saw a beacon in the night. Wally's All Night Grocery was lit up with its many neon signs. This would be the perfect place for any pedestrian to get warmth. Automatic doors swung open as he approached the entrance. Once inside, he noticed a neighbor sitting down at a table in the delicatessen. It was Will Blessing, a friend for many years. Will was looking down, obviously depressed. His elbows were on the table with his hands clasped, leaning against his forehead. It looked like the big man was praying.

Floyd was concerned and walked up to Will. "Are you okay, Will?" he asked.

Will looked up and was relieved to see Floyd. "I am so glad to see you!" he said. "I came here to buy some groceries. I didn't realize that my bank account is overdrawn, and I don't get paid until next week.

Floyd knew what to do. He pulled out his wallet and opened it. He took out the fifty-dollar bill and handed it to Will.

Will's face lit up with a big smile. That money represented enough food to feed his family until payday. He *had* to accept it. He looked up at his friend and said, "Thank you, Floyd. We needed this bad."

Floyd chuckled and said, "You are a good man, Will. Besides, now I can shop with you and get warm!" The friends laughed with a handshake.

Will got up and walked to an empty shopping cart. "I know what to do," he said. He pushed the cart to the section that had the marked-down food. He filled the cart with enough perishables and frozen items to equal the fifty dollars, including tax.

The two went to the checkout line. It seemed that they were the only customers in the store as the clock struck midnight. The clerk inspected the expiration dates on the food and looked directly at Will. He then said in a joking matter, "I have some good news, and some bad news."

Will was scared. His household was out of food. The clerk introduced himself as the manager and said, "As of midnight tonight, all of this food cannot be sold by our store because they have now officially expired their shelf life. He then leaned over and whispered loudly to Will and Floyd. "But that doesn't mean I can't just give it to you. The food is still good for quite some time, and the frozen food is probably good for at least another year! Why don't you go back to the discount bins and take all of it home with you? I need to get it off of my hands anyway."

Will was flabbergasted! "You have a deal, sir!" he said. Will and Floyd quickly pushed the cart back to the discount section and took the remainder of the marked-down items.

Frozen steaks, hamburger, hotdogs, cheese, with many canned soups, boxed dinners and pastries were waiting to be taken. They left the store as the friendly manager waved, wishing them a good night. When they reached Will's station wagon, Will handed Floyd back the fifty dollars. "I won't be needing this, my friend!" said Will. The men emptied the cart into the vehicle. "I will be sending you a care package real soon," laughed Will.

"Well, that's great," replied Floyd. "We can always use some extra food." He placed the bill inside his wallet and put it back into his coat pocket.

Will then extended his hand and shook Floyd's. "Let me give you a ride home," he offered.

Floyd knew that it was late, but still felt that he didn't get his nightly walk in. "I appreciate that," he answered. "I need to walk more; I have too much energy in me to sit still anywhere."

"Okay," said Will. The big man gave Floyd a bear hug and said, "I think I know why everyone loves you so much." Will closed the gate to his station wagon and entered his car. He tooted the horn as the relived provider started the car and drove home.

Floyd was alone and surrounded by the quiet darkness once again. He continued his walk with the full understanding that God had heard his initial prayer, and answered it. He pondered over the fact that he spent the fifty dollars three times, and still had it!

He trudged through the icy terrain until he reached Willis Street. He stopped and took out his wallet. He pulled out the fifty-dollar bill and held it up to see if there was anything unusual about it. At that exact moment, a gust of wind kicked up and blew the paper money out of his hand. It resembled a dry maple leaf as it flew over the icy street. Floyd sprinted after it. The bill glided with the wind, until it finally rested up against a metal mesh screen.

The tuckered-out man grinned at the money that seemed secured against the barrier. As he bent over to grab it, he noticed a sign. Beyond the screen was the stairwell that led to the subway. He was staring directly at a small strand of red fiber that was hooked around a bent screw that supported a handrail. It gracefully swayed in the gentle breeze, as if to serve as a reminder to Floyd.

He dropped his hand and stood back. The fifty-dollar bill was in the exact spot it was when he found it. At that moment, it occurred to him that the money had already served its purpose; it took care of his family that night. It was now returned to its rightful place, to be discovered by another struggling family.

Floyd's mouth dropped with this realization. He stood up looking to the heavens. Laughingly, he spoke to God. "Okay, I get it," he said. "You really do hear prayers and help others. Lord, I want to thank you for being with all of us this evening. I know that soon, there will be someone else just like me who also needs your help. Please guide them here safely and take care of them, just as you took care of me. I love you!"

Floyd Matthews was enlightened. It was now time to return home. Soon, grace would find another cold, dejected soul wandering through the subway station, looking for a prayer to be answered.

Chase: A Special Person

The Guardian Angel Report

Golden rays channel through fluffy clouds, creating a prism of rainbows. Shimmering silver outlined a universe of crystal vapor as the earth turned below. Angels danced on an infinity of mist that was often referred to as 'cloud nine'. The heavenly crowd resembled playful otters at feeding time, with some doing cartwheels and somersaults. The festive moment began to change into one of concentration. Their jurisdiction on planet Earth was about to have light shed on it.

It was now time to get mentally prepared. These special angels were given the greatest task that our Creator could issue. They were anointed to spiritually guide and protect a specific mortal on Earth. Their efforts could sway one's path to Heaven. They are an elite force under our Creator known as the Guardian Angels.

Guardian Angel Sir Nigel Lennon was most fortunate. He got the 'pick of the litter'; he was assigned to Chase Mansfield. What a simple task! Chase was a superior being by many standards. He possessed a natural purity that spread compassion. He was above deceiving others and exposed his honest traits throughout every facet of life. The planet he survived on was greatly flawed and mislead. It had a high population of misfits that invented a standard to be judged by. To many, acquiring possessions and establishing leverage over others gave the highest rating. It was clearly a case of 'the blind leading the blind'.

Guardian Angels were needed here, and they had to be good ones. It was their mission to strategically place these wonderful, sincere, caring souls throughout the planet. They would serve as a way to set an example for the many less fortunate. The irony was that there were those who viewed such wholesomeness as a weakness or handicap. Some even placed a stigma on it.

Looking over a silver-edged cloud was the humble figure of Guardian Angel Sir Nigel. The four-hundred-year-old soul was deep in thought as he glanced down toward the mortal population. Floating toward him was the illustrious figure of Guardian Angel Robert Hershel Hollingsworth IV. A soul that was once royal blood in a past life.

"Good morning, Sir Nigel," greeted Robert Hershel Hollingsworth IV.

"Good morning, Robert," replied Nigel.

"May I ask a favor of you, my good man?" asked Robert.

"Sure," answered Nigel. "Anything you want."

"I seem to be getting little progress with my student, Patrick Chesterfield," said a dejected Robert as he looked down. "I realize that he usually means well, but he has this quirk about wanting to rule others." Robert then had a frightening thought and looked up at Nigel. "I hope that I was never guilty of that when I lived down there."

Nigel was quick to respond. "You were just like the rest of us when we lived there. It was all about living, learning and understanding that we were there to serve our Lord and help others. You made the grade, Robert; and that's why you are now up here with us."

Robert looked proud as he stood tall and puffed out his chest.

"Do you mind if I have my Patrick Chesterfield spend some time with your Chase Mansfield today?" asked Robert. "The lesson would benefit him greatly."

"Forgive me for interrupting, but I was thinking the same thing about my foster human." Nigel and Robert looked up to see Guardian Angel Philip Hydes hovering above them. The lanky street sweeper from the 1700s had been assigned to Earth's Professor Richman.

Philip continued. "My project has the same character flaws as yours does, Robert. Why, he can get overbearing to the point of being pompous."

The Guardian Angel team of brother and sister Malcolm and Grace Whitney glided in. They held a wonderful position, being guides for Chase Mansfield's mother, Julia, and her brother, John. Malcolm and Grace glanced at Nigel, realizing that the immediate group would be spending their day together.

"Isn't today their Friday?" asked Philip Hydes.

"Friday?" questioned Malcolm Whitney. "That always meant fish and chips in our neighborhood."

"Isn't there a quaint fish and chips stand in their town that Chase loves?" asked Grace Whitney.

"Why, I do believe so," answered Nigel. "If I recall, it's more than a stand – and they even went there for Chase's birthday last year."

"How about arranging a gathering there today and see how it plays out?" suggested Philip.

"Splendid idea!" remarked Nigel.

An immaculate sensation was about to set in. One that would mysteriously round up a few needy souls and migrate them toward Chase Mansfield.

The objective? To be humbled.

The playing field? Wally's Broiler, the town's best fish and chips.

The time? Now.

◀◀ ◀◀ ▶▶ ▶▶

Professor Richman sat at the breakfast table, wearing his majestic red bathrobe and matching slippers. His renowned silver hair and trimmed beard showed signs of a good night's rest. The rising sun peered through the kitchen window, causing him to close his eyes. The soothing rays gave the professor's body a tingling sensation.

Like a turtle on a warm rock, he directed his weathered face to the medicating light. His special blend of coffee would perfect the moment. Intellectual crystal-blue eyes looked over at the counter and saw that it was brewed, with its aroma enticing the entire kitchen. Looking at the stainless steel coffee pot, a forgotten memory of yesterday made its presence known.

The cupboard behind the pot was slightly opened, exposing a gift that his mentally challenged grandson, Chase, made in school. It was a thick, uneven coffee mug that was painted with the same craftsmanship. In bold mismatching letters was an inscription: "For Grandpa - Love Chase." The grandfather was distracted by this hidden labor of love, as if it was crying for life.

Instinctively, the professor left the table and walked toward the counter. He reached into the cupboard and took out the dusty mug. He felt guilty realizing that it was made just for him. Chase was indeed special to him. He was the only family member who never asked for anything. The only one who just wanted to see him whenever he could. Chase was handsome, with his blonde, curly hair and defined face. More important, he also inherited the blue eyes that personified the Richman trait. The grandfather felt a presence as he held the keepsake. He washed and dried it over the sink and poured his first cup of coffee into it.

There was a strength that accompanied Professor Gerald Richman at that moment. With pride, he admired the beautiful gift as his favorite drink gave steam off the top. The mug was heavy for its size, because the thickness would not allow its hot contents to burn his hands. "What an ingenious design," thought the Rhodes Scholar. He cautiously sipped the hot coffee. His senses took over, serving testimony that this was the best cup of coffee he'd ever experienced in his life.

The prominent man expanded on this sensation by reflecting on his life with Chase.

He was more than just Professor Gerald Richman; he was also a grandfather. But not just any grandfather; he was Chase Manfield's grandfather. The most respected person in that entire town. The professor took another sip from the earthy mug and grinned with pride. "What a legacy . . ." he thought to himself. "I think I will call my daughter Julia today. I want to take her and my grandson out for lunch."

The morning sun cast its nourishing warmth through the windows of the Security Building.

Patrick Chesterfield leaned over his desk to analyze documents with his back facing a window. Behind him, the radiant healing powers penetrated his spirit. The short, overweight man with black hair and bald head felt the heat relax his entire body. It was as if he was being massaged. Leaning back, he stretched and glanced straight ahead in thought. A candy stain on the far corner of his desk came into view. It jarred a fond memory that took his mind off his task. A memory that changed his life forever.

The stain was not a blemish; it was a trophy. The most wonderful person he had ever met left that mark there. Chase Mansfield remembered that Patrick didn't hand out candy on Halloween that year. The conscientious boy secretly placed some of his candy on Patrick's desk, to make sure that he was not forgotten. That was the only time in Patrick Chesterfield's life when someone showed that they actually cared about him. When the building Patrick worked in upgraded with new furniture, he demanded that his desk not be replaced. He considered the discolored polish as an heirloom that marked a milestone in his life. It was his goal to take the desk home with him when he retired.

Patrick's expressionless face started to turn into a smile. It dawned on him that he could leave the office early and do something special. He and John Mansfield had been working many extra hours on a project that was completed the night before. They could work a half-day and go out to lunch with Chase. Patrick clasped his hands behind his head and looked at the discolored mark, marveling at his genius . . .

John Mansfield sat attentively at his desk with the door slightly opened. This signaled that anyone was allowed to visit the middle-aged man with fine brown hair, matching eyes and mustache. The loyal employee was reviewing the latest project that he and his boss had just completed. A distinct knock pushed the door opened. John knowingly looked up to see his boss, Patrick Chesterfield, enter the room.

"And how is my good friend John Mansfield this fine morning?" greeted Patrick.

John was taken by his boss's exceptionally good mood and leaned back in his chair. "Did you just win a lottery this morning?" asked John in a humorous tone.

The boss continued with his happiness. "You know," responded Patrick as he placed an index finger on his chin, looking off into the distance. "Maybe I did!"

The jolly fat man continued. "First of all, I need to thank you for the long hours you put into our last assignment. You did the great job you always do, and again, made me look pretty good. We are ahead of schedule now and might as well reward ourselves by taking the rest of the day off."

Just then, the phone rang. John maintained the festive pace by answering it through the intercom.

"Hello?" called out John in a laughing voice.

"Well, it seems that the entire world is happy today!" answered the voice of John's sister, Julia.

"Hello, sis," responded John. "I am under the impression that this is not an emergency call."

"Oh no," said Julia. "My dad dropped by, and we were going to take Chase out to lunch. We were just wondering if we could bring you anything?"

"Why don't you turn on the speaker phone so that we can all think out loud?" asked John.

"Okay," volleyed back Julie. "Is this better?"

The background sounds from each phone could now be heard, with a considerable volume increase.

"Yes, much better," said John.

Patrick's eyes lit up. Going out with Chase and his loved ones would fill a void in his life. "How about all of us meeting somewhere for lunch?" he suggested.

"That would be great!" came the prestigious voice of Professor Gerald Richman himself.

"Is that you, Professor Richman?" asked a surprised Patrick.

"No, it's not," answered the regal voice. "Professor Richman is that man in the suit who gives lectures. This is 'Gerald Richman' and I want to go out with my grandson, Chase, and his friends!"

Patrick was impressed with the professor's 'regular guy' attitude. "Do you mind if I tag along?" asked Patrick in a friendly voice.

"Mind?" questioned the professor. "Why, you are one of Chase's most favorite people, you'd better come!" he said in a definitive tone.

Patrick was further moved; he was just accepted by the famous Professor Richman. "Well, then I guess I'd better be there!" replied Patrick.

"Good show!" quipped the professor.

John openly asked out loud, "Where do we want to meet for lunch?"

There was a long pause, then all at once both rooms said, "How about fish and chips at Wally's?" The intercoms went silent as everyone looked around in shock. There seemed to be a touch of magic in the air.

Finally, John spoke up. "Then Wally's it is! We'll meet you there in half an hour."

"Okay," said Julie. The phones were disconnected, with lunch thirty minutes away.

"Since we're off work now," said John, "I'll meet you there."

"Sounds good to me," replied Patrick. John grabbed his coat from a coat rack in the room as Patrick walked down the hall to get his coat and hat. Within twenty minutes, they arrived at Wally's and entered. They were immediately greeted by the hostess. "Table for two?" asked a young blonde–haired, blue-eyed woman dressed like a pirate.

"We'd better make it for five," said John.

"Right this way," replied the hostess as she grabbed five menus from a stand. She led the two men into the dining room and sat them down at a varnished table that resembled a door to a schooner of yesterday. Maritime memorabilia from the 1800s surrounded the dining room. Ropes on pulleys, nautical stained glass and brass candle holders gave one the feeling that they were on the high seas a century ago.

Moments later, Julia and her father showed up with the man of the hour, Chase Mansfield. It was plain to see the brother and sister resemblance between John and Julia. She too had beautiful thin brown hair with matching eyes and a medium build. Julia also shared his humbleness. A friendly exchange took place with handshakes and hugs. Immediately, all were strategically seated with the three men sitting together, facing Julia and Chase.

The server came by to take their orders. All were in agreement that nothing sounded better than fish and chips with a drink. The drink cups arrived first, with the party leaving the table to the self-serve soda fountains. Within minutes, the meals arrived in the traditional baskets lined with paper.

The ball was now put into play.

It was now time to prove one's superiority. The food gatherers needed to provide the final ingredient to make fish and chips complete: tartar sauce. There was more to this task than just returning home with the bounty. It had to be presented in style!

John went to the condiment station first, with Patrick and the professor close behind. He saw the small paper trays stacked on top on of one another that were used to carry tartar sauce. John took the top half portion of the tiny paper trays and started to pump tartar sauce into each one, until he could carry no more. It was obvious that he got enough for Chase and himself.

Competition had set in. Patrick upped the ante by bringing his hat and cleverly placing the filled tartar trays outlining the rim. Like a party clown, he wore the ridiculous hat and pranced back to the table.

Professor Richman raised the stakes with his ingenuity. He spotted a candle holder that held ten small candles that were the same diameter as the paper trays. He removed the candles and set them off to the side, replacing them with full trays of tartar sauce.

Like the three wise men, they returned to the table with their sacred gifts.

The audition was underway, with each witty candidate using his gimmick to win over Chase. The smiling threesome reminded the boy of television characters he always enjoyed watching: Curly, Larry and Moe.

Chase, however, didn't choose one surplus over another. He instructed his mother to take her basket and follow him. He led her to the condiment station and went to work.

Without thought, Chase meticulously parted the fish side by side and poured tartar sauce directly on top of the fillets. He then exchanged baskets with his mother and repeated the process.

Returning to the table, he saw his uncle with stretched-out arms that held a series of filled tartar trays, lined from his wrists all the way up to his shoulders. He noticed Patrick wearing his hat outlined with more paper trays filled with tartar sauce. A proud Patrick leaned his head forward to make the sauce more accessible. His grandfather conveniently held the candle holder with one hand, accompanied by his patented smug.

Chase looked at the adult males and shook his head in disappointment. Displaying his engineering talents, he placed his basket in front of them for all to see. "You should never use those small paper holders," he scolded with authority. "Now you're going to make a big mess and will have to clean it up!"

The *stooges* froze momentarily as they absorbed the advice. Slowly they turned to look at one another, realizing that they had some developing to do. Chase sat down with his mother and added another thought-provoking idea. "Let's say grace before eating." The mentally challenged teenager bowed and led the table in prayer.

◀◀ ◀◀ ▶▶ ▶▶

"Oh, that Chase is a bright one!" cried out Robert Hershel Hollingsworth IV as his hands pressed against his stomach.

"He certainly has a way about himself!" giggled Grace Whitney.

"Bravo, bravo, my good man!" shouted out Sir Nigel as he rolled through the clouds, shaking in tears.

A chain reaction of comments followed by hysterics raced across the sky.

Cloud nine shook the heavens with echoes of intense laughter. Angels from all directions turned and looked toward the jubilant eruption. A saintly voice could be heard off in the distance saying, "I don't know what's going on over there, but I bet it involves Nigel's man, Chase!"

The Discovery of Teddy Downing

The West Hill Doughnut Shop

Harold and Mary Barton felt fortunate as they counted the days to their retirement. This milestone would be bittersweet, due to the fact that they loved operating their famous doughnut shop. It was their wonderful customers that helped make it so special. Soon the retirees would start their golden years, with something missing . . .

A young nephew by the name of Teddy Downing traditionally spent part of his Christmas holiday with the elder couple. Teddy was consumed by an identity crisis. He was an adopted child who didn't know his parents. This made him feel outcast—as if he was never suppose to be born. What he was about to discover was that he did belong in this world. He would also unveil his aunt's secret pain; and cure it. She was approaching old age and felt that she'd failed, not having children of her own.

Mary Barton bent over to open the industrial-sized oven. Her padded kitchen gloves grabbed the first sheet of glazed doughnuts. She carefully removed the hot treats and placed them on the counter above.

Mrs. Barton looked up and saw a wool mitten wiping off frost from the shop's window. It moved in a circling motion, until a smiling face with red cheeks could be seen peering through. Soon, many huddled in front of the small opening like a choir ready to sing.

The Bartons were the most loved, charitable people in West Hill. Every morning, their first tray of warm doughnuts was shared with those waiting at the bus stop. Hot chocolate and cider would also accompany this act of goodwill.

Their kindness didn't stop there. Often, their small dining room was opened for those who were too cold to wait outside. As always, a fresh, warm doughnut and a hot drink was provided – free of charge.

The kind old woman put on her coat and picked up a tray full of fresh doughnuts. Her husband donned his jacket as he took a thermos of hot cider, along with Styrofoam cups, and joined her. They opened the front door to their shop and went outside. It was time to serve their first customers of the day, with the news out on the street that they were about to retire. Eager hands in leather gloves and woolen mittens surrounded the happy couple.

"Thank you, Mr. and Mrs. Barton," said an eleven-year-old girl. "I am sure going to miss you."

"You are very welcome, and we will miss you," said Mrs. Barton. "I hope this keeps you warm."

"Thank you so much, Mr. and Mrs. Barton," said John Hightower, a middle-aged African American man. He gracefully accepted a warm doughnut and a steaming cup of cider. "We are sure going to miss you when you retire."

"Why, thank you, John," said Mr. Barton. "We will miss you, and everyone else, very much."

"Mr. and Mrs. Barton, I appreciate this very much," said fourteen-year-old Jay Turner. "You two have been great to everyone, ever since you opened your shop. We are all going to miss you two."

"Thank you, Jay," said Harold Barton.

Many hands were filled with treats for the final time. This was always the best part of Harold and Mary's day. It was now time to return to the shop and focus on their last day in business.

Upon entering the shop, Harold made a distracting sound by clearing his throat. This intentionally got Mary's attention. The husband pointed at the calendar on the wall.

Using his index finger, he pointed at the following day. She nodded her head with understanding. That was the day they would close their shop of forty years and retire. There was also something special that were looking forward to. That morning, they were expecting a visit from Mary's sister, Elma, and their nephew, Teddy. It was an annual tradition to have Teddy spend this week with his aunt and uncle.

The business partners started to roll dough and prepare their pastries for the oven. The rhythm of their production was interrupted by a jingling sound.

The bell on top of the door signaled its opening. The aging couple looked over at the lobby to find a twelve-year-old boy bundled up in a wool coat with matching neck scarf and ear muffs. He was holding a vintage plaid suitcase and had an enormous grin. A woman in her sixties was dressed identically, standing beside him. Their nephew, Teddy, and Mary's sister, Elma, had arrived.

Teddy placed his suitcase on the floor and yelled, "Hi, Aunt Mary and Uncle Harold!" He ran behind the counter and hugged both of them at once. "Can I help you make doughnuts today?" asked the nephew.

"Why, sure you can," said Mary.

Harold and Mary walked over to Elma and gave her a hug. "It's so good to see my sister again!" said Mary.

"I missed you too," said Elma.

The guests took off their heavy coats, neck scarves and earmuffs, and placed them on a coat rack that occupied a corner of the lobby. The four sat at a booth in the dining room and visited until an oven timer sounded. "I have to get back to work," said Harold. The sixty-five-year-old, gray-haired man with glasses got up and went to the kitchen.

"I need to get back there too," said Mary. "Please, have some doughnuts with something to drink," she offered. The aunt got up and went behind the counter. Teddy's eyes were wide open as he rolled his tongue across his lips in anticipation. Mary arrived in a minute with a tray full of pastries and two cups of milk. The relatives thanked her and began to eat the warm treats.

Afterwards, Mary visited with her sister Elma for a half hour while Teddy assisted in the kitchen. Harold pulled double duty as he worked with his nephew and served customers.

It was getting close to eight o'clock in the morning, and Elma commented that she had appointments that day. She said that she had to go, and would return by the end of the week to get her grandson. Elma hugged Mary and Harold, and thanked them for having Teddy over that week. "He has so much fun when he's here with you two," said Elma.

"We love to have him here!" said Harold.

The grandmother bent over and addressed Teddy. She hugged him, saying, "I am going to miss you!" She kissed him on the cheek and said, "Have a wonderful time with your aunt and uncle." Elma went to the coat rack and put her winter garments on. "Goodbye," she said as she waved her hand. The sixty-two-year-old woman open the door and left.

Teddy looked at his aunt and uncle, and said, "Hey, we need to make doughnuts!"

They laughed at their nephew, with Harold saying, "You're right, boss!" They went behind the counter and instructed Teddy what to do as a constant flow of customers were being served.

Throughout the day, Teddy heard customers express to his aunt and uncle how happy they had made them through the years, and how much they would miss them. Everyone who entered the shop congratulated them on their well-earned retirement. At one point, flowers were delivered with a large balloon that read, "*Happy Retirement*". They were signed 'from your happy customers'. Teddy saw his aunt and uncle get teary-eyed as they marveled at the thoughtful display.

The doughnut shop had a busy day, with their five o'clock closing time moments away. The last customer had left the establishment a half-hour ago, with the utensils having been cleaned. It was now the final ten-second countdown until quitting time. The old clock on the wall that a flour vender had donated to the shop over thirty years ago ticked the final ten seconds. The trio held hands and counted the last ten seconds out loud. "Ten, nine, eight, seven, six, five, four, three, two, one!" Immediately, Mary turned the cardboard sign that dangled over the front door from 'open' to 'closed' and locked the door. Harold turned off the majestic red neon sign that was on the roof, reading, "The West Hill Doughnut Shop." The forty-year enterprise that became a landmark was officially closed.

The married couple who had weathered all those years with their hard work hugged in relief. They had challenged the American dream and got it! Teddy could hear the sniffling of tears as they embraced with the realization of what they had accomplished.

It was time to count the money in the register, empty the safe, clean counters and sweep floors. Like clockwork, they quietly attended their assigned chores. In twenty-five minutes, they were finished. It was now a simple task of gathering their coats, jackets and other apparel, turn off the lights, and lock the back door.

Once they were outside, Harold inserted the key into the deadbolt that protected the back entrance of the shop. He turned it smoothly and secured the metal door. Looking down the block, he saw a light on the top floor of a high-rise apartment. That was home, and it served as an additional surveillance for the family business.

It was time to celebrate with dinner out on the town. Teddy's favorite restaurant was selected, and there he would have his favorite meal: a bacon cheeseburger with French fries. The nephew was also paid for his labor. "Thank you, Uncle Harold!" said Teddy as he received the token of appreciation. Dinner was enjoyable as life's stress and anxiety left the Bartons' life. Home would be the next stop.

It was eight o'clock in the evening when they entered the apartment on the top floor. Teddy was accustomed to staying in their guest room. He entered his dwelling with his luggage and closed the door. Moments later, the bedroom door opened with Teddy entering the living room in his pajamas. His aunt lit up the Christmas tree lights, making the room festive. The happy nephew sat on the sofa and admired his surroundings. He was always grateful to be staying with his aunt and uncle. There were even times when he wanted to stay there forever, with his grandmother included.

"Teddy, would you like some hot chocolate before bedtime?" asked Auntie Mary.

"Mmm, I'd love that!" exclaimed the excited boy.

"So would I!" remarked Harold.

Teddy was warm, happy and simply enjoying a quiet ending to a great day. His Auntie Mary returned with three cups of hot chocolate topped with whipped cream. She placed three coasters on the coffee table and rested the hot cups on them. The three picked up their cups and made a toast to their retirement, and to having Teddy staying with them. The precious moment was savored, with funny stories rotating amongst them. Soon the thick white porcelain mugs were empty, and it was time for bed.

Teddy went into the bathroom and brushed his teeth. He returned to the living room and hugged his aunt and uncle goodnight. The tired guest went to his room and climbed into bed. He said his goodnight prayers and fell fast asleep.

Mary woke up at four o'clock out of habit. She was quiet, being hopeful that she wouldn't wake up her husband. He too was already awake, trying not to disturb her. Each became aware of the other and laughed.

"Well, I guess we're up," said Mary in a humorous tone.

"I'll make some coffee," said Harold.

Mary put on her bathrobe and followed her morning routine. She would first go to their deck and inspect their shop down the street. She slid open the glass door that allowed access and stepped on the deck, closing the plate glass behind her. Mary leaned over the railing and looked at the aging brick structure on the corner. Harold slid the glass door open and joined Mary, closing it behind him. He arrived with two cups of hot coffee, handing one to her.

Together they looked at the Christmas lights that lit up the neighborhood as their dark doughnut shop sat in silence.

This was the best time of the day, where silence reined. Only a gust of wind was allowed to contribute, with swaying branches and the scratching sound of dried leaves whisking on the pavement below. Soon birds would follow, with the haze of dawn greeting a new day.

This morning was different, with no schedule to keep. They could have another cup of coffee, kick back and relax. It was now five in the morning, the time when their shop usually opened.

A movement down below caught their attention. A car slowly pulled in front of their shop and stopped briefly. Its driver must have read the sign on the front door: *Out of business due to retirement.* It quietly drove away.

Soon, the regulars gathered at the bus stop. A scout left the party to carefully look through the dark windows of the vacant pastry shop. There were no signs of activity inside. Slowly, the dejected pedestrian returned to confirm the bad news. The small gathering at the bus stop seemed to have changed. They appeared to be individually secluded and impersonal.

Harold and Mary didn't know how to feel at that moment. It wasn't that they didn't like to bake or get up early in the morning. Unbeknownst to them, Teddy was also up and watching them from the living room. The mature boy felt that they were going through an adjusting period and knew to respect their privacy.

The sun began to rise over the distant mountains, with the city coming to life. Traffic lights on the roads leading to town increased as the noise of the city began to take over. It was time for the elders to go inside and start breakfast.

"Good morning, Teddy," said his aunt with a surprised tone. "Did you sleep well last night?" she asked.

"I slept fine, Auntie Mary," said the nephew.

"I bet you would like a bowl of oatmeal with raisins and brown sugar," said Harold.

That was Teddy's favorite meal for breakfast. "I'd like that a lot!" answered the boy.

Breakfast seemed more quiet than usual. Teddy noticed that his aunt and uncle seemed to be running out of things to say to each other. It seemed that they wanted something to do, but didn't know what. Whenever Teddy made a comment, it seemed to perk them up.

After breakfast, each went a different direction. Teddy went to his room, changed into his clothes, and watched the television set provided there. Harold went into the living room and watched the news. Mary got out all of her old high school annuals and photo albums. The lonely senior placed them on the dining room table and started to thumb through them.

This first day of retirement didn't seem significant at all. In fact, it was boring. The couple did their daily chores as mundane conversations arose. It was as if they had nothing to do; or worse yet, nobody to share anything with. Teddy sensed a depression developing between his aunt and uncle. He noticed how they would stare at one another as if they were trying to ask, "Now what?"

Teddy was already fighting a depression of his own. It was the holidays, and he could only notice the happiness that normal families were having. He saw parents playing with their children and felt all alone. He felt denied, not knowing his parents, and questioned if he was even meant to exist.

Teddy decided to soul search. He knew the neighborhood and many of the shop owners. He would take a walk and wisely reach out to seek advice.

He asked his aunt and uncle if he could go outside and walk the neighborhood. He promised to be back before dinner time. "That's all right, Teddy," said his aunt. "Make sure that you bundle up and stay warm," she said.

"Be sure to stay safe, Teddy," cautioned his uncle.

Teddy was enthused, now that he had something to do. He knew that such visits usually brought a touch of adventure and taught lessons. "I promise to stay out of trouble," said the responsible nephew. He hugged his aunt and uncle, put his coat on, and left for his walk.

Teddy's journey started by walking down the street and evaluating himself. He knew that he was different from all the other kids. He felt awkward being bigger, heavier, and only being able to afford clothes from thrift stores. He felt a stigma being raised by his grandmother, without any contact from his real parents. It also bothered him that they often had to relocate to cheaper housing to survive on her fixed income. This always put him at the status of being the 'new kid in school'.

The young man was in deep concentration over these hardships. All at once, his thoughts were interrupted by someone yelling out his name.

"Teddy!" called out a familiar voice. It was, Gregor, a local rock-and-roll musician who worked at the gas station across the street. Gregor had a gift for relating to younger people like Teddy. He would be the perfect guy to get advice from.

Teddy was at a corner with no cars traveling nearby. He crossed the street, and in a loud voice said, "Hi, Gregor!"

Gregor was happy to see Teddy. The long blond-haired man with rich brown eyes and a barrel chest gave Teddy a man's handshake. "I was hoping that you would come by to see me," the grown man said. "I know that you always stay a week with your aunt and uncle this time of year."

A black air hose that lay across the lot had a car drive over it, signaling a bell. This alerted Gregor that a customer had arrived. "I have to go for a minute," said Gregor. He approached an old Pontiac driven by a gray–haired, sixty-five-year-old woman wearing a flowered hat from the 1950s. "What can I do for you today, Mrs. Willows?" asked Gregor.

The spunky woman answered, "I need three dollars of regular gas." The senior handed Gregor three dollars and leaned back in her seat.

Teddy watched Gregor pump gasoline into her gas tank as the revolving numbers kept pace with the amount owed. The three-dollar figure was passed at maximum speed, with more fuel being pumped into the gas tank. Gregor randomly stopped, with the balance at seven dollars and fifty-eight cents.

"We're all done here, Mrs. Willows," said Gregor in an accommodating tone.

The gray-haired woman on Social Security started her car and leaned toward the fuel gauge. "Mercy!" she exclaimed. "I have more gas than I realize."

"Well, good!" remarked Gregor. "You have a nice day, Mrs. Willows."

The woman was smiling and said, "You do the same!" She cautiously drove off.

Teddy looked at Gregor, nodding his head in approval. "You bought Mrs. Willows extra gas because she needed it," commented the boy.

"Well, not exactly," said the tenant. "My boss will cover that, but I do extras in return." Teddy focused on his older friend and wanted to hear more.

"This is a small town, and we need to help each other out a bit to survive," said Gregor. "If you go a little further to make things nicer for someone, it makes everything better for everyone."

The forty-two-year-old man bent over and looked at Teddy. "It's like your family's doughnut shop. They are known for giving out to everyone in this neighborhood. In turn, people go out of their way to pick up any litter that's around it. They also shovel the snow off their walkway during the winter, and they are always seated first in any restaurant they go to around here. It's called *respect*, and it doesn't always have to cost money."

Gregor continued, "I always wanted to be a famous musician. My dream got to the point where I forgot about caring for others. That made me go nowhere. Now, I am actually a member of this community and have a job. I also get to play my music at weddings, parties, street fairs, and taverns. People even give me small change when I perform. I actually achieved my goal as a musician when I accepted that I would never be rich, but could still care about others."

Teddy was absorbing this lesson. It reminded him about his own life and what he had to accept. Gregor had more to say. "Do you want to know what I do with the money I get for playing music?" he asked. Teddy nodded his head up and down. "I spread it around, just like your aunt and uncle do," said Gregor. "I tip the barmaids in the taverns I play at. If someone needs a small handout, I might be able to give a bit. I even take my boss out to dinner sometimes, as a way to thank him for having this job. There were times when I was broke in this town, but I was never hungry or homeless."

Another car drove up to the pumps. Gregor said, "I have to go now. It's been nice talking to you, and I hope you come by again." He patted young Teddy on the shoulder, giving reassurance. With dignity, the musician approached his next customer.

Teddy had food for thought, realizing how important it was to care about others. He continued down the street to the malt shop to visit another friend, Walt Evans.

The visitor needed no introduction. "Teddy!" called out the proprietor. "I heard you would be in town this week. I am so glad that you dropped by."

Teddy loved Walt, and trusted the short, jovial man with the crew cut and waxed mustache. He took the fight to Walt.

"Walt, can I share a problem with you?" asked Teddy.

Walt erased his smile and walked up to his young friend. With sincerity, he got close to Teddy and patted two bar stools that faced his counter. The shop had no customers, and the setting was perfect for a heart-to-heart. They sat down next to each other and swiveled the stools, facing one another. With direct eye contact, the shop owner whispered, "What is it?"

Teddy began to explain that he always felt *different* from all the other kids. He used his appearance as an example.

Walt said, "I think I know what you are talking about." He asked Teddy to turn around for a moment. The boy followed the instructions. "Now turn back around," said

Walt. Teddy spun one hundred eighty degrees and faced the malt shop owner. Walt was leaning over with his hands pressed firmly on the counter. His paper hat was shifted off to one side, covering his left eye. "What color are my eyes?" Teddy stared at his right eye and saw a blue eye concentrated on him.

"Blue," said Teddy.

"Now turn around until I tell you to look at me again," said Walt. Teddy followed the instructions, spun in the opposite direction and stopped.

"Now turn around again and look at me," said Walt. Teddy pivoted around.

This time his hat was repositioned, covering his right eye. "What color are my eyes now?" asked Walt. This time Teddy was staring at a brown eye.

Teddy said, "Brown." The boy realized that Walt's eyes had just changed color, or so he thought. "How did you do that?" Walt removed his hat, which gave the answer. His eyes were different colors!

"You see, Teddy," explained Walt. "In one way or another, we all are different; and that makes all of us the same."

Teddy was amused by the demonstration. It also made him feel better about who *he* was.

"Now, I have a problem that I need to share with you," said the kind man.

"What is it?" asked Teddy.

"I need to get rid of some ice cream," said a happy Walt. "Why don't you help me with this problem, and let me make you a sundae?"

Teddy sat up tall with a smile. Walt continued, "If my memory serves me correctly, you like hot fudge."

An anxious Teddy nodded his head up and down.

A hot fudge sundae was served, with a pile of swirling whipped cream topped with a cherry. It also had a small candy cane sticking out of it. "Thanks, Walt!" exclaimed Teddy.

"You are quite welcome, my friend," said the jolly man. "I want you to enjoy that while I make an important phone call."

Teddy savored the treat and finished it just when Walt returned from his call. "I have another surprise for you," said Walt.

"What is it?" asked Teddy.

"Do you know the Heyden twins?" he asked.

"No, I don't think so," said Teddy.

"You know Sam, don't you?" asked Walt.

"Sam the barber?" asked Teddy.

"Yes," said Walt. "Sam also has a twin who's visiting him at this very moment. I shared with them the problems that you and I have about feeling *different*. They feel the same and want to share their story with you."

Teddy got excited and said, "Neat!"

A flock of customers entered the ice cream parlor. "I am going to leave now, Walt," said Teddy. "I will visit you again this week."

"Thanks for visiting me," replied Walt. "You are always welcome here. Bye, Teddy!"

"Bye, Walt!" said Teddy as he walked out to the sidewalk. His trek would only last a few seconds, because Sam's barbershop was only two doors away. It appeared that another wise old friend would give guidance and share advice.

Teddy entered the barber shop to meet the Heyden twins. The room was empty, except for a woman who was visiting with Sam. "Hello, Teddy!" exclaimed Sam. "Do you want a haircut today?"

"No," said Teddy. "I just dropped by to visit. Walt told me that you have a twin, and that you wanted to share a story with me. Is your brother here?"

"I don't have a brother," said the barber.

"But Walt told me that you have a twin?"

"I do," said Sam with a smile, "and she's right here!" Sam pointed at the woman. "This is my twin sister, Samantha." Teddy had a confused look on his face.

251

"I thought that you would have a twin brother," he said.

"Don't women count?" asked Samantha.

Sam spoke. "A boy can have something sacred like a twin, but it doesn't mean that your twin can't be a sister."

"Or a brother," added Samantha.

"You see, Teddy," explained Sam. "Everyone and everything is different, and that's not always a bad thing. I do have a twin, and she's the best sister I could ever have."

Samantha reciprocated, "And my twin is the best brother I could ever have."

The twins with matching sweaters looked at each other with respect. They were always family and proud of it, just like Teddy and his grandmother. Teddy felt warm inside.

It was getting close to dinner time, and Teddy needed to start walking home. "It was great to meet you, Samantha," said Teddy.

"It was nice to meet you," she said. "I've have always heard wonderful things about you." Teddy blushed.

"It's nice to see you too, Sam," said Teddy. "I have to go home now.

"Thank you for seeing us, Teddy," said Sam. "Don't be a stranger."

Teddy walked toward the apartment he was staying at and saw the old doughnut shop that was a block away from it. He noticed a familiar car parked out in front of it. It was the small station wagon with 'Choy's Bakery' on the door. It was his friend's father, Benard Choy!

He ran down the street as he saw Benard getting into his car, "Mr. Choy!" he yelled. Benard heard Teddy and turned around.

"Teddy, is that you?" he answered back. Teddy waved his arms and got his attention. "What are you doing all the way out here?" he asked.

Teddy caught up with Benard and caught his breath. He explained who his aunt and uncle were, and that he was visiting for the week. He also pointed out that the doughnut shop was theirs.

"I didn't know that," said Benard. "I saw an ad in the paper about a doughnut shop being for sale in this town. I called the number and agreed to meet your uncle here, to see if I wanted to buy any of his baking utensils. He even gave me this box of old things that he wanted to get rid of." Benard looked at the young boy staring down into the box. "Why don't you take a few items as memorabilia?" suggested Benard. "They will always remind you of your aunt and uncle." Teddy nodded his head up and down and took their old aprons, kitchen gloves, a rolling pin, and a tarnished set of keys.

Teddy realized that Benard was a good man who always gave good advice. He asked if he could share a problem with him.

"Why, sure you can, Teddy," said the compassionate soul. "You can always talk to me about anything." There was a picnic bench in front of the vacant shop. Benard pointed at it and said, "Let's sit over here."

Teddy sat with Benard and looked down as he gathered his thoughts. He then explained the pain he felt not knowing his real parents. He went further and questioned if he should consider himself a part of anybody's life.

Benard understood the feeling and had something to say. "Much of my family lives in Korea, including my mother. When I finally got to return home to visit her, it was as if we never had a gap in our lives. Our phone calls, emails, and letters, along with our memories, kept the closeness alive."

Benard had more to say. "When I arrived, it didn't even seem that far away, even though it was on the other side of the world. I realized that it didn't matter how much time had passed since I last saw her. It doesn't matter if there is a mountain range, or even an ocean that creates distance from any loved one. That love keeps you close for life, as if you were seeing them every day."

Teddy was taken by this discovery. He did have a *different* type of upbringing, just like Benard, and others. He was starting to feel pretty good about himself.

Benard then said something that broke Teddy out of his depression. "The same holds true with all people. You don't have to be related to anyone, if you want to be family with them."

That statement served as the last antidote needed to cure his identity crisis. It occurred to him that he *was* just like everyone else in this world—and it felt wonderful! Now it was time to shed the light for his aunt and uncle.

"I have to go home now," said Teddy.

"Okay," said Benard. "It certainly was a pleasant surprise to run into you, Teddy; and Merry Christmas!"

They said their goodbyes and parted in opposite directions. Teddy no longer thought about his complex; it didn't exist anymore. He could only think about his aunt and uncle, and the happiness they deserved.

Teddy realized what was missing in their life; it was loved ones. They didn't, however, need children of their own. Everyone in that community was family! It was now his turn to spice up the holidays, and he knew what to do.

The nephew returned to the apartment, hiding the artifacts under his coat. He knew that the Christmas wrapping paper, bows and ribbons were in the closet of his room. His desk also held tape and scissors in the drawers. He would wrap them up immediately and secretively slide them under the tree.

He was greeted by his aunt and uncle. "Did you have a good walk through town?" asked Mary.

"Yes I did," said a reinvigorated Teddy.

"I bet you ran into old friends," remarked Harold.

"I did!" exclaimed Teddy. "This town is as nice as ours is back home."

"We have another surprise for you," said his aunt. "Tonight we are having spaghetti and meatballs!"

"Yummy!" said Teddy. The youth ran into his bedroom and closed the door. He took off his coat and placed the gifts on the floor. He got out the wrapping paper, bows and ribbons, along with the scissors and tape. He quickly wrapped the presents and opened his door slightly to see where his aunt and uncle were. They weren't in view, but the Christmas tree in the living room was. Like a cat burglar, he quietly entered the living room, got on his knees and slid the gifts toward the back of the tree. Next, he raced to the bathroom and washed up for dinner.

"Dinner will be ready in five minutes," called out Mary.

The dining room table was set for a feast. Spaghetti and meatballs was served with salad and garlic bread. Once again, it was Teddy's presence that added life to their evening. The married couple started to communicate openly with laughter. It was obvious that they felt empty when left alone for too long.

Teddy learned a lot that day from his older friends. The nephew conjured up a strategy that would direct their life to the happiness they once knew. "I have an idea," he said.

Harold's eyes lit up as he asked, "What is it?"

"I think that we can invent a tradition that will last forever," said Teddy.

The adults sat back and wondered what he was thinking. "What's your idea?" asked Mary.

"We can bake Christmas cookies shaped like Christmas trees and sprinkle colorful sugar on them," said Teddy.

Harold thought and said, "That idea has been done everywhere for years."

"But we will have a rule attached," said Teddy. "These cookies can't be eaten by the person we give them to; they can only be eaten by who *they* give it to."

The elders sat back and digested the idea. It was brilliant! It emphasized the concept of giving during the holidays. It *would* start a tradition, right there in this very town.

"That's a wonderful idea!" exclaimed Mary.

"I have to agree!" said Harold.

"We can start baking right away, we know so many people in this apartment," said Mary.

"I have another idea," suggested Teddy.

"What is it?" asked Harold.

"I'd like you and Auntie Mary to open up a few gifts I got you. It didn't cost me anything, and I'd like you to have it now."

The request stimulated the room further, bringing excitement.

"That sounds fun!" said the aunt.

Teddy got out of his chair and ran to the living room. His aunt and uncle followed. The excited boy got on his hands and knees and crawled under the tree to retrieve the presents. He pulled out two small gifts that were beautifully wrapped in blue paper with silver ribbons and bows. He handed them to the elders and said, "Go ahead and open it up."

Like excited children on Christmas morning, they opened the gifts. "Ohhh!" came the response. They each held up their gift to display it to the other. They were holding the aprons from the doughnut shop that they'd worn for the past forty years.

The couple then looked at one another holding the heirlooms and kissed.

"How about another gift?" asked the nephew.

"Well, all right," said Harold. Teddy crawled under the tree and fetched two more gifts, wrapped the same.

"Here," said Teddy as he handed the gifts out.

The intrigued couple looked at each other and began to open the gifts.

"Ohhh!" came the response. Mary was holding a rolling pin from their bakery, and Harold was holding two pairs of used kitchen gloves.

"We need to start baking Christmas cookies," said Mary. "There are so many people in this apartment complex to make them for. This will keep us up all night."

"I know where a much bigger kitchen is that would serve a lot more people, you know," said the nephew. "And it would make everyone happy!"

He presented another gift that was in a small box. It was wrapped in white paper and had red ribbons with a matching bow. "I want both of you to open this together," instructed Teddy.

The aunt and uncle sat together and opened the small gift. It was the original keys to the doughnut shop.

Teddy made a comment. "I saw you two this morning, watching everyone pass by the shop. They all seemed sad." Teddy's wisdom continued. "It's as if they lost the mother to this entire community," he injected.

Mary's face slowly grew to a warm smile; *she* was that mother. It also occurred to her that she had left her post.

"Let's go there first thing in the morning and bake Christmas cookies!" said Mary.

"That sounds good!" agreed her husband. They embraced, having found what was missing.

Teddy remained quiet as he gleamed at his aunt and uncle. They were cured!

"We need to get to some sleep," said Mary. "We are going to have a busy day tomorrow."

They each changed into their night-time clothes, used the bathroom and went to bed.

The next morning, everyone got up before their alarm clock went off. Mary made a quick breakfast, and within twenty minutes, the trio left for the doughnut shop.

The short distance allowed them to arrive at the back of the shop within moments. Harold unlocked the back door, and they entered the small building. He turned on the kitchen light, with everyone knowing their stations.

Harold immediately turned on the industrial sized oven. Mary spread cooking sheets on the counter as Teddy started to grease them.

Dough was being rolled in flour, with Christmas tree cookie cut-outs brought out to commemorate the holidays.

At the bus stop, life carried on with a pall. On occasion, a head would turn to look at the empty doughnut shop. Tim Rollins, a fifth grader, took an extra-hard look at the empty shop. Its dark windows seemed to make the streets colder, with familiar faces becoming strangers. "There's no use looking over there," said John Hightower. "The Bartons have closed up shop and gone away. All good things come to an end," he said with sadness. The child felt disowned as he looked up to the tall man in despair.

"Do you smell that?" asked Jay Turner.

"These streets will always have that wonderful scent that the doughnut shop left here," said John. "It will remind us of how wonderfully the Bartons treated everyone."

"But it smells as if something is baking in there," insisted Jay.

"That's all in your mind," said John. "We will all smell that faint smell that was here every morning for the rest of our lives. Everyone would love to have a warm doughnut, a cookie, and that hot cider they always gave us. More important, it would be great just to say, "Hello," to Mr. and Mrs. Barton."

The red neon sign started to flicker with a low buzzing sound. All at once, the landmark glowed to life as its light pierced through the early morning fog. It now served as a beacon for those who felt abandoned. The streets started to fill with the unmistakable sweet aroma that only their ovens could produce. Brisk faces with cold hands felt a renewed spirit as the West Hill Doughnut Shop opened its doors again. Like a peace march, the spirited masses walked in unity toward the corner of Main Street and Forty-Second.

The soul of that corner had returned, with the aroma of fresh-baked cookies carrying for blocks. Noses were awakened by the sweet smell as ice-cold faces broke into smiles. It was five o'clock in the morning, and the West Hill Doughnut Shop was open for business.

Mary had made thermoses of hot cider as the kitchen timer dinged, signaling time to remove the baked goods from the oven. Teddy operated his portion of the assembly line by sprinkling red and green sugar on them. The first batch of holiday cookies was complete, with additional trays being placed in the oven. Harold made a grunting sound to get Mary's attention. She looked and saw him pointing to their shop window. Small porthole-likepatterns covered all across the moist glass, with happy faced peering through. The trio kept producing cookies until the counter was full of hot cookie sheets. It was now time to introduce the holiday cookies to the community, and the custom that would go with it.

The bakers donned their coats and prepared for the masses. Harold rolled a small table on wheels and placed five thermoses of hot cider on top, along with many Styrofoam cups and napkins. Mary placed the many cookies in a large wicker basket, outlined by a large white cloth that folded over the baked goods. She would carry them when she marched out of the shop. Teddy was given the honor to unlock and open the front door. He would also introduce the sparkling shortbread cookies to the community—and the new custom that went with them.

Like Hollywood celebrities arriving in a limousine for an awards ceremony, they were flocked by their fans. Teddy led the procession, with Mary following and Harold rolling the table behind.

Teddy took charge. "We have a new tradition that we want to share with everyone," he announced.

Everyone silenced, with all eyes on Teddy. The proud boy reached into the basket of cookies and pulled one out. He raised it in the air and like the town crier continued. "These are our holiday cookies, but you can't eat them."

Everyone looked at one another with a puzzled expression. Again, they stared at Teddy. "The rule is that you have to give this cookie to someone else, and *they* get to eat it. When someone gives you one, then you can eat it."

The crowd shook their heads in understanding. The many smiles showed that they liked this new concept and cheered with approval. At once, a line formed in front of Mary as she passed out cookies to her *children*. The spirit of giving took off like wildfire as those that received, immediately gave. It started a frenzy, with "Thank you" and "Oh, how sweet" traveling around the community.

The news spread quickly by word of mouth. Practically everyone in town made their pilgrimage to the famous West Hill Doughnut Shop that day. Harold baked continuously as Teddy roamed back and forth, helping his aunt and uncle. Mary was in her glory, serving the many that congregated around her. Regular customers, familiar faces, and old friends paid a visit, thanking them for their everlasting kindness.

Teddy felt a light tap on his shoulder. He turned around to see his friend Gregor handing a cookie to him. "This is for you, Teddy," said Gregor. "Happy holidays, my friend!"

Teddy had a cookie in his hand and reciprocated. "This is for you, Gregor," he said. "Happy holidays to you too!" They each bit into their gift, savoring the warm sweetness.

Teddy saw Sam and his twin sister, Samantha, approach his aunt in matching jackets. He saw each sibling accept a holiday cookie and hand it to the other. The brother-and-sister team looked at one another and took a bite at the exact same time. Teddy laughed to himself as he remembered what they told him about *everyone and everything being different*.

An old friend approached his Aunt Mary who remembered her from their high school days. The woman accepted a holiday cookie and gave thanks. A brief conversation arose. "I thought that you two retired and would probably spend the rest of your life close to your children," said the woman.

"We are retired," said Mary, "and we're doing just that!"

The adopted nephew felt the same, realizing that it didn't matter where he was. All that mattered was *who* he was. He was Teddy Downing, and he'd discovered something about himself, just like his aunt and uncle did: As long and he loved and gave, he would always have family everywhere.

Teddy stood back and admired the harmony that his aunt and uncle had with the entire neighborhood. He was also grateful to be a part of it. Like a young child at a carnival, he just wanted to join in with everyone else. He weaved through the small crowd and continued helping his Auntie Mary hand out their holiday cookies.

It did Teddy good to see someone who was a little hungry and a little lonely receive a cookie from a new friend they hadn't met yet. It would serve as that little push they needed to jump in, introduce themselves, and wish everyone a Merry Christmas.

Fun Spacey Stuff

V=ac::t/[^^i<>/on .<^^E]].a._rt><]h
(*Vacation Earth*)

Somewhere off in the distant future; far, far away in a timeless galaxy etc. etc.- stands a group of teens on what will always be know as 'the planet Earth'.

These struggling students were not without merit however. Despite a heated debate, they valiantly agreed to not skip class as originally planned. Instead, they agreed to embark on a mandatory field trip to gain the necessary credits needed to graduate.

Before them stands an ancient computer that still functions- if allowed enough time to warm up . . .

and now our story begins!

Contorted faces watched in amusement as a primitive form of communication *woke up*- attempting to recite vital information they already knew.

```
    ]]'>[:^^*/  /.[]]_\:-<<.^*/  ::/.[\_=<^^.  ::]*^[]=  **-
//_-/_>R[.*u^_n<'].                              .^/S:/p-
.>>o^t_//r[.u.      ./n^.      ]]>S^'e\.e      :^]D<.ic)_k
^^<[wi_t[::/h=_>< <'J^ane. ^^]._-><*_..]
    ))H*/_er[/^^e          \||c_[o[]_-me=/s          [[]
S'/a/^^[ll=. .y\........
```

*H=-_e=_*re][[c=)om.<e>>*s []ou_-^r .f((ath_:er . .a \\|nd mo^*_]t_her.

The automated orientation was clearing its throat with static bumps and groans spitting out a diffused language that dissipated eons ago. In the meantime, bodies began to stretch and twist as the monotonous presentation continued.

^^*[W/^^^:/*e),.]lco).>m<-e to]]^* th^<e Int-<\erplanet\|>ary Vaca^_/tion >//- Cor_^-porati>/|on.-**^[[/.))

All at once the vintage recording was aligned and zeroed-in crystal clear.

"The Interplanetary Corporation welcomes you to planet Earth! We thank you for your patience while we programed our tour. This was to channel the once dominant language of this planet to the one you speak."

"Great . . ." muttered the captain of the chess team. "Another boring day at a museum." The handsome boy with wavy blonde hair and chestnut eyes continued his antics by faking a yawn and pretending to fall asleep.

Immediately a cheerleader responded with theatrics of her own and laughed out loud. *It was her way of showing approval to the boy she had a crush on.*

The script continued.

"We have done this so that you can further experience the pioneering life your forefathers lived over fifty million years ago. A primitive form that through time- evolved into the society you've come to know. Today's tour evolves around visiting a planet they once frequented to monitor its progress: the *planet Earth*. We are proud to say that our tour goes into great depth by having our customers referred to as an 'Earth name' for the duration of their visit. Boys will go by the name, *Dick;* girls will answer to the name, *Jane*."

Eyes looked at one-another with peculiar expressions.

The orientation continued.

"Many of you are familiar with the Interplanetary-DNA-Encyclopedia-Language-Adapter; (commonly known as *adapters*) that was issued to you upon landing. For those of you who have never used one before; don't worry-its quite simple. Like any camera or telescope; simply point to the object of your choice. From there, your adapter will identify what you are looking at and tell its entire history. Remember, your DNA adapter will address specific information meant for *you* only.

Metal fragments, rock, dirt, modified caves, and altered stone are the only remains of the many cultures that once survived here.

It's much like the demonstration we displayed when we took what was once known to this solar system as the planet *Uranus*. We started off by placing it on one of our deserts to thaw out for one million years. Once all moisture evaporated- we split it in half. This exposed the thousands and thousands of civilizations that once lived on that planet when it was within proper range of a given star.

This *Earth* has only one such layer of civilizations. It was cursed by being the third planet from a star that wasn't very big and burning out at an inconsistent pace. This pulsation had Earth constantly being drawn towards larger nearby masses or pulled closer to their tiny sun. This caused ice ages and global warming trends with occasional earthquakes and tsunamis.

However; like all civilizations it had its share of unique life which unfortunately, has gone extinct long ago. Lessons were learned though, which is why this visit is deemed so important. The human life on this planet had a non-stop history of battles over land, religion and politics. There were always a few; if not many such battles going on at the same time. These senseless acts slowed down their development as a species and served as a contributing factor of why human life existed here for only a short time. Life here was further complicated with different societies using their own language and customs. This caused a 'Tower of Babel' effect throughout their tiny world.

It is up-most important to remember that the minerals from this planet eventually became contaminated and are not compatible with other elements. Obviously, we are restricted to how long we are allowed to stay. For that very reason, everyone must also be free of any speck of Earth dust before leaving this atmosphere- or we will all dissipate and become part of this deceased planet. To ensure that such a disaster won't happen, we have employed a mineral disinfectant chamber to remedy the situation. This chamber exists in the very spaceship that brought you here and is automatically used upon entering and leaving this planet.

And now comes the fun part: It is crucial for everyone named, 'Dick' to partner up with anyone named, 'Jane' and work as a team. Enjoy your stay and have fun!"

It was the moment of truth for Jane. The bubbly blonde haired blue-eyed *Miss Congenial* had done everything she could to win over the high school heart throb. Her *sources* informed her about the *all day* field trip that Dick would participate in. From there, a *mysterious* set of circumstances resulted in Jane sitting next to Dick on the lengthy twenty minute flight.

True, this sacrifice did not set well with anyone- except for Jane. The mode of transportation was a necessary evil to set the stage on how rough things were for their ancestors.

A vintage craft once referred to as a *spaceship* was taken out of mothballs to personify the hardships encountered by their pioneering forefathers; which was the soul purpose of this field trip. It did come at a price however:

It was an eye-sore. An embarrassing relic that no impressionable teen would ever want to be seen in. *The Edsel of the free universe.* "Why don't they just use a transporter and let us click our heels three times?" was the boy's remark when being seated.

Jane was on top of things and would utilize the situation as a trump card. Knowing that all on board would be a bit perturbed she brought a tasty treat to help tip the scales even. With impeccable timing, she offered Dick a Snickers bar- a universal treat that *no one* could ever turn down!

"Wow!" he said with bulging eyes. "I love these things. Thanks!" She handed *her man* the candy and assumed the liberty of patting him on the back in the process. Her nonchalant advancement was accepted giving her goosebumps.

The ball was in Dick's court- but it was a *no-brainer*. He naturally went with the current. Looking at the girl who was dying inside, he popped the question:

"Well how about it, Jane; would you mind putting up with me for a day?"

Wedding bells rung in her head with love swimming throughout her entire body and projecting through her eyes. "*I'd love to!*" came her reply.

The arrangements to continue the history project had been made with the team embarking on their assignment. They were to scout around this desolate dirt ball out in the middle of nowhere that once sustained life and write a report about it.

Men are from Mars and women are from Venus.

A mother doesn't need to complicate things when explaining to a daughter that boys don't always have a full understanding about reality. They 'get it'...

Jane and every female she ever knew was all too *familiar* about the male ego. The situation presented now called for some massaging. Her intuitiveness let her know that it was critical for their relationship to let Dick be the protector and food-gatherer. In essence: *the man.*

Age-old tactics like saying, "Oh, you're so smart!" and pointing her adapter at a useless rock for him correct would be necessary if they were to have a future. It was also a good idea to have him lead and *believe* that he was doing all the thinking . . .

With adapters in hand Dick barked out the command. "Let's go!" He then leaped high in the air with Jane following and glided over what now appeared to be a junkyard in the desert. One that went as far as the eye could see. Looking behind, he motioned Jane to join him as to travel abreast. She answered the call and was soon inches away from the boy she always dreamed about.

The adapters began to narrate what was all around them. It mentioned that the dried out planet was once covered by approximately two-thirds of liquid that were thriving with diverse forms of life.

The lesson continued.

It pointed out that intense heat from an eroding atmosphere caused life to eventually cease with an inversion following. This inversion had the planet's surface push any foreign entity to the surface as a way to refortify its once nourishing soil.

The invisible voice then gave instructions.

"Let's test our adapters by pointing at the two metal objects that are in front of us."

Without thought, the team of Dick and Jane followed orders and aimed at two massive mounds that had many pieces scattered about.

"As you can plainly see, this was once a vessel that traveled over water. It was the largest moving man-made object when it was built. It made history when it was considered unsinkable and still managed to sink on its maiden voyage. It collided with a floating mass of ice and sustained enough damage to sink; breaking apart in stages. This disaster also resulted in the loss of life for over half of the passengers on board. This mighty ship at one time rested at an estimated two-and-a-half miles below the water it once traveled on. Today, it lies on what would have been known as *desert sand.*"

"Wow!" *exclaimed, Dick.* "Let's check it out!" Without hesitation he banked a turn and landed on the deck of the fabled ship with Jane close behind.

The phenomena that shrouded the planet's natural inversion provided a great geological service in the process. It stopped the deteriorating process to where it fortified what was left and put a shine to it. Some scientist even speculated a theory:

the possibility that many structures actually reversed their decomposition to a degree and looked closer to the day they found their final resting place.

Such was the case for the ill-fated HMS Titanic. A once mighty statement of mankind's march after the Industrial Revolution. One like their Apollo 1 project: a hastily, speedy advancement that was beyond their actual capacity-with disaster to follow.

The mighty steamship still had its name readable with all forms of rust and algae removed centuries ago.

The adapters gave a more in-depth account on what happened on that fateful night with an actual footage showing the disaster take place. Dick took notes as he scouted about the broken vessel with deep fascination.

This find was more than a landmark, it was a grave site. Upon that realization Jane shed a few tears for the many souls who met their passing. Soon both she and Dick bowed their heads in silence to pay respect. Eventually they left quietly as the automated tour guide continued to give information as they traveled.

"Throughout this tour you will notice narrow- metal cylinders that range from one-inch in length, to sometimes over a foot. They are scattered about ranging from being isolated miles apart from others; to being in clusters of thousands and thousands. These were known as *bullets* and used a primitive form of propulsion known as *gun powder* to travel through the air and penetrate their target. They were primarily used to hunt for food or to eliminate forms of human interference."

"What a way to live . . ." commented Jane as she shook her head in disbelief.

The adapter continued to point out things of interest.

"What you will notice is that the original structures made of stone proved to be of a superior technology and stood the longest. The Pyramids from their *Egypt* still stand and serve their real purpose. The Roman aqueducts are another prime example that still stand today, though dry. The industrial revolution spawned new designs with newer material that was actually a step backwards. 'Big

Ben' deteriorated many, many centuries ago as did the Empire State Building, Statue Of Liberty and other later-dated man-made landmarks."

"Look!" exclaimed Dick as he pointed at a rock formation identified as *Stonehenge*. "They have one of those too!"

Jane saw what caught his attention and knew *exactly* what he was talking about. In perfect formation was a circular stone structure found on many planets that focused on its closest star. What made this special was that throughout history; such creations have been known to be dismantled- only to naturally re-position themselves and continue to serve the function it was initially designed to have. It was as if the 'pull of the universe' was all it took.

Both were in awe and jotted down a few notes with Jane being a few steps ahead. "Hey, I brought us a lunch if that sounds good," she called out.

Her suggestion was music to Dick's ears as he slowly turned around with a look of approval.

Soon the team was sitting on the ancient altar. Jane then opened her backpack and coincidentally brought out Dick's favorite sandwich: peanut butter and preserves. That along with juice and chips made her man look at her in a more endearing way.

Eyes met with Dick at a lost for words. Something came over him realizing how special he had been treated that day- and the many other times she had made a difference.

At that moment there was no choice- but to kiss her. The normally confident BMOC started to stutter and found himself at a loss for words.

He was now under Jane's spell. At that moment a mild breeze kicked up – but was not the reason why Jane showed signs of a mild tremble. She was fidgeting over the excitement of having her knight in shining armor finally notice her in the right light. "Here," said Dick as he took off his jacket. Jane leaned forward and soon she wore his coveted Letterman's jacket.

Before Dick could gather his thoughts, the girl who was now getting giddy said, "Wait here; I'll be back in a minute." Instantaneously, Jane leaned back and charged into the sky like superman (superwoman). She then activated her friend locator and was guided to their whereabouts. Beeping them continuously, she flew over where they were huddled as hands waved in acknowledgment.

Jane was proud as a peacock and slowed down to a stop, spreading her arms for all to see her prize. Turning around, she posed like a model displaying the latest in fashion. Her friends were happy for Jane and cheered her on! The lady in the sky took a bow and in an instant- blurred back to her man.

In moments they were drifting through the airstream together and looking for more treasure. The audible lesson resumed.

"On occasion, a craft will be seen from a different galaxy. Some arrived damaged and couldn't return home; others were sent here to stay. Specific explorers came here to study the primitive life that once existed here. Scientists from far away would visit to monitor their slow moving progress."

Dick was such a species; as were most men. But today's outing gave him a 'railroad spike' on the growth chart. *Progress;* and in time their romance would blossom into a happy family! Leaving things the way they ought to be . . .

Today however, was *now*; and it was time to assemble at the old spaceship that brought them there.

Their reports were complete and automatically transposed into a fax that would convey their notes into perfect language. From there they would be electronically delivered to their teacher's mailbox. The passing grade needed to earn a diploma!

Upon realizing that they officially passed high school, a 'high-five' was exchanged with ear-to-ear grins that spelled *freedom*! Their flight to the base camp was underway and full of exhilaration.

Dick and Jane were happy to see that Dick and Jane were already there. Soon Dick arrived with Jane, and the rest were soon accounted for. Amazing stories were now shared about the many interesting artifacts that each had come across.

"Did you see that enormous, primitive wall outlining that ancient civilization?" cried out Dick in amazement.

"We sure did!" replied, Jane. "Wasn't that something?"

"Did anyone see any of those stadiums that had players wear helmets that represented eras they were suppose to have evolved away from centuries ago?" asked Jane.

"How could you miss one?" replied Jane in a puzzled voice. "Those things are scattered throughout this entire planet!"

"It was probably just another form of human sacrifice- without the inhabitants realizing it," commented Dick.

"You're probably right," replied Dick as he shook his head in disgust.

"What gets me is that this is the place where we got our hamburgers and pizzas from," said Dick.

"And don't forget their *Beatles*," added the girlfriend wearing his awards jacket. "They're still 'number one' throughout the entire universe!"

"Hey; I have an idea," said Dick. "Since we are now considered a contribution to society; why don't we go to Albert's Asteroid for some burgers and shakes tonight and celebrate?"

"Count us in!" said Dick as he held his future fiancee's hand.

"There's a film festival later; should we go to it?" asked, Dick.

"What's it about?" asked Jane.

"Its Science Fiction Night!" he replied.

Science Fiction Night at the theater was a hoot! It was a marathon showing films from primitive societies that went extinct long ago- and their backwards concept about intelligent life from other planets.

Immediately, Dick got on his knees and pretended to scan an object over the dirt, as if he were leaning over someone. Looking up he said with a sincere expression:

"He's dead, Jim."

Jane jumped in and began to sway her arms in a frantic, uncontrollable motion shouting:

"Danger, Will Robinson, danger!"

"I can't believe how stupid they were!" exclaimed Jane. "They were so proud when they started to use robots on dangerous jobs and never credited us for doing the same thing."

Dick chimed in. "They should have realized that the so-called aliens we used were just advanced robots that had hearts and veins instead of just electrical wires."

Jane had something to say. "What kills me is that if those droid astronauts were *real* human beings; who in their right mind would ever want to marry one? I mean; did you see what some of them *actually looked like?*"

Everyone laughed in agreement.

And soon our spirited teens with a bright future entered the space craft to reverse the process that allowed them to visit Earth- assuring a safe trip home! Once buckled in, The Law Of The Universe was immediately announced- and to be enforced if necessary:

"Be sure to say your goodnight prayers before you sleep tonight!"

That's it and thank you!
Matt-

/-T^_<]*h:.-e[:_E^-/.n>_\d.

Personal Life

Midnight Grace

It just turned midnight as Steve Smith awoke from a deep sleep. He looked at his left foot and saw a hand wiggling it back and forth. The groggy man turned and was startled. His son, Allen, had pulled up a chair along his bedside to intentionally wake him. It was all in fun. The son had been gone for a while, and he dearly missed his dad. His absence was further compounded by Steve being a trucker who would be gone for long durations. A visit was long overdue.

"Hi, Dad," whispered a lanky nineteen-year-old with brown hair and matching eyes.

Steve leaned over to one side, resting on his left arm. He recognized the voice and now had a better look at his visitor. "Well, this is worth getting up for!" said the father in a very soft voice. "Let's go downstairs so that we don't disturb your mother."

The son nodded his head with the understanding and skipped toward the open bedroom door. He then proceeded down the stairway. Steve got out of bed quietly and put on his bathrobe, following the teenager's trail. He quietly walked by his daughter Jessica's room as she slept. When Steve entered the dining room, there sat Allen with his traditional ear-to-ear grin. "Have a seat, Dad," said the youthful soul.

"Let me get us something to snack on first," suggested the dad. Steve left for the kitchen and returned with a partial bag of chocolate chip cookies and two cans of root beer. He set them on the table as Allen grabbed a pop. This was late night, with the rest of household asleep. Plates were no longer required, just bare hands.

The father and son team would now share one of those secret midnight meetings that would always be remembered. Allen kicked it off.

He told a story of a friend that paid an unexpected visit to his family late at night. He initially scared the daylights out of them, even though he didn't mean to. "I can just imagine the looks they must have had on their faces," laughed Allen.

"Like you did to me this evening?" chuckled Steve.

Allen couldn't hold in his laughter. With both hands pressing against his stomach, he leaned back in his chair and said, "Well, something like that."

Steve nodded his head sideways as he giggled at Allen. It was now Dad's turn. He told a story of a harmless prank that he pulled on his best friend at work. Allen interrupted and said, "I think I heard about this. Go on, Dad."

Steve tried his best to tell the story without laughing. "You know who Kim is," said Steve.

"Sure I do, Dad. I love him very much," said Allen. Steve started to explain about how Kim was a creature of habit and always showed up at work the same time. He also pointed out that he took great care of his car. When he arrived at work, he would park in the same stall and go to the break room to put his lunch in the refrigerator. He would then clock in and return to his car until it was time to start his shift.

"This one particular morning, I brought a smoke bomb to work," said the dad. "When Kim parked and left to do his routine, I placed the bomb near his car and lit it when I saw him coming. I then yelled out to him that his car was on fire." Steve bent over laughing. "You should have seen the look on his face when he came running!"

Allen laughed along with his dad and said, "I was told about that. That's pretty funny!"

275

"It wasn't funny to Kim at the time," said Steve as he doubled up and started to hyperventilate. "But when he saw that it was just a joke, he laughed harder than any of us."

Humorous stories volleyed back and forth as they tried not to wake up the boy's mother and sister.

Allen switched subjects and said, "I have to go now, Dad."

"That's okay, Allen," he said. "Keep in touch."

Allen looked at his dad with a frisky expression and said, "I will, Dad." They got out of their chairs and hugged. Steve returned to his bedroom undetected and went back to sleep.

At precisely one o'clock, Steve felt a jolt and was wide awake. He threw the blankets off to one side and silently began to step out of bed. In doing so, he bumped into a chair that was positioned at his bedside. A chair that was normally in the far corner of the room.

The dad got out of bed and put on his bathrobe. He left the bedroom and wandered downstairs into the dining room. He approached the entry to the dining room and stopped with his arms extended over the door jamb.

There stood the dining room table with two empty pop cans, an empty cookie bag and crumbs scattered on top. Two chairs facing one another were pulled back at an angle. He looked up at the wall and saw a series of Allen's grade school pictures that progressed with age. Next to it was framed memorabilia of the many accomplishments the boy achieved during his short life.

Steve smiled at the pictures and felt compelled to walk through the kitchen and open the back door. Once doing so, a gentle breeze filtered through the trees, giving Steve a warm sensation. The father felt a tranquility of peace. It was a grace that let him know that he was not alone and had nothing to be afraid of.

It was now time for him to continue his walk through life. He returned to his room and went back to sleep.

Frank Loves Vyerl

I feel it's safe to say that, in life, we encounter those events that seem to have no explanation. Such phenomena definitely occur in all families. Maybe it's just me; but have you noticed that usually when such stories are told, it's from a senior member of the family? Back in 1975, my mother shared such a story.

At this point I need to back up a bit and give some history about my parents.

My father, Frank, lost his father in 1934. Dad was an eleven-year-old child with no siblings. From there, he and my grandmother would survive the Great Depression together.

WWII sent Dad to the West Coast to train at Fort Lewis in Tacoma, Washington. This is where he met my mom, Vyerl. My dad was a loyal son who wrote his mother every week until her final day. The first round of letters expressed how proud he was to be a soldier in the United States Army. Soon the letters changed tempo and were about being introduced to Vyerl, and spending all of his free time with her. They were in love. The sentimental son would write home to cover the week's events and mail it promptly.

In 1975, our grandmother, Maggie, had completed her life at age seventy-nine. It was necessary for my parents to travel all the way to the East Coast and rummage through the house my dad grew up in. The place needed to be prepped for sale while addressing important documents. My parents stayed there briefly to take care of business.

The house was a typical grandmother house. It was old, having been built in 1917. It was a two-story house designed for two families; one upstairs and one down. The front door opened into an enclosed room with two doors. The one on the right gave access to a flight of stairs. The left door allowed entry to the first floor. The configuration of such a house created its share of nooks and crannies. Maggie owned the entire structure.

It was hard work that required many trips to the local dump. Finally, the house was empty; or so they thought. It was time to leave where Dad grew up and drop the keys off at the Realtors. Once in the car, my mom had a sensation and asked for the keys. They were handed to her, and she got out of the car and entered the house. Instinctively, she picked "door number one" and entered the main floor, walking directly to my dad's old room.

This bedroom had an obscure closet that was enclosed directly under the stairwell. My mom opened the door to the closet and immediately walked its short length where it followed the path of the L-shaped stairwell above it. There in a forgotten nook was an old chest. She pulled it out of the closet, having to open it. To their delight, it was filled with letters that Dad had written his mother throughout the years.

It seemed to be a finalization of the changing of the guards. Some of the letters dated back to the war. Dad wrote his mother, telling her how wonderful my mother was. That moment reminded them how much they were, and still are, in love with each other.

What about the chest? They eventually closed it with every letter left inside. That artifact was part of the bond my father had with his mother. It was returned to where they found it. My parents left the house and locked the door for the last time.

This finding did not make any of us rich. However, the chain of events that led up to this discovery was priceless.

For myself, it served as testimony to why everyone should keep all of their loved ones in their thoughts and prayers. This also includes the ones that have gone on before us.

Thank you,
Matt Shea

Epilogue

I appreciate the fact you took the time to read my stories and hope my overall batting average met your satisfaction. This is my eleventh book, and is mainly an updated rendition of Kindle projects I released some time ago. This book is my answer to those who wanted all of my stories to be available in paperback.

For those of you who have read any of my past writings: I am grateful beyond words!

It's now time to reflect on the three main stories this book centers around.

The Mouse That Roared:

No one could ever argue that life is quite an acid test. This is especially true for those who started off behind the eight ball — with our star, William Randall Stokes IV, serving as a prime example.

This young man — who was small in stature and excessively meek — knew pain. His childhood was full of rejection. Even after receiving a material gift every peer would want; he was still denied in the long run because *he just didn't fit in*. William's new truck *did* briefly get him in the *in-crowd*. However, he failed his audition when he refused to degrade others the way the popular kids did.

Wisely, he gained the respect of elders and leaned on them for advice.

The result?

William Stokes was mysteriously guided to the needs of our Lord and found his true calling in life. From there, he seemingly became a drawing card who brought the entire community together. In fact; his faith would soon make him the most popular guy in town. In time, our Lord did reward young William by allowing him to receive everything this young man could ever hope for:

He was granted the gratification of becoming a pastor and got the girl of his dreams!

Yee-haw!

◄◄ ◄◄ ►► ►►

Let's get to *Lauratown*:

In this story we get the pleasure of meeting the town's oldest citizen. Travel back in time with her, and get the *real* story of the town's roots.

To our surprise, Laura O'Shea was actually just a common, God-fearing person. The magic was that she knew all of us are dealt a winning hand by our Lord in order to serve Him.

Laura did what we are all naturally meant to do: she prayed and followed her heart.

The result?

Their small settlement gained national prominence from its God-given central location and grew into a boomtown appropriately named *Lauratown*!

Equally important: it united the town with brotherhood (*Laurahood!*).

Let's take a closer look at the *Laura O'Sheas* in our world today and access the lessons waiting for those who dare!

◄◄ ◄◄ ►► ►►

Aren't senior citizens great?

They are actually youthful people with lots of intensity, fire and spirit. They have just lived a little longer and traveled down your path a little further. Don't let the age difference or battle scars fool you; they actually make great friends. At moments of disparity, their experience with life will comfort and give direction.

I challenge you to initiate a conversation with any neighbor who falls into that category. Be fair about it and make it longer then a token five minutes. You'll be amazed at the many things they'll have in common with you and what they have to teach. I also guarantee that they *will* make you laugh!

My stories are all about exposing the beauty behind the average person. Once this takes place, a new friendship is available for the taking. I encourage everyone to say, *Hello* to that familiar face they always seem to cross paths with. That moment could transpire into one of the greatest gifts your life will ever receive.

I promise!

◀◀ ◀◀ ▶▶ ▶▶

Let's go to *The World's Greatest Rock Star*:

There is something special about underdogs that we love. They are usually misunderstood souls who are the victims of being misplaced. Such individuals inspire others as they put forth a valiant battle in life. Everyone secretly relates to their pain as we cheer them from afar. When they succeed, we feel a personal victory that comes with it. After all, wasn't that an accomplishment from someone *who also feels the pain of being labeled*?

Milton Livingston's existence was just that. He had no choice but to walk through life being himself and suffer the price that came with it. Grace finally intervened, placing him in a world where he could be himself and live out his dreams.

The ending had the epitome of life: Milt utilized the gift of forgiveness. That would be the only cure that could free his parents of any guilt. The same age-old cure that works for everyone.

◀◀ ◀◀ ▶▶ ▶▶

As mentioned earlier, I am honored that you took the time to read my stories. I invite you to email me with any comments you might have; *whether good or bad*. Your input will allow me to understand your views as well as others. This, in turn, will improve me as an author and, more importantly, as a person.

Thank you, and I wish you and yours the very best!

Matt Shea
worknmatt7@aol.com

Matt Shea Author Biography

Mathew Joseph Shea is one of many authors from the Puget Sound area in the state of Washington. Like many from that region, he appreciates a misty rainy day, Mt. Rainier, and a good cup of coffee.

When it comes to his writings, one doesn't have to read very far to understand where his passion lies.

It's people!

Everyday people like you and me with this message being sent:

The simpler the better.

AND:

It's a good thing you are the way you are!

It's that common man (and woman) who keeps our country flowing and compels Matt to write his stories. A spotlight for the many unsung heroes who go by unnoticed until their character receives its *spiritual calling.*

The former Catholic altar boy is no stranger to the concept of being self-sacrificing. Later in life, he would become a Campfire dad and volunteer for seniors as well as other worthy causes. Matt always knew that this *right path* would come with its own blessings. What he sent out as a labor of love, always seemed to returned in the form of nurturing shortcomings of his own.

"I caught on years ago that when you follow your heart and crusade for a good cause, you can only 'then' receive what you actually need . . ." says Matt.

Matt believes in the power of prayer. Like many timeless classics of someone yearning to find love, he wrote a secret prayer story of his own titled:

Secret Radio Man

A message in a bottle to get a knight in shining armor by means of a radio personality. One who would grant him an interview.

Prayers do get answered and dreams often come true. At age sixty, author Matt Shea had made an important discovery:

His special prayer story had already been answered *several interviews ago* by legendary talk show host Ric Bratton and his multi-award winning talk show, *This Week In America*.

"Ric became such an instant friend that I forgot he was a delivery from our Lord; the answer to my secret prayer!" said Matt.

Matt's story about the radio man finding an unknown, is on a publication that Ric Bratton himself interviewed!

So far, Matt Shea has published eleven books with many, many more to be added. All of which encompass the common man/woman: *people* we see every day. This includes at work, in our neighborhood; and who you see when you're brushing your teeth in the morning . . .

Matt loves feedback and encourages anyone to write him. His website not only has many free stories, but a place where you can write him. Matt promises to do everything he can to return your message. He does this so he can thank you for taking the time to digest his writings, ask you for ideas- and, most importantly, *to say, "Hello!"*

Thank you and may God bless.

Matt

www.mattsheabooks.com

Laura Shea with her dad, Matt Shea.

Books by Matt Shea

 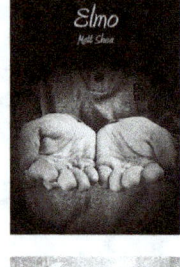 

**More Uplifting
Stories From
Matt Shea Books!**

Matt Shea

286

www.ingramcontent.com/pod-product-compliance
Lightning Source LLC
Chambersburg PA
CBHW070835250626
47159CB00003B/795